DROP-OFF

DROP-OFF

A JOHN RODRIGUE NOVEL

KEN GRISSOM

ST. MARTIN'S PRESS *NEW YORK*

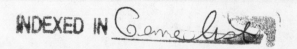
This novel is a work of fiction. All of the events,
characters, names, and places depicted in this novel
are entirely fictitious or are used fictitiously. No rep-
resentation that any statement made in this novel is
true or that any incident depicted in this novel
actually occurred is intended or should be inferred
by the reader.

Editor: Jared Kieling

Copy-edited by Eva Galan Salmieri

Design by Jaye Zimet

Library of Congress Cataloging-in-Publication Data

Grissom, Ken.
    Drop-off.

    I. Title.
PS3557.R5366D76 1988   813'.54   88-11548
ISBN 0-312-02196-8

First Edition

10 9 8 7 6 5 4 3 2 1

TO DEBBIE

The theory of a free press is that the truth will emerge from free reporting and free discussion, not that it will be presented perfectly and instantly in any one account.

—Walter Lippmann

DROP-OFF

CHAPTER 1

Rodrigue was dreaming of raging surf. It was a good dream because it meant he would spend the day hustling the tough Afrikaner barmaids instead of tacking on anodes with an ear-ringing Ramset Tool under ninety feet of cold water. A jangling noise finally hammered into his consciousness and dissolved the Afrikaner barmaids and even the raging surf. There was only the whirring of the ceiling fan in the dark room.

It was more than four years since he quit oil-field diving, but he felt the same faint urgency—as if he had a boat to catch. The phone rang again.

"This is the marine operator," announced a tired female voice. "I have a call for John Rod-reeg, from the motor vessel *King Ghu*." He acknowledged and the line immediately turned crisp with radio static.

"Hi, Rod. Phan here," said a cheerful voice. "We about to sink here."

Rodrigue switched on the light and focused his

1

civilian eye on his Timex. He groaned and fell back on his pillow. It was 4:55.

"Rod?"

Both eyes were open now and staring half-blindly at the flickering reflection of the outside lights on the edges of the fan blades. They were slightly mismatched eyes, hooded and expressionless, and they gave the impression that he was always somehow standing apart, watching coldly, even while he was singing drunkenly in archaic French at the top of his lungs.

"Rod? Rod?" Phan was saying. Rodrigue sighed and lifted the receiver again.

Phan was a shrimp fisherman who had hit a log in the dark and put a hole in the side of his boat at the waterline. They had stuffed a mattress in the hole and then dropped anchor from the opposite outrigger which, as they put a strain on the anchor line, caused the boat to heel and raise the hole out of the water. But it was a pretty precarious situation and Phan couldn't swim a stroke. He hadn't wanted to call the Coast Guard because they were shrimping out of season when they hit the log, so he called Rodrigue.

Rodrigue was running an authorized rescue service but only for nonemergency calls. The commandant of the Coast Guard had decided it was a waste of taxpayers' money to dispatch a forty-one-foot patrol craft each time some outboard skiff broke down in flat-to-moderate seas with no weather in sight—something that happened frequently out of a busy sportfishing port like Galveston. Rodrigue had been doing some light salvage and he had a suitable boat, so he got the local "seagoing wrecker" franchise.

A lot of people saw it as a license to steal, especially when they got back to the dock and some smart aleck showed them how to knock the sludge out of their fuel filter and get going again. Rodrigue didn't do repairs and

2

he didn't carry spare parts and he didn't carry extra fuel. He towed—and then only when he had been paid in advance or adequate collateral had been transferred aboard the *Haulover Queen*. Car keys. Wives. Whatever. People said his boat should've been named *Haulover Coals*.

He ought to charge Phan twice his usual $75 an hour, he thought grumpily as he pulled on a pair of worn mechanic's coveralls. The little gook was stupid to have been running at night with the Gulf full of debris from the swollen Mississippi. Besides, he could use the money.

Business was terrible. After months of hard rains over the central U.S., the entire northwestern Gulf had a surface layer of chocolate-colored water six feet deep. Fishing was lousy and at the peak of summer, when Rodrigue should've been the busiest, the Galveston Yacht Basin was like a ghost town.

He was drawing $905 a month disability pay from the navy, but his utilities, garbage pickup, and so forth ran him around $350 a month in the summer and his boat slip at the yacht basin cost $195 a month. He had a whopping insurance note for liability on the boat. And with gasoline at $1.15 a gallon and beer $5.40 a twelve-pack—well, the money just went. He wasn't eating as well as he liked nor drinking as much.

It was being on the edge of poverty that give him that old familiar sense of urgency he thought he had kissed good-bye. Working because you had to was a bitch. Yet he was a lot better off than most of his friends on B Row, charter captains with either a mortgage or a nervous owner hanging over their heads. For them, dirty water was like drought to a farmer.

At the yacht basin, Rodrigue turned left toward the bait camp. There were only half a dozen boats parked along A Row and it looked permanently abandoned in the weak light of dawn. Many of the big boats had been sent down to Cozumel or over to the Bahamas for extended fishing trips. Others were stocked with cases of Cuervo and Bacardi and maybe some coke, loaded with twenty-year-old secretaries and maybe an important client or two, and piloted just offshore where the girls could complete their tans. If dirty water was a hindrance, they were taking it stoically.

The morning light shone on four huge cranes at the container-ship terminal across from the yacht basin. They loomed over the vacant public parking lot like a herd of lank dinosaurs. The lazy stirring of the marsh-smelling breeze off the bay provoked a forlorn clanking from a hundred aluminum masts on the sailboat docks.

The bait camp was open because the owner had nothing else to do. Rodrigue parked, went in, and picked up a six-pack of Miller Lite. It would've been cheaper at a grocery store but he liked to patronize the place. He got as much towing work on referral from the owner as he did from the Coast Guard. Still feeling a little sorry for himself, he opened a beer for breakfast and drove around to the other lot and parked at the foot of B Row.

Dub Brezinski was up already, changing oil on the *Prettiest Sally,* an old Chris Craft Commander. He had a look of determination about him, like an airborne commando packing a chute.

"Y'all using the *Prettiest Sally* next week?" Rodrigue asked, guessing. Brezinski and Jerry Taylor usually fished tournaments aboard Taylor's twenty-seven-foot Black Fin, which more than made up in speed what it lacked in air-conditioned comfort.

"Yeah, *I* am," he said, with a trace of bitterness.

"You not fishing with Taylor?"

Rodrigue didn't mean to rub it in, but he was having trouble digesting it. Brezinski and Taylor were like soup and crackers.

4

"Fuckin' Taylor's fishing with Glasscock."

"*Glasscock?*"

Julian Glasscock was a Sugar Land car dealer who sold pickup trucks like McDonalds sells hamburgers, almost. He fished not for relaxation—pickups sold themselves in that part of the world—but for that old team spirit, that sense of heroics on display which had evaded him in high school and college. It had evaded him in fishing, too. But with the dirty water offshore, the tournament would hinge on sharks and red snapper, neither of which were bothered by a murky surface like the more nomadic king mackerel and ling. And Jerry Taylor knew more about catching red snapper than any ten other fishermen in Galveston.

"Hired him on, eh?"

"Bought our numbers is what he did," Brezinski said angrily. "Numbers"—the loran coordinates for rocks and wrecks and other unseen snapper havens—were the currency of B Row.

"You don't think Taylor's going to let him see the numbers, do you?"

Brezinski shrugged helplessly. These were tough times.

"Well, I've got a little job and I'll give you half of the take if you'll run out with me and tend my hose."

"Half starting right now. Gimme one of them beers."

Rodrigue peeled off a Lite for Brezinski and the two of them trudged down the pier to where the infamous *Haulover Queen* hung high and dry in nylon slings. "What is this job?" Brezinski asked as he helped roll the low-pressure compressor aboard.

"Tack a patch on a shrimper holed at the waterline."

A breath of resignation blew out of Brezinski. "So my half'll be half of a box of shrimp or something."

"You know my rates," Rodrigue said gruffly.

5

"I have never heard of you taking a dime off a shrimper."

With the shrimp they got from Phan, Rodrigue cooked a big oily gumbo that afternoon, the catalyst for a much-needed party. Lawn chairs were scraped up and Judge Albert Castillo broke out his last two cartons of snapper fillets, cut them into fish fingers, and deep-fried them for hors d'oeuvres. There were blenders humming aboard nearby boats, the happy rattle of beers being pawed out of full Igloos, and Rodrigue made friends with an errant bottle of Ron Potosi, which he took in an iced tea tumbler with soda, fresh lime, and lots of cracked ice. It was almost like old times, except for the fight.

Brezinski was coming out of the restroom at the foot of the dock and Taylor was going in, and they cracked foreheads at the door. Brezinski took it personally and he rared back and hit his old buddy square in the face. Taylor backed away, rubbing his nose vigorously. He recovered from the blow quicker than from the surprise of it, but when he did, he plowed into Brezinski.

They were both so drunk that it was actually comical— both of them waltzing mightily, locked in a bear hug, neither with enough leverage to throw the other. Everybody was laughing except Rodrigue and Jackie Taylor, Jerry's wife, and Bruce Phillips, a Galveston County deputy sheriff. Phillips was over fifty, a crackerjack investigator but a frail, dry-boned fellow who couldn't have relished the idea of mixing it up with tough young men like Brezinski and Taylor. He made it a rule to look around small infractions at the yacht basin anyway, because that was where he went on his time off, to relax on his thirty-one-foot Bertram.

Rodrigue was watching the scuffle coldly through a gathering rum fog. Finally Jackie leaned forward in her chair and touched his thick forearm lightly.

roughneck and he had a lot of Permian Basin sand in his craw. If you didn't need furniture or fish for marlin, Buck Greathouse didn't have any use for you.

But people who wouldn't have any use for Rodrigue often wound up needing him anyway. Greathouse said he wanted to come over for a private talk. Emphasis on private.

"Where are you now?" Rodrigue asked, hoping the answer would be Dallas. Or, hell, Denver.

"Just passing Clear Lake. I'm on one of these new cellular phones."

Rodrigue sighed and it hurt down in his shoulder blades. Clear Lake was halfway down the Gulf Freeway from Houston. As usual, Greathouse hadn't intended to take no for an answer. "Okay," he said finally, "take the 61st Street exit to Seawall Boulevard and turn right. Go—"

"I know where you live. Put some coffee on, I'll be there in forty-five minutes."

Rodrigue hung up and sat on the side of the bed waiting for the familiar throb to find his head again. He shouldn't have been surprised that Greathouse knew where he lived. After all, he was known far and wide as the notorious modern-day pirate of Galveston. He had seen to it himself.

He padded barefoot across the itchy sea-grass and put on a big pot of water to boil in the kitchen. He stepped in and out of the shower and slipped into tan corduroy shorts and a faded cotton Hawaiian shirt with orange palm trees against a black sky from the diminishing stock of shirts Rosa had ironed the last time he could afford her. He came back in the kitchen just as the water in the pot began to roll nicely, charged a big twelve-cup drip pot with dark-roast Community, and poured the boiling water into the receptacle on top. As the water trickled into the grounds Rodrigue leaned on the counter with his chin in his palms and his eyes closed and let the aroma seep into him like a steam bath.

From early June, typically, until well into October and sometimes even November, Rodrigue lived in a gray crackerbox of a house on tall pilings at Sea Isle, one of the resort villages that served as suburbs on Galveston Island. It was on the low-lying western end where the barrier island was only about three-quarters of a mile across. The houses were scattered from the seashore over the arid spine of the island to a small private marina complex on the shallow bay.

Rodrigue's house was in the row on the khaki-colored, tar-stained beach that sloped gently into the Gulf of Mexico. In the shade beneath the house lurked a black '78 Blazer with Rancho suspension, Dick Cepek off-roaders, and rust spots on the hood and doors. Out in the sandy yard was a tandem-wheel EZ Loader boat trailer.

The Galveston *Daily News* was resting faithfully on the concrete driveway. Rodrigue grabbed it as the pot finished dripping, went back and poured himself a cup, and then wandered out to the broad sun deck to greet the flat sea, which was about the color of his café au lait.

The chairman of the joint chiefs of staff was saying there had been some discussion of using U.S. troops as a peacekeeping force in the Falklands. The Astros took a four-to-nothing clubbing from the San Diego Padres, their fifth loss of the last seven games. Rodrigue read it all dispassionately. To him, current events were the stuff of soap opera.

Here was someone saying that the unusually wet winter and spring were caused by a pool of warm water that generally appears off the Pacific coast of South America in December, prompting Latin Americans to name it El Niño, after the Christ Child. It had grown way out of proportion last winter, affecting the equatorial trades and throwing weather patterns out of kilter all around the globe. A great swath of western Africa had been turned into a kiln where thousands were starving each week.

Rodrigue shook the creases out of the paper. Here was something that touched him. He knew that the people quoted in newspapers were in the habit of laying blame on sunspots or the ash cloud from Mount St. Helens while at the same time scientists were blowing holes in the aurora borealis just to see what would happen. He knew that aerosol sprays were dissolving the ozone layer and giving everybody skin cancer, and that pollution of the Saragasso Sea and clearing of the rain forests were threatening the world's oxygen supply. Man was to blame for all that and Rodrigue was just enough of a primitive to believe that every now and then nature got even.

The hushed perfection of a Mercedes door being slammed below announced Greathouse's arrival. Soon the stairs were creaking under considerable weight. Rodrigue wondered why Greathouse was hanging around Galveston while most of the serious billfishing boats had long departed for Cozumel or Islamorada or Chub Cay. The multimillionaire walked onto the sun deck and bluntly appraised the purloined café table and Cinzano umbrella.

"Cream and sugar?" Rodrigue asked, hoisting his empty cup.

"Black," said Greathouse.

Rodrigue fetched two brimming cups and they sat under the umbrella. Greathouse was egg-shaped with a face full of little red veins and he talked in gusts, like Broderick Crawford. He screwed up his face when he tasted the dark-roast Community.

"Christ!" he said without the slightest trace of diplomacy. "Got any Jack?"

"How about some rum?"

Greathouse made a flat mouth, the look of a man accustomed to finding things not quite to his satisfaction. Rodrigue went inside and found his coveted bottle of Pusser's behind the empties in the liquor cabinet.

"Ice?" he called from the kitchen. "Soda?" And, getting carried away: "Pineapple juice? Grenadine?"

"Just bring the bottle."

Greathouse splashed some of the Pusser's into his coffee and tasted it with every square inch of his tongue, like a dog eating peanut butter. Rodrigue shuddered involuntarily watching him. Then Greathouse set the cup down deliberately and turned to the business at hand: "I need you to do a job for me and I need you to keep your mouth shut about it."

"I tell you wot," said Rodrigue, tired of playing the congenial host, "I'll keep my mouth shut about anything up to the point I say yes or no. And if I say yes, I'll keep my mouth shut about anything after that. And if I can't keep my mouth shut about anything after that, I'll say no. Fair enough?"

"That's fair enough. I want you to go out to the One Seventy-four, pick up a boat that's tied off out there—nobody's on it—and take it out to the Claypile and sink it. I say the Claypile because I don't want some goddamn shrimper to come along and find it with his nets. If you can think of someplace better that'll do the job, that's fine with me."

Rodrigue took a sip of his coffee. The One Seventy-four was an oil production platform out in the Gulf, and the Claypile was a rocky outcrop on the bottom *way* out in the Gulf.

"I can't do anything like that unless I know why," he said finally.

"You don't want to know why. The less you know the better. If you get caught towing it, all you know is that some fucker called you and told you to tow it. You're sharp enough to work out some excuse why you can't say who it was or where to find him. Just don't get caught *sinking* the goddamn thing."

"Let me say it again, Buck. I ain't gonna do it until I find out why. If you don't feel like you can say why—and if it's bad, don't, okay?—then just take that for a no, all right?"

Buck Greathouse didn't know how to negotiate with grace. He had a temper that tended to rare up and obscure his objective. His face glowed and his knuckles blanched, and it looked for a moment as though he were about to launch himself off the chair. Then he visibly shrank as the anger hissed out of him.

"Friend of mine owns the boat," he said. "He was out there, fishing I guess, and he started having trouble with it. He's been having a lot of trouble with it. So he hitched a ride in on another boat. Now he wants to get rid of it for the insurance."

"Fishing, eh? Gonna report it missing from the rig?"

"Right."

"Great. And two days later, someone'll report seeing it under tow behind a Boston Whaler Frontier, of which there's only one in Galveston that I know of. What is this somewhat risky job worth, Bucko?"

"A thousand dollars. Look, there's no one out there right now. The One Seventy-four is an unmanned plat-form, no standby boat or nothing. They fly a pumper out there two or three times a day, on the average, but I did a little checking around—quietly, you understand—and found out that he won't be back out there until late this evening. You got plenty of time."

"Two thousand and we'll talk."

"Two thousand," Greathouse said without hesitation.

"What kind of boat is it?" Rodrigue asked.

"Hell, I don't know. Little. Some kind of center console outfit. There ain't gonna be but one boat tied up out there—sink *it.*"

"Buck, these little boats ain't like *Wahoo Too,* you know. Most of them, all the newer ones, have flotation in the hull. You could cut my boat into a dozen pieces and they'd all float."

"Well, then pour gas all over it, stand off, and fire a flare into it. Burn it to the waterline. Goddamn, I *know* it'll sink then."

After Greathouse left, Rodrigue poured himself another cup of coffee and wandered absently back out on the deck to consider his options. He could tow the boat back inside through San Luis Pass and keep it hidden at a ramshackle landing he knew about up Chocolate Bayou, where one little fishing boat more or less wouldn't attract attention. Trying to sell it himself would be risky, of course, but there might be a finder's fee coming from the insurance company. Nothing they love more than making a good case of fraud.

Rodrigue thought of these things perfunctorily, as a matter of course, but they didn't tempt him. He knew the danger of greed. Besides, if he had to screw somebody to make a buck, he'd rather screw an insurance company than just about anyone, even a steamrolling fat cat like Buck Greathouse. And Greathouse had paid in full—cash money, 100 percent tax-deductible.

Resolved, Rodrigue leaned back and poured a little of the dark, heavy rum into his coffee and tasted it. Not bad, he decided.

CHAPTER 2

Rodrigue found one of the wheelbar-rowlike carts and loaded it with a five-gallon jerry can of gasoline from the back of his Blazer. He pushed the cart quickly down B Row. All the crushed beer cans and stomped cigarettes from the night before had been swept away. The only signs of the party were an empty bottle of Cuervo Especial upside down in a rod holder on the *Fine Fin,* a sickening streak of pink-flecked gray down the side of the *Prettiest Sally,* where it looked like Brezinski had thrown up everything he had eaten since Christmas, and an open smoker behind *Mac Attack* giving a sour, ashy smell to the still morning. It was shabby and sad, like a Saigon whorehouse in the glare of day. It wasn't the usual midweek scene.

It was nothing for B Row to whoop it up on a weekday but it was normally the earned, honest kind of party that would make a good Old Milwaukee commercial. Somebody would mince a fresh school dolphin for ceviche. Someone else would smoke a sow snapper or two, and someone else would boil the crabs or shrimp they had traded for beer with a shrimper out on the Gulf. Everybody went home buzzing—but satisfied and happy and ready to get up and hit it again the next day.

Nobody was stirring that morning, which delighted Rodrigue since he didn't want to have to explain why he was piss-anting gas to the *Haulover Queen* in her slip instead of taking her around to the fuel dock. She had a fuel capacity of 140 gallons, which would take a while to fill from a five-gallon can.

The *Queen* was a twenty-five-foot fiberglass boat powered by twin outboards. It was actually two hulls, one inside the other and the space between them filled with foam. The result was a very rigid and virtually unsinkable craft. It had a tall pilot house and a aluminum mast and lifting boom that made it look like a small shrimp boat, and a special towing package that included a heavy rail around the outboards to fend off objects and keep the towline from hanging up on them. With its two 150-horsepower Evinrudes, it would run forty-nine miles an hour and pull a small island—lovely virtues for a seagoing wrecker.

His thumb on a big green button, Rodrigue lowered the *Queen* into the water and kept the electric motor running until the heavy slings sank far enough for the Evinrudes' props to clear. He hopped aboard and started the outboards, the cold V-6s spewing an oily fog. He cast off the stern line and rumbled slowly out of the yacht basin into the Galveston Channel.

Out in Bolivar Roads, the eighty-two-foot Coast Guard cutter *Point Monroe*, which was normally stationed down the coast at Freeport, was hove-to with a couple of forty-one-foot patrol boats nudging at her like suckling pigs. Another forty-one-footer stood alongside an oil field supply boat in the channel halfway out the jetties. It had

16

the earmarks of a big dope-sniffing operation. They would sit there and board incoming vessels, giving each one a quick shakedown and escorting the suspicious ones back to the Coast Guard station for a more thorough search. It had been a long time since they blockaded the Roads like that.

Pissing in the wind, thought Rodrigue. Wasting tax-payers' money. There were too many oil-field vessels coming and going all the time—and it wouldn't take a Houdini to hide a *bunch* of dope on something like a 200-foot supply boat. An inbound tanker marched by without challenge.

Rodrigue eased the *Queen* past the Coast Guard blockade, shoved the throttles forward, and skipped off the long, low swells rolling in over the bar—stopping briefly to secure the big gumbo pot Jackie Taylor had returned all clean and shiny. He passed a ship at anchor waiting for a harbor pilot, and a crew boat veering off to the east, and then he was alone. It was a sorry sight—a sluggish chocolate sea.

The One Seventy-four was twenty miles beyond the sea buoy on a southeast heading. It wasn't a popular spot with anglers. The snapper had been fished out years ago. It occasionally attracted big ling when they moved through in the spring, but it had never held any king mackerel to speak of. Rodrigue couldn't imagine anyone fishing there now, except maybe for sharks.

When the platform came into sight on the horizon, Rodrigue eased the outboards into neutral, went outside and hopped up on the gunwale, and trained his great-grandfather's old brass telescope on it. Beneath the tall, skeletal structure a white sliver gleamed from the shadows. It looked as though the boat had been swept into the platform by the current, which was a likely fate for any craft left unattended. Surface currents sometimes

17

reversed themselves overnight. Rodrigue walked onto the *Queen*'s foredeck and slowly swung the telescope in a full circle—no other vessels in sight.

Arriving at the platform, Rodrigue searched the horizon again—empty—then he stood off, bumping the Evinrudes into reverse occasionally to hover near the abandoned boat. There was no wind and a moderate eastbound current. The boat, an eighteen-foot center console Wellcraft with a 150-horsepower Mercury Black Max, was wedged lightly beneath a diagonal brace—a steel pipe two feet in diameter—on the northwest leg of the platform. It had been tied up short by the stern with a rig hook, a length of aluminum conduit crooked at one end like a shepherd's staff with a line fixed to the other end. The hook was placed over a crossbeam and the line made fast to a stern cleat, a common method of tying up to fish but hardly the way a prudent skipper would leave a boat unattended. If it hadn't have been so calm offshore, the Wellcraft might've been battered pretty badly.

Two short, stout fishing rods with bulky nine-ought Penn Senator reels were stuck in holders on the Wellcraft's starboard gunwale, their green Dacron lines bellying in the current. Rodrigue balanced himself on his gunwale and looked down into the derelict—blood was smeared all over it.

Shark fishermen, all right, he thought. Dirty water didn't hurt shark fishing. He backed off and circled to the landing on the opposite corner of the platform, where the current would hold the *Queen* off. Expertly lassoing a bollard on the landing, he tied the Whaler up short by the stern.

The landing was a steel grate ledge where workers could get off and onto a waiting crew boat by swinging on knotted ropes suspended from the overhanging top deck of the structure. It was designed to be more or less the same height as the back deck of a big crew boat, but it was a good foot over Rodrigue's head as he stood in the Whaler's cockpit. Stretching, he could just reach one of the two-inch nylon swing-ropes. If there had been swells to lift the boat it would've been a snap, but there were no swells. With the frayed end pinched in his fingertips, he stepped up on the gunwale and edged up to the pilot house, pulling the rope with him. The Queen was sitting at enough of an angle for him to swing from the top of the house without hitting her mast. He gave a mighty lunge and swung like Tarzan's fat uncle to within an inch of the landing . . .

Then he swung back to within two inches of the Queen . . .

And back again to within three inches of the landing . . .

Four inches of the Queen . . .

Five inches of the landing . . .

And finally he just hung there, at least four feet from anything.

The nearest object was one of the black rubberlike bumpers, heavy vertical ribs installed to protect the platform and crew boats from each other in sloppy seas. Rodrigue stretched out his right leg, toe outward, and tried to snag the bumper. The shift in weight caused him to pirouette with agonizing slowness, like a dancing bear in a tutu. Sweat was stinging his eyes and his arms began to quiver. Once his toe brushed the bumper—then he finally got a grip on it and pulled himself over. He sat on the grate wheezing mightily until he got his breath back.

Underneath it was dark and cool while the day blazed white-hot all around. Rodrigue paused to savor the familiar damp, sweet-oily hollowness, like a cavern that ran on diesel. Below, the Wellcraft suddenly shifted with a groan and the sound, transmitted up the hollow leg and into a hollow framework, seemed to come from everywhere. He balanced himself on slippery crossbeams, shuffling along until he was directly over the abandoned boat. Then he dropped heavily onto its cockpit, one foot slipping on a bloody spot so that he came down hard on his bad knee.

After the blinding flash of pain, he became immediately aware of the stench. The sickening smell of rotting carcasses overpowered the odors of diesel and rust from the platform. This was no way to treat a hangover. He barely made it to the rail in time to vomit over the side.

He took off his shirt and bunched it against his face to mask the smell. There were drying pools of blood and bloody footprints everywhere. The starboard gunwale was smeared with the blackening stains in two places, forward and aft of the central steering console. Something big, he thought, to leave all that blood. Big bull shark probably. Or tiger.

He bent down and looked carefully at the cockpit sole—there were brown crusty lines where blood had run aft in the stern-heavy boat, but no drip spots in between. *Two* sharks—one back there, and one up here, Rodrigue decided. But why would anyone drag a big shark over a stainless steel handrail instead of walking it back aft to the console where the gunwale was lower and there wasn't any rail to get in the way? Probably there were two fishermen—and two sharks being boated at the same time?—so there wasn't enough room in the cockpit aft for both of them?

Holding his breath against the smell, Rodrigue reeled in both lines and found bare sixteen-ought Mustads—hooks the size of small anchors—each connected to about ten feet of braided steel leader. The bare hooks were to be expected. Triggerfish would've cleaned them of bait. But if, as Greathouse had said, the fishermen had intended to go in and their outboard wouldn't start, why were the lines out at all?

Okay, so they catch two sharks, decide to go in and show them off (in Mexico it would be to sell, but sharks had only bragging value in Galveston), and then the Mercury doesn't start. There's nobody else around, nothing to do but keep fishing. Then along comes someone who offers them a ride but not a tow—either can't or won't tow the Wellcraft—so they dump the sharks back overboard and, maybe in haste, maybe in disgust, leave the baited lines out.

A battered forty-eight-quart Igloo against the port gunwale aft wasn't shut securely. Rodrigue looked inside and the sour odor hit him like a hot wind. Inside was a gray jack crevalle—prime shark bait—floating in slimy water. Fighting nausea, he lifted the ice chest and shoved the whole thing overboard.

Cans of beer bobbed in tepid water in the seat-cooler forward of the console. There was a near-empty beer can lying on the casting deck forward and another, half-full, in a gimballed holder on the console near the wheel. Two cans for two fishermen. Rodrigue lifted the seat again: two six-packs of Lone Star just like they came out of the store, and a solitary can with the plastic six-pack holder still attached. No other empty cans anywhere. They were chunking the empties overboard.

It meant he had to worry about at least two people besides Greathouse keeping their mouths shut, but he should have expected that. Few people came out in the Gulf alone—and no shark fishermen at all that he knew of. Even out of the water, a big shark was damned dangerous.

Rodrigue checked the hull for damage. On the starboard side there was a small puncture surrounded by a spiderweb crack in the gel coat. It looked too much like a bullet hole to actually be one, he decided. It could have happened when the boat shifted against the platform just now. Otherwise the Wellcraft was sound. Lucky. Much larger boats than this had been sunk by slamming against offshore platforms in rough weather.

Of course this one wouldn't sink easily. It was small enough and new enough to have Coast Guard–required flotation built into the hull. He would have to burn it, as Greathouse suggested. But first he had to figure out how to get back aboard his own boat.

Rodrigue looked at the rig hook hanging on the crossbeam overhead. Might hold him. Sure it would. But did he have the oomph to shinny up it? He looked down into the tan water. If one trait characterized former commercial divers it was that they did not jump overboard at the slightest provocation. And even a bold diver wasn't likely to linger on the surface when the visibility was bad—especially around a platform. That was asking for a nasty, V-shaped bite from a lurking barracuda that might mistake him for a big fish. A 'cuda wouldn't eat him, but there he'd be, spilling blood where a lot of blood had already been spilled. And where big sharks had been caught—

The Wellcraft's ignition key was still jutting out of the switch in the console. Rodrigue gave it a twist and the Mercury started right up.

He didn't like it but he hadn't expected to like it. Even very rich men like Buck Greathouse didn't pay people two thousand dollars to enjoy themselves. Maybe the outboard had been flooded.

There were a lot of loose maybes floating about and Rodrigue simply quit worrying about them. He eased the Wellcraft out from under the platform and took the up-current route around. If the outboard quit on him, he would drift back toward the platform and the *Queen*. It would not do to be adrift in somebody else's bloody boat.

In the anchor locker in the bow there was about a hundred feet of half-inch polypropylene—fine for a light-weather anchor line had there been enough of it, but not so great for towing. Rodrigue passed it through the two bow cleats and tied a loop with a bowline, then he hopped onto the Whaler with the coil. It would serve until he could put some distance between him and the platform.

Before casting off he made another sweep with his ancient telescope, picking up a crew boat heading in from another field to the east. Unless its skipper was watching his radar closely—and there was no reason for him to in the middle of a clear day—he wouldn't see the two small boats leave the One Seventy-four. Rodrigue plodded southeast with the Wellcraft in tow for a half hour. Then he got out the telescope again, saw some shipping and an ocean-going tug with a barge but nothing to worry about, so he hopped back aboard the Wellcraft and quickly fitted it with a bridle that encircled the hull and a nylon line for some high-speed towing, his specialty.

It was nearly four o'clock when Rodrigue reached the spot he had picked, a place that satisfied all of Greathouse's requirements without being anywhere near where Greathouse had suggested. Once again, he glassed the horizon. It was crucial this time—the gas in the Wellcraft's tank would go off and probably send a flame thirty feet in the air. When he was satisfied it was still all clear, he hauled in the derelict and boarded it with the jerry can.

The Wellcraft's deck was still sticky where the blood was thickest, and it still had a smell like putrid bacon despite the considerable airing-out he had given it. Rodrigue didn't feel good about this boat. Somehow blowing it to little glass splinters seemed the right thing to do. He salvaged the Lone Stars from the cooler and sloshed the Wellcraft steam to stern with gasoline.

Back aboard the *Queen* he set the Wellcraft adrift and

unceremoniously hit it with a twenty-five-millimeter flare. It went up with a hot, roaring *FOOM!* In three minutes the weight of the outboard lifted the melted, blackened slab of hull from the water at a forty-five-degree angle. Exposed to the air, it continued to burn for another minute or two and then slipped beneath the surface.

Rodrigue idled forward and ran a tight grid pattern, shifting his attention between the loran's digital read-out and the Lowrance X-15 chart recorder. The stylus burned a narrow band, representing the Gulf floor on the moving ribbon of paper. Suddenly it became excited and sketched what looked like a denuded Christmas tree, and Rodrigue noted the coordinates on the loran. As he had expected, the hull was sticking bow-up. If the currents left it alone, it might be a good place to pick up a few snapper when he was in the neighborhood.

He fetched his loran log from its hiding place within the padded seatback of the helm seat. In it he recorded both the Wellcraft's state registration—the TX number—and the loran coordinates using his usual code, adding two to each digit and discarding the extra ones when the total came to ten or eleven. To decode, he would simply insert ones before each one and zero, and subtract two down the line. It wouldn't fool a CIA computer long enough for its tubes to warm up, but certain unscrupulous charter boat captains and spearfishermen of his acquaintance were dense enough to sink in a parking lot.

He hid the log again, smoothing the hidden Velcro seam. He opened one of the salvaged Lone Stars—it was warm, but what the hell—settled on the seat, and shoved the throttles forward. Favoring his sore knee, he positioned himself to use his weight on the wheel, fighting the torque of the big Evinrudes as they hummed along at 5,000 rpm.

The *Monroe* was still wallowing around in the Roads.

Her skipper hailed the speeding Whaler on Channel 16 and at the same time Rodrigue saw a forty-one-footer break off and head toward him. As it drew near, he was surprised to see an investigator he knew, Charlie Hagan. Rodrigue had occasional dealings with Coast Guard Investigations—friendly dealings usually, and he considered Hagan a friend, although they didn't go to each other's parties. He was in his early thirties, with a thick dark-blond beard that parted down his chin and a close-cropped Ivy League haircut. He fussed over his pipe like a professor and he had a sense of humor like a pallbearer, which Rodrigue figured was just part of being from Maine.

"Where the devil have you been, Rod?" Hagan asked when he boarded the *Haulover Queen*. The familiarity eased the tension and the petty officer who had boarded first lowered the short, ugly snout of his Winchester Model 1200 riot gun. Rodrigue had boarded boats when he didn't know the score and he felt almost as good for the young coastie as he did for himself.

"I've been out looking for something that resembles the goddamned Gulf of Mexico. Seen it?"

Hagan laughed humorlessly. "You didn't happen to run into a ghost boat out there, did you? About an eighteen- or twenty-foot open outboard?"

"*Ghost* boat?"

"Nobody on it. Possibly adrift."

Rodrigue's guts were churning and he had flutters in his upper arms. "Don't you suppose I'd have lassoed such a vessel and claimed salvage on her? What's the deal?"

"Can't go into it. Not our deal."

A third coastie boarded, glanced at the jerry can lashed to the mast, then ducked inside the *Queen's* house for a look around. A gas can shouldn't seem out of

25

place aboard a rescue boat, Rodrigue thought. The petty officer with the shotgun stood back by the idling motors, keeping the weapon handy.

"Well, you see what we're into here," Hagan said. "We think the guys in the ghost boat were involved somehow. Something turns up, you let me know, okay?"

He turned and stepped back onto the forty-one-footer and disappeared inside. Rodrigue saw him again through the windows on the bridge with a coffee mug in his hand, talking to the skipper.

The two coasties remained aboard and continued the search. Finding nothing they went over the usual check-list of life jackets and other required safety equipment, then they cut him loose and the forty-one-footer turned back for the *Monroe*.

Rodrigue's hand was shaking as he reached for the control binnacle. The sky over the Bolivar Peninsula was growing dark. He jammed the throttles forward, shot up on plane, and went airborne over the wake of the forty-one-footer, rounding Fort Point into the Galveston Channel in a skipping slide.

The careless ride cooled him off. By the time he throttled back and rode his own wake past the yacht basin's breakwater—just as the first fat drops of rain spattered on the windshield—Rodrigue was able to assess the situation calmly:

He had been stupid. Sloppy. Too damned anxious to make some cash.

And Buck Greathouse had played him like a fiddle.

CHAPTER 3

It was more than the usual evening thundershower. The rain had wind in it. It swept across the vacant parking lot in big gray sheets and rattled loudly on the high steel roof over the pier. Rodrigue liked it. Bad weather was a good excuse for some craziness.

He didn't have any particular craziness in mind, but that was okay too. Rodrigue knew he had a tendency to rush headlong into bad situations. Better to bat it around awhile.

He hosed the saltwater off the *Haulover Queen* with deliberate care. With a hydrometer he checked the Sears DieHard deep-cycle battery that ran the *Queen's* loran, VHF and CB radios, and both chart and digital-readout depth finders. The Evinrudes had only six-amp alternators and Rodrigue preferred to reserve their output for the two twelve-volt starting batteries. If he was going to run out of juice at sea, he preferred losing his electronics to losing his outboards.

The battery checked out 50 percent so he hooked up the trickle charger and stood for a minute trying to think of anything else that needed doing. There was nothing, so he strolled slowly, favoring his sore knee, around the dock to A Row.

Greathouse's boat seemed vacant. It was a fifty-foot Hatteras convertible with a full tuna tower, outriggers, and fighting chair—a plush summer home where you could catch a thousand-pound fish off the back porch. Rodrigue stepped lightly—as lightly as he could—into the cockpit. The thundering rain on the metal overhead deadened any noise he made. He tried the door to the saloon. It was locked. To the right was the bait-rigging station, a counter with drawers that contained the big plastic trolling lures and other tackle for marlin fishing. In the top a small sink was full of coiled monofilament leaders and hooks. Rodrigue picked one up and examined it thoroughly, then another. The thick plastic line had dozens of small nicks and cuts in it. The leaders had both been used, changed out, coiled neatly, and set aside.

Against the bulkhead was a wood rack that held a half dozen thin-bladed fillet knives. Rodrigue absently slid one out and tested its edge with his thumb while he gazed around. Abruptly he replaced the knife, leaned out of the cockpit, and rubbed his finger around the fuel fill. If the boat had been recently topped off, it would be greasy with spilt diesel; it wasn't. Topside, the bridge was enclosed in clear vinyl weather curtains, all zipped up and buttoned down.

He was looking for anything that suggested the *Wahoo Too* had been readied to go fishing. If that had been the case, he knew all he would have to do was wait and Greathouse would come huffing and puffing into his clutches. But it looked more like she was battened down for the winter. Wormed into his corporate labyrinth in Houston, Greathouse wouldn't be so easy to ferret out.

28

And what would he do with him when he found him? Ask him some hard questions. Anything beyond that would depend on the answers. Go *slow,* maan, Rodrigue reminded himself in his Belizean Creole.

He went to the pay phones near the bait camp and got the number of Greathouse's main store from the information operator. He finally reached a secretary who said Mr. Greathouse was not available. She wouldn't give out any other numbers, not for the car phone nor his home. Rodrigue gave her his name and number. No urgency, he said, just an old friend trying to get in touch. He tried information again, just in case, but Greathouse's residence was unlisted at the customer's request. Naturally.

Rodrigue went into the bait camp and helped himself to an icy beer from the old-fashioned metal cooler in the back, the kind that used to dispense soft drinks at filling stations on two-lane country roads. Except for Brezinski, Taylor, and Ed Smedstad, another B Row bum, the place was empty. Rodrigue joined them at the wooden picnic table and listened to speculation on whether the rain would clear the water or just dump more muddy runoff into it. Brezinski and Taylor were divided (but amicably) and Smedstad couldn't make up his mind. Nobody mentioned anything about an abandoned boat or a drug shakedown—nobody had been offshore lately. Finally he got another beer for the road and went into the downpour, still limping slightly.

He drove slowly along the seawall, enjoying the texture rain gave to the rising swells. It quit abruptly as he turned into Sea Isle so he walked to the water's edge to enjoy the righteous anger of the Gulf as it can only be enjoyed from solid ground. It was like standing at an open refrigerator, but he missed the tang of salt. He trudged back, hurrying to beat the new wall of rain sweeping down the beach. He kicked off his sand-caked shoes under the house and went up for a long hot shower. He pulled on a pair of dark gray slacks, a crisp white guayabera, and slipped sockless into a dry pair of leather Top-Siders. Whether it rained for a day or a week—and whatever Buck Greathouse might have done—there would be a broiled flounder waiting for him at Hill's Old Original Seafood House.

The wind had died and the rain was cascading, giving Seawall Boulevard a fuzzy glow under the streetlights. Probably because of the rain, the restaurant was nearly empty. Rodrigue was disappointed. He craved the clatter of silverware and the tinkle of ice and the soothing hum of about two dozen conversations with his supper. He detoured into the lounge for a little cheering up.

A small crowd of office types over in the corner appeared to be stranded and using the rain for a little craziness of their own. Someone said, "Plug it in! Plug it in!"—apparently the punchline of a running joke—and the thirtyish men and women were reduced to gasping and wiping away tears. Rodrigue watched them over his shoulder, grinning.

From the other side of the bar came a high, musical, "Hi!" He turned back and looked into a friendly face with a dazzling smile, and eyes that crinkled at the edges and seemed so unguarded and bold, searching his face with questioning that seemed to go beyond wadayawant—high cheekbones, short light brown hair that took care of itself—an instant of beauty frozen in the twinkle of bar glasses.

"Beer," he said, because he had to say something.

"Sure," she said, patting the space on the bar in front of him comfortingly. She turned and expertly drew a draught in a tall glass. No bored spiel of brand names. Man wants beer, man gets beer. Rodrigue was impressed.

She frowned with the concentration of keeping the foam down, and he could see then she was nearing forty. That interested him too. A woman doesn't keep such a fresh smile for nearly forty years by having a bad attitude. Great tan too, the kind that takes years to accumulate. It probably caused her to look older than she was sometimes, like when she frowned. That and the hair and the unleashed smile told Rodrigue that here was a lady who lived for today. His kind of gal.

She slid the beer before him and smiled again. It seemed wonderfully unselfish of her.

"You have an interesting face," Rodrigue said.

"You do too," she said in a tone of mild surprise, as though an interesting face was the last thing in the world she expected to encounter at work today. "I haven't seen you in here before. What's your name?"

"John Rodrigue." He offered his hand and she simply held it, softly, for a moment. "I live down at Sea Isle." Island residents always identified themselves up front. It was a useful form of snobbery.

"Rod-*reeg?* Is that Spanish? Like Rodriguez?"

"Several hundred years ago it was Rodriguez. Some of my relatives had a falling out with Spain during the Inquisition. They were in the Caribbean for a long time, then Louisiana. Rodrigue is just a French version of Rodriguez. My great-great-great-"—he counted on his fingers—"great-great-great-grandfather changed it. To thumb his nose at the king of Spain, I suppose."

"Oh, you're a Cajun then, huh? I wondered where that accent was from."

"Creole actually, but it's an awfully small difference. It has to do with where we started and not where we are. And you? I say Florida."

A faint look of panic washed through her face. Rodrigue had said Florida because that's where all the strangers with great tans came from—there or California, and she, God bless her, was no California girl. The look said she was on the run. He resolved to keep all the usual innocent questions out of his small talk.

But business was slow and she volunteered the answers—or at least answers. Her name was Sandra Carson—Sandy, which went with the hair. She and a friend named Sarah had moved to Galveston three months ago. From Florida, naturally.

The lounge got busier and the new customers drew Sandy away from him. Gazing appreciatively at the flare of her hips as she served a table, Rodrigue had an inspiration. He always did his best thinking when his brain was deprived of blood, he imagined. He rose to find a phone.

The public phone inside the restaurant was *too* public. It was right between the cash register and the maitre d' station. He went outside, dug a slicker from beneath the seat of the Blazer, and splashed across the parking lot to the pay phones out by the street. Huddled against the rain, he dialed a number from memory and gave the operator his own for billing.

"City desk," an impatient voice answered.

"Mike Ferguson there?"

City desk had nothing more to say to Rodrigue. He heard the voice, away from the phone, yelling for Ferguson. There was a click and the phone went dead for a second, then Ferguson answered, "Yeah."

"It's Rod."

"Hey, Rod," Ferguson said irritably. "You just caught me. I'm trying to get out of here before the goddamned parking lot floods. What's up?"

"Could be I'm in a little trouble here. I need a little research done without any questions being asked for the time being."

The phone was silent.

"Well?"

Ferguson was not the kind who did favors. But he was nosy. He had made a profession of being nosy. "Is there anything in it for me?" he said finally.

32

"Very probably. There's what you might call a mover-and-shaker involved."

"My meat."

"Uh-huh."

"So?"

"So find out about a couple of guys missing in the Gulf. Shark fishermen in a small boat. Probably overdue today sometime. I don't have any idea where they would've launched but I would assume Galveston or Bolivar or Texas City. Write down the TX number." Rodrigue gave him the derelict's registration number from memory. Then: "You know Charlie Hagan?"

"I don't believe I do."

"Well, you need to. He's in Coast Guard Investigations. I got stopped coming in the jetties this evening along with every crew boat, shrimp boat, and supply boat in Galveston. Dope shakedown. Charlie told me the boat was missing and that it might be tied up in a dope deal somehow. He did *not* tell me the TX number, though, so be careful, eh? Could be the news isn't out yet. When I get myself clear of it, I'll let you in on how the mover-and-shaker's involved—once I find out for sure myself, that is."

"Isn't that more in my line?"

"It is but like I said, I've got to get clear of it first."

"Where can I reach you? Tomorrow around noon, say."

"I have no idea," Rodrigue said. He had another inspiration: "If you've got something and you need me to call you, leave a message with Sandy in the lounge at Hill's on Seawall Boulevard. You know, the restaurant. But don't go into any great detail, now. I should be home by evening."

Mike Ferguson made a living out of embarrassing the rich and powerful, inasmuch as his newspaper would let him. He also liked to fish when he didn't have to buy the bait and to drink when he didn't have to buy the beer, so he was Rodrigue's buddy. Rodrigue went back to the bar and drew a few more beatific smiles from the mellow Florida beach bunny before ambling into the dining room for his flounder.

In the gray dawn of the next morning, a clap of thunder woke him up. He felt the weight of a long brown leg on his, an arm over his chest, and soft, shaggy hair cuddled against his neck. She had been hungry, practically cannibal, and it would have scared him if it had not been for the smile. And the little crinkles around her eyes. And the eyes—green-flecked gray with just a touch of almond shape to them. Twice she had stared at him and the eyes went serious and he felt like she loved him more than anything else on earth. But of course that was silly. They didn't even know each other.

He would have been perfectly satisfied to put in a few more appearances at the lounge before making his move. She had picked *him* up, using as a pretext an insatiable desire to sit out by the Gulf.

"At night, when there aren't many lights, it's like the ocean rises up and envelops you," she had said, heaving a sigh.

"Yes," he said slyly. "It draws out these atavistic passions."

"Atavistic?" She shrank back in mock suspicion.

"Primitive," he promised, loosing his broad, even grin.

"Hmmm, I *am* a passionate woman . . ." Now teetering on feigned indecision.

They had gone by her apartment, and she ran in and told her roomie she had scored, then they went out to his place and sat under the Cinzano umbrella in the rain-washed air, drinking a too-sweet wine she liked, and then finally they fell into bed as through they had been engaged for a month. But they were still total strangers.

He gave her a hug and she stirred, turning sleepy gray eyes up at him. "Hoo!" she said. "I *slept!*"

She stretched and Rodrigue rubbed her back.

"You hit me pretty hard last night," he said. They had been physically intimate. Now he just wanted to be intimate.

The soft shaggy mop raised and the eyes focused. *"Hit you?"*

"Staggered me. Grabbed me by the soul. I don't know what I mean. Instant attraction, I guess."

She laid her head down again and he could feel the smile broadening against his chest. "And you were thinking, is she this sweet to everybody?"

"Uh-huh, I guess so."

She looked up again. "Define 'everybody.'"

He laughed.

"C'mon now, this is a test."

"How about 'anybody special'?"

"Maybe," she said, teasingly, running her fingertip around his nipple. "Depends on what you call 'special.'"

Rodrigue sighed. "I guess I'm hoping to fall somewhere between 'love of your life' and 'la cola de la cola'— the tail end of the line."

She smiled, and anything she said afterward would've been okay.

"You're in luck," she said. "Actually, you kind of struck me too. I mean it. You have this way of cocking your head and staring funny, like you don't *believe* what's going on. It's cute. Sort of like a little boy all made up like Bluto or something. Remember Bluto?"

Rodrigue chuckled.

"He was the big bully on the Popeye cartoons, remember that? I think he even had a tattoo on his arm like you. 'Course you don't have the beard—"

"I have a glass eye," he said.

"C'mon!"

"Well, actually it's acrylic. My left one. Look, it's brown and the right's this muddy-looking green. That's why I hold my head that way sometimes, because my peripheral vision doesn't go past my nose."

She rose on her knees and looked at one eye, then the other. The truth was evident. She squealed with laughter and put her face in her lap, gasping and turning red down to her shoulders.

"I'm so *embarrassed!*" she said when she finally had breath. "God, I hope I didn't hurt your feelings."

"Nah. Hell, I used to pop it out and drop it in people's drinks, just for kicks. They'd go to take a drink and there'd be this eye staring at them. I had to quit it, though. Burned too much when I put it back in."

She was in hysterics again. Rodrigue pulled her over himself as he would the covers, rocking with her laughter and tasting the salt on her cheeks. She grew quiet and molded her body to his.

"Mmmmmmmmmm," she purred, stretching her arms out along his until her fingertips reached his palms. His erection filled her as it formed and soon they were making love again, in slow motion. In stop-action.

"It was the smile," he said, "that got me."

She folded her arms on his chest, propped her chin up, and poured those velvety gray eyes all over him. "I think you're going to be a 'somebody special.'"

And then she kissed him so tenderly that he almost believed her.

He gave her the abandoned Wellcraft's registration number and in just a few seconds she gave him a name and an address in Baytown, a community nestled among refineries on the Houston Ship Channel. Through long-distance information, the name produced a phone number. Rodrigue dialed: busy. He dialed: busy. He dialed: busy. Finally he called the operator, who switched him to another operator who told him the phone he was trying to make ring was in use and was his call an emergency?

No, he said, and hung up. He went back into the store and bought a twelve-pack of Miller Lite and a bag of ice. He iced the beer down in a small Gott cooler he kept in the Blazer and set a course for Baytown.

On the causeway leaving Galveston Island, he noticed an orange Duster topping the rise over the Gulf Intracoastal Waterway less than a quarter of a mile behind him—big wheels bulging out at the sides. It got his attention because that Duster should've been way out front by now, and because what the hell was a car like that doing coming out of the Bob Smith Yacht Club in the first place? He rode the rearview all the way to the turnoff at Highway 146.

But when he took the exit, the Duster kept going up the Gulf Freeway. So he figured . . .

There were only three ways off Galveston Island by car: the Bolivar Ferry, which put you on the road for High Island and points east; the toll bridge at the western end leading to Freeport; and the causeway, which spawned the Gulf Freeway to Houston and the world. Probably 90 percent of the traffic came and went on the causeway. That narrowed the coincidence somewhat.

So maybe the driver of the Duster had to stop and make a few calls himself and that's why he had fallen behind.

Or maybe there were *two* orange Dusters with big wheels in Galveston. And maybe one of them belonged

41

to the son of a member of the yacht club. There's no accounting for taste. And in any case, who cared? What did he have to fear from anyone who drove an orange Duster with big wheels?

He opened another beer and tuned the radio to KTSU-FM. The static didn't turn to jazz until he was nearly to Baytown.

The address the woman in Austin had given him was in an old neighborhood of narrow streets, frame houses with big trees in the yards, and pickup trucks driven by refinery workers in faded Levis and cowboy shirts with mother-of-pearl snaps. In front of the house was a patrol car of some kind, local police or sheriff's office—Rodrigue couldn't read the door emblem—parked behind a five-year-old Ford LTD. There were two pickups in the driveway. Rodrigue stopped in the next block and watched.

Another car arrived. A couple got out and walked slowly up the lawn—the short, thick woman forging ahead in a wobbly stride, the man holding her arm and taking measured steps to match hers, his face aimed at the ground. He was close to sixty, with a gray crewcut and crisp-looking slacks and sport shirt. She wore a dress and carried a big black purse as though it didn't weigh much—Sunday clothes, both of them, and this wasn't Sunday. They looked glum. Rodrigue put the Blazer in gear, hooked a left, and went on back to the highway.

They were having company at that house and it wasn't a bar mitzvah. He stopped at a convenience store and bought a Bayton *Sun*—two men were in critical condition after an explosion and fire at a local chemical refinery; an earthquake measuring seven on the Richter scale hit El Salvador, damaging the U.S, embassy and killing at least a dozen Salvadorans in the capital city. But there was no mention of Baytown citizens missing at sea. No missing boat, no dope investigation, nothing. Nothing to do but head for home.

The only thing Rodrigue knew for sure was that Greathouse had lied to him. He might have a friend who owned an eighteen-foot outboard boat, but not one who lived in a blue-collar neighborhood in Baytown.

Something bad had happened out there in that little boat. It might not have had anything to do with dope but it was bad, whatever it was. And the newspapers either didn't know anything about it, or—

Bingo. Rodrigue emerged from the Baytown Tunnel and accelerated onto the stretch that wound south along the western bayshore toward Galveston Island. He reached back for another beer and popped it in celebration. When he got home he put on his tropical khaki suit and the British regimental tie he had taken in trade for his South African naval officer's cap one drunken evening in the tiny bar at the Hotel Mopan. He had finally come up with something crazy to do.

CHAPTER 5

Petroleum Helicopters, Inc., operated from a small clapboard building in a jungle of oleanders beside the new terminal at Scholes Field—or Galveston Municipal, as the former army air base was officially called. Rodrigue moved into the yellow light of the porch and knocked on the door. It opened and a man in clean faded khakis stood in the doorway, leaning on a large push broom. He couldn't have been much older than forty but he looked wasted, with a wino's rutted face.

"Mike Ferguson," Rodrigue announced. "Houston *Post.*"

The man at the door turned his head and said into the room, "Some newspaperman from Houston." His body blocked the view inside. Rodrigue heard a reply but he couldn't make it out. He looked back at Rodrigue and said, "Wadaya want?"

"I want to ask the dispatcher some questions about dispatching helicopters," Rodrigue said.

He looked puzzled.

"We're doing a story on night dispatchers. Police. Ambulance. Fire trucks. Cabs. Helicopters. I just want to ask a few simple questions."

"Sminit."

He left the door and Rodrigue stepped inside uninvited. The man in khakis was leaning over talking to a man with long scraggly hair seated at a table lined with radios. Then they both looked up at him and Rodrigue could see the dispatcher's beard and the bored eyes that showed age. On his T-shirt was a circle with a toes-down crow's foot in it—the peace symbol of the sixties. Block letters above it said FERGIT HELL!

A *hippie!* Rodrigue thought with a surprising rush of nostalgia. There were some free spirits around the yacht basin, white pseudo-Rastamen and calypso rednecks in the Buffett mold, but he had wondered where all the real old-time genuine card-burning hippies had gone. Well, here was one who still showed the colors, even though he was dispatching establishment helicopters to establishment oil rigs.

The hippie evidently didn't have the same tender feelings toward him. With a look of disgusted resignation, he motioned Rodrigue in. He clumsily worked his chair around to face the visitor, and Rodrigue saw he had but a leg and a half.

"'Nam?" he guessed.

The dispatcher lowered his eyelids for an instant. It served as a nod. In a quick motion Rodrigue took out his prosthetic eye and popped it into his mouth. From long practice he held it in puckered lips with the phony brown iris looking out, so that he had a peculiar, lopsided stare.

"Nangh," he said around the eye.

The dispatcher liked the trick so much he nearly fell out of his chair.

Rodrigue had left the regimental tie knotted loosely

because that's the way Ferguson wore his ties. But he had gargled with Listerine to erase the beer smell while Ferguson often smelled like a bar rag at closing time. Rodrigue figured a helicopter dispatcher would expect a reporter to be a little sloppy, but he wouldn't expect him to reek of beer.

Especially when he reeked of beer, Ferguson liked to lecture on investigative reporting. The night shift was a good source of information, he said, because all the office restraints were relaxed after the day workers went home, and because often the night crew harbored a little resentment against management. And you could better capitalize on this if you were there in person—best of all if you could wrangle a cup of their coffee and look like you needed it—than if you were just a voice on the telephone.

When the dispatcher recovered, Rodrigue softened him up a little more with some alumni talk, not about war but about R&R in Hono. Happy times.

And he softened himself up in the bargain. He couldn't bring himself to continue the Ferguson charade, so he told the dispatcher, who was still smiling at some long-buried memory, that he had lied, that he was a private citizen with a private reason for wanting to find the man who flew pumpers out to the production platform in Galveston Block One Seventy-four.

The smile vanished. "I ain't gonna be able to help you much," he said, making a nervous move back to the company's radios. He halted and looked up at Rodrigue with earnestness in the tired eyes. "It's looking pretty bad, though. You just remember—you ain't been here."

"Don't even know where this place is. What do you mean it's looking pretty bad?"

"It's looking like those dudes are dead. And now that boat's turned up missing. You're playing with someone that plays hardball, man."

"Not me. I was just hired by a guy to find out what's going on. He was headed in from offshore and saw a boat with nobody on it tied at the rig, but he just kept on going. Didn't even call the Coast Guard. First thing they do is instruct you to stand by, and you know how long that can take—or, hell, maybe you don't—but anyway this guy got to feeling guilty and wanted to find out what happened. Without getting mixed up in it."

Ferguson hadn't needed to tell Rodrigue that honesty was always the best policy, even if you had to fake it.

But the hippie wasn't buying it 100 percent. He cocked his head and looked at Rodrigue out of the corners of his eyes. "Hey, man, I don't *care,* dig? If you and your buddy're clean, go talk to Virgil Chapman. But if you were expecting a package, stay the hell away from Chapman. And keep *me* out of it in any case."

"Virgil Chapman?"

"One of our pilots. Flew all the trips to that platform, including the extra one with the Coast Guard."

Rodrigue felt his palms getting damp. "Coast Guard went out there? When?"

"Start of my shift yesterday." He looked at his log. "Left the ground at 1742."

Rodrigue thought back to the moment Charlie Hagan stepped aboard the *Queen.* Was there anything off-key in his manner? No, he decided, nothing he could recall. Hagan was a pretty cool character, but Rodrigue wouldn't expect him to be *that* cool if he suspected something. Besides, the Wellcraft was on the bottom by the time the chopper went up.

"This Chapman guy—Vietnam vet?"

The dispatcher grinned wearily. "Probably Korean War. Solid fuckin' citizen. Deacon in the church and the whole bit."

"How about giving me his home phone and address?"

"No problem, long as you don't say where you got it."

"Don't worry about that. And you remember too—I ain't been here, eh?"

Chapman lived on Tiki Island, a bayfront development on the mainland that was a labyrinth of canals. Every home had a boathouse or landing behind it. Rodrigue called first, stopping to use a pay phone on 61st Street. With the beer buzz gone, he had lost faith in his ability to impersonate a journalist, so he changed his story. He told Chapman he was an investigator named, whimsically, Throckmorton, doing legwork for Ferguson. He apologized for the hour, blathered about deadlines, and asked if he could come over. Chapman wasn't exactly delighted, but he agreed to see Rodrigue if he could make it to his place in thirty minutes.

Chapman owned a Grady White, a center console fishing skiff like the Wellcraft but larger, fancier, more expensive. Rodrigue could see it hanging in slings, pearly white in the yard lights, as he rounded the house to meet Chapman out back the way he was instructed. Rod holders on the side of the boat's steering console were full of what looked like custom-wrapped trout rods.

The wind had shifted back to light southeast. The night air was muggy and a violet bug zapper was steadily humming with the impact of mosquitoes. Rodrigue was raking them off his neck.

"Here, use this," Chapman said, stepping out of the shadow of a short covered walk between the main house and a utility room. He had a can of Deep Wood Off in his hand. Rodrigue took it gratefully.

Chapman's face was two-toned from wearing a cap and sunglasses all the time. He had a square jaw and slits for eyes. Eyes like Roy Rogers. Eyes that looked like they meant business. He wore cardboard-stiff khakis and a big stainless Rolex and his iron-gray hair was cropped in the military fashion. His bearing made Rodrigue instantly uneasy.

He looked about Rodrigue's age. He had probably seen 'Nam, all right, but Rodrigue sensed they might not have the same feelings about the experience—might not have had the same experience, period, because of the enormous gap between the enlisted mess and the officers' wardroom. So instead of the alumni bit, Rodrigue admired the Grady White and drew him into a conversation about fishing, trying to put him at ease without making him feel the pinch of time.

It was working. Chapman loosened up a little—he apologized for making him come around back, said he still had young ones at home and it upset their routine if visitors came late. Rodrigue could imagine a young, very pretty wife and a home "routine" like the plan of the day at Pensacola Naval Air Station. He decided to get on with it.

"Actually, Mike already has the story," he said. "But his boss is a careful one and he wants me to get some more corroboration. To *my* satisfaction, he said, so I don't have to speak your name to a soul. I wouldn't come out here at this hour for an interview, but if the facts all jive, I'd love to put this baby to bed." Newspaper talk.

"Yes, I suspect Ferguson's editor *would* be a careful one. I'm familiar with his work." It wasn't a compliment.

"Well, if you don't mind, let's start with what you saw out there."

"I noticed the boat when we came in, and I thought it was odd. The water was dirty and there weren't many boats that close inshore—you seldom see one at that platform anyway. The fishing's apparently not that good there. I don't do any offshore fishing myself. At any rate, Alley went down to do his work and I remained topside with the aircraft. Alley came back and said there wasn't

49

any personnel on the boat, and they didn't seem to be on the rig either. I hadn't noticed that the boat was unmanned, being kept fairly busy as we made our approach."

"And this Alley is the pumper, right?"

Chapman's mouth broadened by a quarter of an inch. "Alfred McWherter. Jesus, what a case of short cables."

"Short cables?"

"Nervous. Jumpiest individual I've ever seen. I've always suspected it was the flying, but apparently he had something to be nervous about."

"Yeah? What's that?"

Chapman's slit eyes bored into Rodrigue for a moment. "You haven't gotten very deep into this, have you?"

Rodrigue felt what remained of his confidence oozing out so he did just what Ferguson would do under the circumstances. He got huffy. "Look, it's real complicated. It involves some angles that you're probably not aware of. I'm afraid that what you're doing is assuming some things that really aren't the way they seem. If you would please stick to what you *know* for a fact, I'll be through in just a second."

"Yes, well, I know for a fact that McWherter is AWOL," Chapman fired back. "And I know for a fact that the Drug Enforcement Administration and the Federal Bureau of Investigation as well as the Coast Guard are looking pretty hard at this thing. Especially since when I hauled them back out there for a look, the boat was gone. You didn't know *that* did you, Ace?"

"Gone? Uh, no, I didn't know that. You say McWherter went over the hill? Tell you the truth, I didn't know that either. What's he look like?"

"Nervous. Tall and—"

Rodrigue guessed: "Skinny and redheaded?"

"That's him."

"And he's from Galveston?"

"Pearland. We're not *corroborating* very much here, are we?"

"Sure we are. Lots of stuff. Have any idea where this McWherter might've gone?"

"I believe we're going to put this in the hangar right here, Mr., uh, Throckmorton. I've lost sight of your purpose."

"I told you, my pur—"

"Good-*night*, Mr. Throckmorton."

He stood there looking like he had slid down intact from Mount Rushmore. Rodrigue smiled, saluted languidly, and turned without another word.

On the way out of Tiki, he saw that same orange Duster parked in the shadows under one of the houses. It could've belonged there, but he didn't really believe it. The house was dark and the Duster was backed in, ready to roll. Rodrigue eased on out and instead of heading for Galveston, he took the Gulf Freeway north toward Houston. The freeway was lighted along this section. Rodrigue checked his rearview mirror and saw the Duster rolling down the overpass about five cars behind.

Rodrigue flashed his shark-grin. Big tires or not, no Plymouth Duster can stay on the tail of a Chevy Blazer. Not when it's been raining.

CHAPTER 6

The Duster stayed well behind. Rodrigue got a glimpse of it as he changed to the inside lane, then lost sight of it again as he crested the overpass where diverging highways wrapped themselves underneath the Gulf Freeway. Just up the freeway was a deep, gullylike median of sodden grass. Rodrigue geared down, kicked the Blazer into four-wheel drive, and careened dangerously down the grassy slope, cutting deep ruts up the other side but merging smoothly with the southbound traffic.

The Duster was just cresting the overpass. The driver must've spotted him—the Duster's brake lights winked on and off and the car yawed a little before picking up speed again. There was nothing else he could do. He sure wasn't going to get that Duster across that soupy median, and it was two or three miles up to the next crossover.

It had to be some goon Greathouse hired to keep tabs on him. Greathouse was rough-hewn and ruthless but if

It reopened, wider, and Sandy appeared. She sighed and looked exasperated and amused at the same time. They stared at each other through the screen.

"I was beginning to think I had scared you off," she said finally.

"Arr, I don't scares easy," said Long John. (Or was it Bluto?)

She banged the screen door open and molded herself to him. "I missed you," she said into his neck, giving him a tight squeeze.

He held her close and spoke to the dusty spiderwebs on the ceiling of the wide porch. "I kind of missed you too." He felt a puzzling urge to draw back, but he conquered it.

She looked up and smiled. "I didn't know if I had put out the right kind of signals, you know?"

"I love it when you talk dirty," he said, figuring she would say what she meant eventually.

"C'mon in, I want you to meet Sarah."

"Are you sure? She seemed pretty shy."

"She wasn't dressed. Sarah, you dressed?" Sandy yelled.

Sarah was struggling with the last button of a pair of tight blue-jean cutoffs. High, firm breasts were molded in her white T-shirt with enough detail to attract Rodrigue's lingering gaze. But she seemed awfully young.

They were living in one of those tall frame houses in the old part of Galveston, a neighborhood of wide verandas sloped with age, shuttered French windows, and jungles of bougainvilleas—the look of some of the seedier neighborhoods in the Garden District of New Orleans. Inside, the apartment was a mess, clothes and records and books scattered all over.

"We used to live aboard a boat where everything has its place and now we're inclined to spread things out," Sandy said without apology.

"Are you really a professional diver?" asked Sarah.

Rodrigue recognized the diver-as-hero syndrome cultivated by the scuba boys. But the girl was plainly suspicious. What kind of hero has gray in his hair and a built-in inner tube around his waist?

"Retired," Rodrigue said.

"Oh," she said, disappointed. She spat on an electric iron. The ironing board seemed part of the decor.

"I tried to call you last night," Sandy said suddenly. "I was horny." She smiled seductively.

For once he wanted to explain, but he knew better than to start that. He was a conquistador, Rodrigue. Suddenly his mind was filled with a lecherous vision of her splayed beneath him in dazzling sunlight on an open beach.

"You working today?" he asked.

"Just until eleven this morning. Some office work."

"You want to go for a boat ride? I know a secluded beach down the coast a ways." It would be like a much-needed vacation.

"I'd love it! But, uh . . ." She looked at the raven-haired girl with the iron. "I hate to leave Sarah alone. She doesn't know any—"

"Forgive me," said Rodrigue. "Of course Sarah's invited." He turned and lifted the girl's free hand to his lips. Sarah's mouth dropped open and then she looked at the hand Rodrigue had kissed as though it might have changed somehow. "We'll cook hotdogs or something," he said.

Sarah gave him a pouty look and Sandy smiled. "Sure," Sandy said, answering for both of them. "Why not?"

Well, great, thought Rodrigue sourly.

CHAPTER 7

The day was still and hazy and hot. Suffocating. Rodrigue grew uneasy again. There was nothing to do.

Waiting was a bitch. He wasn't suited for it. But it was somebody else's move, either Greathouse or the FBI or somebody. What if Greathouse had skipped the country, along with the redheaded pumper—what was it? McWherter. Here Rodrigue was assuming that Greathouse was hanging on Ferguson's every word and all the while he might not be reading anything more absorbing than menus in Grand Cayman or someplace.

Ferguson was turning the whole mess into a big career move, and the good ol' boys from Baytown were dead as King of Norway sardines. Rodrigue thought of the .45 in his glove compartment and kept his eyes on the rearview mirror. Hadn't he seen that light blue Ford earlier? Couldn't be sure. There were a lot of light blue Fords.

He went by B Row to check on the *Haulover Queen*,

then to the bait camp for a beer and some companion-ship. He had really been looking forward to nailing Sandy to the beach in broad daylight. Maybe they wanted to go three-way, which would be okay except—well, some-thing was wrong with it.

Jerry Taylor had picked up a single-sideband transmis-sion from the *Prettiest Sally* at the West Flower Garden Reef, a coral outcrop 130 miles offshore. The water wasn't exactly blue, Dub had said, but at least they were catching bull dolphin. Maybe there would be a party on B Row after all. In high spirits suddenly, Rodrigue decided to pass by the restaurant early.

The lounge was empty of customers. At the bar, Sandy was head-to-head with a slender man who looked to be in his twenties. They were going over a tape that spilled out of a large adding machine and talking good-naturedly. Rodrigue felt an unfamiliar pang. He would've backed quietly out the door but she spotted him and beamed a smile.

"C'mon in," she called. "I want you to meet Larry. Larry, this is John, the guy I was telling you about."

Larry offered a disdainful smile beneath a thin mus-tache. A real sleaze-ball. Rodrigue would've welcomed an excuse to hit him.

"Beer?" asked Sandy cheerfully.

"No, thanks. Am I interrupting?"

"No, no, not at all," she said. Larry's head wagged smugly. "But I'm afraid this is going to take longer than I expected . . ." She had taken his arm and was steering him toward the door. "The other girl is sick and I have to work the whole shift. Can we go first thing tomorrow? The restaurant's closed on Mondays, you know."

Rodrigue nodded soddenly. He suspected the worst.

When she had maneuvered him far enough not to be overheard by Larry, she said, "I can come out to your

60

place when I get off at ten, though." A naughty wink from the smiling gray eyes.

Great, he thought. The three of them could sleep in his closet—Sandy, Rodrigue, and Rodrigue's big pistol.

"Well, I tell you wot . . ." he said, playfully mimicking the late Bob Marley while his brain concocted lies. "See, I thought we'd be at the beach so I promised an old friend he could use the house to screw his secretary. I was taking too much for granted and I'm plumb sorry."

She laughed and kissed him, a quick peck on the lips. "It's okay. Why don't you just spend the night at our place tonight? We can go from there."

He was relieved and uneasy and anxious and disgusted with himself for letting his emotions run away with him—all at once. Now all he had to do was figure out how to keep from being tailed to her house.

He knew he had no business messing around with a woman at a time like this. He also knew that any time you could was the right time to mess around with a woman like Sandy. There probably wouldn't be any action out of the goon in the orange Duster until Ferguson publicly put the finger on Greathouse. Still, there was no point inviting trouble. He told her to pick him up at the Holiday Inn.

Rodrigue swung down to Sea Isle and hooked up the big EZ Loader behind his Blazer. He rushed back to the yacht basin to beat the Sunday evening crowd and then remembered there was no Sunday evening crowd these days. There were all of three boats ahead of him. He wouldn't have even had to wait except that one guy backed in crooked and took up the whole ramp. But in a short while Rodrigue pulled the *Queen* out and parked it dripping by the back fence. Then he sauntered back to the bait camp under the steady gaze of Bruce Phillips and Jerry Taylor.

"Damn, I'm glad I didn't put my money where my mouth was," Taylor said cryptically.

"It'd get Copenhagen all over it," Rodrigue said. "And then what if I had to tow you someday? Uck!"

"Yours is paid for," said Phillips, squinting through the cigarette smoke that billowed out with his words. He held up his can of beer.

Rodrigue moved quickly through the cool gloom of the bait camp and dug a Lite out of the beer box. He rejoined Phillips and Taylor on the bench outside, waddling his butt to squeeze between them.

"Dub *said* you wouldn't take much more of this before you packed up and headed south," Taylor went on.

Phillips sucked on the last inch of his cigarette in silence. He never pried on his own time.

"Nah," said Rodrigue. "This is the rainy season down there. The only thing good about the rainy season in Belize City is it washes the shit out of the gutters. Literally."

"Hell, divers don't care about the rain. They're gonna get wet anyway."

"It's the goddamned bugs. It's not so bad out in the islands where all the dive resorts are. But I don't exactly do package tours, y'know. I charter right out of downtown Belize City. You know what no-see-ums are? Little fucking gnats. Make these mosquitoes around here feel like a bubble bath."

And then, because they were curious: "Got a seal leaking in my starboard engine. Gonna haul her up to Dickinson to get it fixed. Guy up there owes me."

He would sit there with Taylor and Phillips and whoever took their places—passing judgment on the trailering abilities of the Sunday joyriders with their "fish 'n' ski" boats, commiserating about the dismal prospects for next weekend's tournament, getting slightly drunk—until the bait camp closed. Then he would melt into the aluminum-mast forest and emerge at the Holiday Inn, where he would hold down the corner of the padded fake-leather bar until Sandy got off work and met him out front. Meanwhile there was nothing to do but drink beer and talk about the blue water, way out beyond the Flower Gardens.

Sandy's young roommate was already asleep when they got there. She was on the couch, covered with a sheet that, in the humidity, clung to her like damp tissue paper. Sandy caught him looking and gave him a sly grin, leading him to bed.

The bed wasn't five feet from where she was sleeping but there was no choice, unless they slept in the kitchen or the bathroom. Sandy planted a long, lusty kiss on his mouth and unzipped his fly at the same time. When he arched his eyebrows and cocked his civilian eye toward the sleeping girl, she put a finger to her lips.

"If I start making too much noise," she whispered, "just stop for a minute. Okay?"

Being drunk helped tremendously. Rodrigue was not bashful, but he had begun to suspect the truth and it bothered him. Yet when she coaxed him on top of her, and then asked him in that so-sensible, matter-of-fact voice to please enter her, the Mormon Tabernacle Choir could've been sleeping on the couch for all he cared.

It was the bed that was noisy. It squeaked with their every move, and once they fell into a steady rhythm there could be no mistaking what was going on. Sarah was *too* still. Rodrigue imagined that she was listening. Then he took for granted that she was listening. And then—he took pleasure in the idea. It was like he and Sarah had a thing going. A good, secret thing. It gave him a rush of excitement and Sandy responded with a shuddering climax.

He woke before daylight, dressed, and then gently shook Sandy awake. She got up without a word and pulled the sheet off Sarah, tugging on her leg. The girl's pale nakedness in the dark room swept Rodrigue with a wave of guilt that mingled with a mild hangover. He stepped out on the porch and sniffed the thick, sweet night air while the lights flicked on inside. Still, he was glad she was going with them.

"Listen, girls," he said as he squeezed behind the wheel of Sandy's old green Triumph, "we'll park around back at the Holiday Inn instead of the yacht basin. The car'll be safer there. Y'all can just go through the lobby and wait out front. I'll walk back to the yacht basin and pick up the truck and the boat and swing by for you."

That way anyone who had staked out the Blazer and then followed him would think he was picking up someone staying at the motel. And if they tailed them down to Port O'Connor, they would be burning Buck Greathouse's gas for nothing.

They drove in silence. Sarah slept in the back.

"She's your daughter, isn't she," Rodrigue said softly.

Sandy nodded silently. The lights of the causeway illuminated her face with steady, rapid flickers, like an old kinetoscope. But there was no motion. Her expression was tranquil, and she looked her age.

Rodrigue stopped on Texas 35 and picked up some little cake doughnuts coated with powdered sugar, coffee for Sandy and himself, and a Pepsi for Sarah. He also got the morning's *Post* from the stand in front of the convenience store and read quickly as Sandy was distributing their junk-food breakfast.

The "Ferguson Files" was about some constable purposely delaying the disposition on property seizures.

64

The fees piled up at the storage warehouse and the constable got a kickback. According to Ferguson.

Spurred by the sugar, Sarah became talkative. She crawled forward and sat between them on the console and they were like a happy little family spinning off to the beach, with an eye on the rearview mirror.

Rodrigue slowed twice and let cars pass him, then he gave up. Nobody looked suspicious so he suspected everybody. If he did have a tail, it wouldn't matter once they got to Port O'Connor anyway. Even if the goon in the orange Duster had seen fit to hook up a boat himself, it still wouldn't matter.

Port O'Connor was a village with more boats than houses, even if you counted trailer houses. Because it was situated near a Gulf pass, and at the junction of big, deep Matagorda Bay and shallow Espiritu Santo Bay, it was a sport fisherman's paradise. Offshore fishing was screwed, of course, but anglers using live shrimp for bait were scratching out limits of speckled trout behind the barrier islands. The ramp at Doc's Dock was fairly busy.

Rodrigue launched the *Queen* and Sandy and Sarah clambered aboard with the nimbleness that comes from living on a boat. With the Evinrudes sputtering at idle, he steered eastward along the Intracoastal, toward Pass Cavallo and the crossroads that led to the Gulf on one side and the vast Matagorda Bay system on the other. One by one, three small fishing boats that had been in line behind him on the ramp shot by on plane, bound for the bay. Rodrigue stuck his head through the side window and told Sarah, sitting forward of the house, to come inside. He shoved the throttles forward and turned the wheel hard. The *Queen* went skipping back down the Intracoastal and both passengers broke out in wide grins.

When he reached the cut, Rodrigue hauled the wheel to port and the boat shot through clumps of grass-covered spoil. If anybody intended to follow, they had better know where they were going. Espiritu Santo was shoal water.

The narrow passage through the spoil bank opened to a shallow lake that with the generous tides of summer the Whaler could easily navigate on plane. The marsh was green and the sky blue. A line of fluffy cumulus clouds looked like snowy mountains in the distance. A startling flash of pink marked the flight of a lone roseate spoonbill.

At the far end of the lake an abandoned canal deadended in the marshy backside of Matagorda Island. The canal had served some long-forgotten strategic purpose during World War II, when the island was an air base. Rodrigue had learned about it from a local fisherman when he was trying to sneak some equipment to the beach to pick the bones of a shrimper that went aground during Hurricane Allen. Only fishermen with shallow-draft boats came back there, and then only in the spring and the fall. In the heat of the summer, the fish were in the deeper waters of Matagorda Bay. At the back of the canal even the Whaler Frontier with its pilot house and mast was hidden from boats in the Intracoastal.

It was just about a mile across the island to the Gulf beach—a little more than a comfortable hike for Rodrigue, whose right knee occasionally nagged him about a decompression stop he skipped during a storm off South Africa. But as usual, it was worth it. They had the beach to themselves. Sandy rolled out a big quilt—and Sarah peeled off her T-shirt, baring her hard young breasts as naturally as if she had been alone in a small windowless room. Rodrigue dove for the ice chest. It was going to be an awkward day.

"Like mother, like daughter," Sandy said, shrugging and smiling that beaming smile. She unfastened her bikini top and dropped it onto the quilt with a self-conscious flourish that the daughter lacked.

Then she wiggled the pants down her long legs and deftly dropped it from her toe onto the quilt beside the bra. Rodrigue was swimming with impressions of the soft brown belly, splayed brown legs, tawny puff of hair . . .

And Sarah, incredibly stacked but just a child, popped the first button on her Levis.

CHAPTER 8

"Wait a minute, Sarah," Rodrigue said in a voice that belied his considerable turmoil. "Do me a favor, will you? Run back to the boat and get that big cooking pot on the V-berths up forward there. Better slip your shirt back on, though, in case there's some fishermen nearby. We don't want to draw a crowd."

She stood scratching her left breast beneath its pale flat nipple. "Cooking pot?"

"Yeah. And there's a bag of limes under there too, somewhere. I hope they're okay. Bring them. And the cayenne. Oh yeah, and the salt."

Sarah shrugged and donned her shirt. When she had disappeared around the dune, Rodrigue redirected his painfully swelling penis. Sandy smiled slyly and stretched on the quilt.

"How old is she?" he asked.

"She'll be sixteen in September."

"Good God."

"She's grown up pretty fast."

"I just imagine."

"Who the hell are you to judge?" she said, sitting up angrily. "Look, I don't apologize for the way I am. I just don't happen to have the usual hang-ups about sex, you know?"

She relaxed, wrapping her arms around her knees. "Would I apologize if I were the one person in ten without hemorrhoids or something? You're the one who's fucked up. I don't mean just you, I mean—"

"You're not talking to some Sunday school teacher here. I've done the ménage à trois thing. But not with any damn kids."

"C'mon! I wasn't suggesting we all roll in the sand together. And Sarah's hardly a kid."

She certainly had a grown-up body. And Rodrigue couldn't honestly be certain there hadn't been a teenager or two in the boozy tangle of toffee-colored bodies he had slept among over the winter.

He watched Sandy lay back on the quilt again. Her smallish breasts sagged and there was a pooch in the flesh of her lower abdomen. Her shoulders were a little bony, her calves too thin, and her feet too big. But Rodrigue was not a slave to the *Playboy* ideal. "Maybe I'm falling in love with her mother," he said, his heart pounding in his crotch.

She sighed and smiled and the crinkles cut deeply into her cheeks. It was a sad smile, Rodrigue thought.

"Maybe you fall in love too easy."

"Uh-huh, maybe."

"We have a problem. Maybe I could fall in love with you someday. But I still have to be me, and that means being free."

"What the hell does *that* mean?"

"Well, for one thing it means not having to keep your

69

eyes on the rearview mirror all the time like you've been doing. How'd you find out?"

"How did I find out what?"

"About Barney."

"Who's Barney?"

"C'mon! You've been watching the road behind us like a hawk!"

"I don't know any Barney. I was worried about maybe being followed down here for reasons of my own. Nothing to do with you. Who's Barney?"

Barney was Barnett Culberson. He was an executive with Southern Bell in Atlanta; a good ol' boy with polish; blond hair in a sixties razor cut glued down every morning with spray; kind of narrow at the shoulder and wide at the hip; a backslapper with a lot of iciness inside; her husband.

They had met 30,000 feet over the Gulf Stream, young Sandra James serving coffee, soft drinks, Bloody Marys, taking her cues from the older gals and accordingly very bowled over by the confidence exuded by a well-dressed man going from someplace fashionable to someplace exotic. Not too attractive in his skivvies in the morning and a little distant most of the time, but bankrolled and respectable and evidently in love with her in his own way. They married, had a daughter, and for six years she was a real Atlanta peach, aging gracefully. Then she succumbed to a quick fuck on the floor of the pool house with someone who was supposed to be deciding where to put the potted palms.

"If I had been in love with the guy, or even overcome with lust or something, it would've been one thing. But he was just being friendly and helpful and I started wondering, just curiouslike, what he'd be like, and I suddenly thought, hell, why not?"

She sat up again to see how he was taking all this. "It had nothing to do with my feelings for Barney, which were shot by then but it wouldn't have mattered. I was not being unfaithful. You know, some people play tennis."

Rodrigue shrugged. He could buy that. He guessed.

"I stayed with him another six years," she said, listening to her own words incredulously. "But it was hard. I missed the beaches, the fun, the laughing. And I was afraid of him."

"Why, did he beat you?"

"No, never. But he had—has—a lot of power somehow. He has connections. He sent someone who found the guy I was living with in Florida and it was a pretty bad scene. I think they beat him up, I don't know. We left."

"You just *left*? You never went back?"

"Left and kept driving until it seemed like it was far enough, and that was here. Or Galveston rather. It was that or back to Atlanta—for Sarah, anyway. I don't think he'd have me. And as for Sig, there was no love lost by then."

"Sig?"

"Sigmund. Like Freud but kinkier. Flies for Eastern. I went back to work when I ran away from Barney. Sig and I sort of took up, you might say. He lives on a motor sailer at Lauderdale so it was a whale of fun at first. There wouldn't have been any problem except I let Sarah know where I was and she ran away too. That's when Barney hired someone to start looking. But we would've had to leave anyway."

"It was over? You and this Sig, I mean."

"Really never started. He was a lot of fun and most important, he could deal with me, the way I am, you know? But then Sarah came and he started hitting on her a lot."

"He *beat* her?" He'd kill the son of a bitch.

"No, no. You know, just trying to feel her up and like that all the time. She didn't like it."

"Well, shit, what do you expect? Letting her parade around like that! And you—why don't you put some clothes on?"

She sighed and went spread-eagle on the quilt as though she had passed out. "Don't you enjoy going nude?" she asked, peeking at him with one amused eye.

"Not really. I'm not crazy about *displaying* myself in front of Sarah, that's for sure."

"Don't flatter yourself," she said, rising on one elbow. "She's seen one that big before."

"Aw, touché, Brute, but it's not her sensibilities I'm worried about. Come on, humor me." He tossed her her discarded bikini bottom.

"Okay, but I really haven't gotten in the habit of telling Sarah how to behave."

"She'll get the idea."

Sarah looked puzzled when she returned with the pot and the ingredients Rodrigue had asked for and found her mother refastening her bra. "We leaving?"

"No, I've just been worried lately about getting too much sun in tender places," said Sandy. Rodrigue gave her high marks for that. She could've turned it into a minor confrontation by laying the blame on him.

The teenager shrugged and whipped her T-shirt off again. In seconds she was naked and Rodrigue was in sympathy with poor Sig. He had done what he could and now he decided that to avert his gaze would be hypocriscy. She *did* have a beautiful body—the kind of unblemished ripeness that lasts an afternoon if it comes at all in most women's lives. She was rounder than Sandy, like a little Italian sex goddess. Rodrigue was amazed that he could appraise her, even enjoy her, without letting himself want her. Incest was a powerful taboo—she wasn't even family.

"So what's this stuff for?" she asked, unfazed by his steady gaze.

72

"Well?" asked Sandy with a knowing look.

"Lunch," he said, rising painfully to his feet.

The surf was alive with big blue crabs, prompted by the unseasonable front. Each wave washing up on the sloping beach left one or two to scamper after the retreating foam. When he first pointed them out to her, Sarah squealed and ran out of the water with high, springy steps, breasts rolling enticingly around her chest. Then he showed them how to block the crabs' progress with sticks of driftwood, how to catapult them back onto dry sand like a golfer making a chip shot and then pick them up, grasping the hind legs as though they were shears, and pretty soon they had the pot crawing with large crabs. Somewhere along the line Sarah had stopped and put on her T-shirt and shorts.

Rodrigue made a driftwood fire and they dodged its sweet, almost rotten-smelling smoke and boiled the crabs in water drained from the ice chest. Then they picked the steaming red crabs apart, licking the salt and cayenne from their fingers and drinking beer to put out the fire in their mouths.

Sandy was quiet on the way home. Sarah sat on the console between the seats in the Blazer and talked. At first it was guarded half-kidding. After a while it was just talk. Then sleepy talk. Then she crawled in the back and went to sleep.

"So," said Rodrigue to Sandy, "you think he's still after you?"

"Barney, you mean. Yeah. No, not after me. Sarah. He's got people looking for us."

"That why you're calling yourself Carson?"

"Yeah. Original, huh? I wonder why aliases are always so close to the real name."

"I didn't know they were."

"Well, on TV—"

"Sandy—"

"I had fun. I'm sorry you think I'm such a slut."

"Are you crazy? I don't—"

"I feel like I've gotten off on the wrong foot with you and I'm . . . I guess I'm scared, for some reason. God, I want to go to bed with you." She reached over and stroked the inside of his thigh.

"So do I, but I just can't handle it with Sarah in the room. I don't know, maybe I'm getting old or something. There's going to be a party on B Row tomorrow—I'll drive you by the place so you'll know how to find it—why don't you and Sarah come on by around three or so. Meanwhile, I'll be looking for a babysitter."

It was past midnight when they got to the Holiday Inn. Sarah slumbered on her feet, leaning against the wall, while Rodrigue and Sandy said good night. Finally they pried away from each other and Rodrigue drove home aching like he hadn't ached since high school.

He lay in bed feeling his government .45 cold and reassuring against his bare leg as he masturbated urgently.

CHAPTER 9

United States aid to quake-stricken El Salvador may mask escalated military assistance to the embattled right-wing government, a U.S. senator charges.

Meanwhile Israel invades Lebanon, Indians protest James Watt cutting back services of the BIA, and award-winning investigative journalist Michael Ferguson has singlehandedly uncovered the kingpin of a Houston/Galveston coke-smuggling ring.

Rodrigue snapped the folds out of the paper. What an *asshole!* he thought, a grin stretching across his face.

There was no mention of Greathouse by name—not even by innuendo. It could've been anyone who considered himself solvent and respected. Mostly it seemed the article was intended to taunt the FBI for coming up empty in its own investigation. Ferguson promised to reveal the identity in an upcoming column, as though it were a trivia contest. Of course it still might flush out

Greathouse. Surely he would realize *he* was the goose about to be publicly cooked.

Or maybe Rodrigue was imagining things. He hadn't seen the orange Duster since he lost it on the freeway after leaving Tiki Island. Maybe they *were* having a bar mitzvah in Baytown. Stranger things had happened.

He had picked up a dozen eggs when he went out for the morning *Post* and he fixed himself an Argentine omelet, with canned asparagus and Monterey Jack. He served himself royally out on the sun deck under his Cinzano umbrella, with chunks of watermelon and fresh pineapple, steaming corn tortillas wiped with real butter, and a pot of the strong Cajun coffee. Such breakfasts made him wonder why he bothered with light beer. Something had to give somewhere, he decided.

About ten thirty he went to answer the phone. The voice—young and brusque—asked to speak to Ferguson.

"You've got the wrong number," said Rodrigue, instantly suspicious.

"He gave me this number. I have some information for him."

"Well, there isn't any Ferguson here. If one shows up I'll give him the message. What's your name?"

Click.

Ferguson came by at noon, as Rodrigue was washing dishes. When he felt the heavy footsteps on the stairs, Rodrigue went to greet him at the door and Ferguson shuffled past without a word, headed for the refrigerator. He always made a big deal out of the drive from his vine-covered brick cottage in the tweedy zone around Rice University.

They had met two years before when Rodrigue was making inspection dives and Ferguson was raking the muck on the Texas A&M research ship that sank at the dock. Today he was wearing a gray sweatshirt with torn half-sleeves and a faded picture of Richard Nixon on the front giving the famous hunch-shouldered victory sign, cutoffs made from *pink* jeans, thongs that made him walk like a bear on skates, and clip-on sunglasses in the flipped-up position on his spectacles. Ferguson found it easier to have fun if he dressed for it.

"Why didn't you bring one of your FBI buddies with you today?" Rodrigue said evilly. "I haven't seen anyone wear wingtips with Bermuda shorts since the time they infiltrated West Beach during the big Russian-sub scare."

"You saw the piece?" said Ferguson between pulls on the can of Lite he had snatched from the refrigerator.

"Uh-huh. What's the matter, you afraid of Greathouse?"

Ferguson jerked the can from his face and glared at Rodrigue with dark eyes that looked like raisins behind the thick lenses. "Fuck, no! Listen, just because the legendary John Rodrigue pronounces someone guilty of a crime doesn't mean it's going to be in all the papers the next day."

"You tell the FBI?"

"Fuck, no. Assholes. We're not communicating."

"I should've guessed it. Your article reads like an application for their shit list."

"Rod, do I come down here and try to tell you how to suck air underwater?" Ferguson opened another beer and looked around the kitchen as though he had suddenly noticed the cabinets covered with slime. "Why is it everyone with the price of a newspaper assumes he can do a reporter's job better than he can? What the fuck do *you* know about journalism?"

"Goddamn, I've been listening to *you* lecture on it for two solid— Yeaaah, I see your point."

Ferguson ignored the taunt. "You can't work with those motherfuckers on a one-for-one basis, you know? You either bully the motherfuckers or you let them use you, one of the two. You *know*? It's like dealing with an umpire in baseball. You've got to keep in their faces, keep in their faces. Then they'll start dealing straight with you."

"Yeah," Rodrigue said.

"Aw, no. They'll deal with you, all right—when *you've* got the goods."

"If you would've told them about Greathouse, you would've had an agent sitting in your lap," Rodrigue said gently.

Ferguson's massive trunk expanded with a quiet sigh. "Yeah, but they're not returning my calls, and I'm not about to throw away that kind of tip on some goddamned secretary."

"Speaking of tips, somebody called here for you just now. Said he had some information."

"Don't they all. I tell 'em to mail me an affidavit. If they won't go for that, I sure don't want to fuck with them."

"He called you *here* is my point."

"Oh, yeah. I left your number on my message machine. Be good advertising for you."

"I'm sure." Rodrigue did not especially relish advertising, even in good times.

"Tell you wot," he said, brightening, "let's just us take a little vacation today, wadaya say?"

He meant every word of it. It was a nice day outside—hot, but with enough of a breeze to whisk away the damp heaviness. It was one of those rare summer days when colors explode instead of fade. The nearby houses were technicolor yellows and blues. The khaki sand looked almost white. Even the water looked an appealing shade of olive, with a hint of translucence. It was the kind of day to savor like a tangy ocean breeze, Rodrigue decided, with no concern for where it came from or where it was going.

Most people thought Rodrigue's life *was* a vacation these days but he would've begged to differ. Not working

78

when you were supposed to be working was not the same thing as a vacation. Just declaring a day off seemed to help, but Ferguson refused to join in the charade.

He watched forlornly as Rodrigue hefted his big Old Smokey into the trailered *Haulover Queen* and then tossed in behind it some chunks from the tangle of mesquite limbs he always gathered on his northward migration. When they came to the seawall, Rodrigue pulled into the right lane and slowed so they could sip their beers and ogle the buttocks swelling from French-cut bathing suits and the firm young breasts bouncing free in damp T-shirts. The journalist looked but he did not enjoy.

Even the prospect of food didn't do it—and Ferguson was a real chowhound. With the *Queen* settled in her slings again, Rodrigue popped the tab on a beer and settled in her pilot house with the VHF radio. Brezinski finally answered from just the other side of the ship anchorage offshore.

"You got the *Prettiest Sally;* go ahead, Rod."

"Aye, mate." (Doing Robert Newton doing Long John again.) "Be it true you got some dolphin aboard, come back?"

"Aye, aye, matey. And they're still on ice. Might be plumb edible."

"Aye, and what be your ETA, matey? Come back?"

"Two-thirty or thereabouts. Water was starting to look pretty good around the Flower Gardens, Rod."

"Great. Break down."

"Uh, thanks but no thanks. Got a deep-frier going?"

"How about a smoker, with pure mesquite, butter and garlic, lime? Come back?"

"Roger-roger, *Queen.* Sounds great to me."

Ferguson had listened to the exchange with morose detachment. He didn't show a spark until Sandy and Sarah arrived and Sandy, using her old sky-aisle wiles, started throwing catch phrases at him from the noon newscast.

It wasn't entirely an act. She, it turned out, was a genuine Kennedy Democrat. Ferguson was a Moynihan Democrat, so they were able to communicate using current events as a sort of pig latin. They pounced right in on poor little El Salvador and then dragged Rodrigue in behind them.

"Hell, you live half the goddamned year in Central America," Ferguson said accusingly. "Do *you* think we're doing those people—the *people* now—any kind of favor by sticking our nose in down there?"

Rodrigue shrugged. Belize was more of a British Caribbean state than a Latin American one. It was an honest shrug of ignorance but Sandy took it for apathy. She looked at him with a coolness in her eyes that surprised him.

"How can you see the pitiful condition people live in down there," she said, "and not understand why they would want something a little better?"

"You know, and if they find it in socialism, so what?" added Ferguson.

Rodrigue popped open another Lite. "Hell, *I* don't know what kind of system people in Latin America want. They've got hospitals and schools for everybody in Cuba now, but they might come and drag you out of your goddamned bed in the middle of the night and ship you off to some goddamned cane field with a Russian-made machete in your hand. I don't know, maybe Latin Americans *like* being had by the balls. I can't think of a time in history when they weren't under a dictator or a king or a fucking Indian chief. Pardon my French."

"Ah, but if they were *real* men like us—"

"Oh, bullshit, Mike. I'm not saying I'm any better than they are. It's just that you have to *be* a Latin American to understand what Latin Americans want and I'm from goddamned Louisiana, that's all."

He had had enough of trying to make things right for people. He would've become very unsociable if the *Meka* hadn't rounded the breakwater at that very moment and distracted everybody with a hell of a catch of amberjack from the Claypile. Shortly afterward the thick dolphin steaks provided by Brezinski's crew came off the grill. Sandy and Sarah and now even Ferguson flowed with the newfound gaity on B Row. Now it was Rodrigue who was in an ugly mood—unfortunately for the crew-boat skipper, who came pacing down the dock in a hurry.

He was a big red-faced man unused to asking for help. "Y'ownt a little job, Rob?" he said curtly.

"What's the problem?" Rodrigue asked without kindness.

"Got some polypro in one of the wheels."

"You know my price?"

"Yeah," the crew-boat skipper said with a derisive snort, "a hundred bucks."

"Aye," said Rodrigue, "a hundred bucks will get me off this chair."

The skipper became aware he was now the center of attention. "What are you saying? In *advance?*"

"Aye."

"You—"

"Where's your boat, skip?"

"In the Roads, with the hook out," he said, calming down instantly. "Engine was heating up. I hitched a ride over on a little sport boat coming off the north jetty."

"Hmm," Rodrigue said. "Wouldn't make it in on the other engine?"

The crew-boat skipper shrugged. "Tide's running pretty good. Oh, I'd *make* it okay, but I didn't want to chance maneuvering at the dock."

"You got a hundred bucks on you?"

"Of course I got a hundred bucks on me."

Rodrigue sighed. "Well, the longer the hundred

bucks stays on you, the longer your boat stays in the Roads."

The skipper glared at the onlookers, then dug the bills out of his wallet.

Rodrigue looked coolly at Sandy. "Be back in two or three hours."

"Can't I come with you?" asked Sarah.

"Do you mind?" he asked Sandy. "Otherwise, I'm just going to have to scratch around for a tender."

"Two or three hours?" She smiled. "It'll be a terrific experience for her. Why don't you just leave me your house key? If you guys get hung up, we'll just move the party out to your place."

Ferguson nodded happily.

"It isn't locked," said Rodrigue, managing a shark-grin. "I'm such a trusting soul."

Glad to be absorbed in a familiar routine, Rodrigue lowered the makeshift gangplank into the *Haulover Queen's* cockpit and rolled the low-pressure compressor into the teak chocks on the deck. He secured the separate volume tank and the figure-eight of hose, got out the Kirby Morgan HeliOx-18B mask and dive control unit, and shut the locker. With Sarah and the brooding captain aboard and the party noise fading behind, he steered for the channel.

He tied the *Queen* alongside and sent the skipper into the crew boat's wheelhouse to kill the engines. With the diesels off, he would have time to get away from the props before someone could crank them up and put them in gear, accidentally or otherwise. He methodically hooked the compressor to the volume tank and connected the hose and carefully threaded on the HeliOx-18B while Sarah watched with out-thrust hip and cocked head.

"Jesus," she said, frowning at the sudden tangle of equipment, "why don't you just use a tank?"

Rodrigue was noticing for the first time the faint freckles on her cheeks, the delicate lines that marked the corners of her mouth when she clamped her lips that way—and when she talked, the whiteness of her teeth . . .

"They're great for sightseeing," he said, "but when you're horsing around down there, and especially when you're in the kinda shape I'm in, you need air." He started the compressor, then held up the mask and turned the black knob to the right of the face plate. The air blasted out in a loud, steady hiss.

"The radio on this thing doesn't work," he lied, "so we'll have to signal each other by tugging on the hose."

Most tenders couldn't resist chattering on the radio, and with the free-flow on, he couldn't hear. He would have to shut the air flow off, ask for a repeat, and wait for the reply. It was a waste of time, so he fell back on the ancient system of communications invented, for all he knew, by Javanese pearl divers.

"If I tug twice on the hose, give me some slack," he told Sarah. "If I tug three times, take up slack."

He put his wallet and keys on the steering console in the Whaler and from long habit handed her his wrist-watch. She looked at the replica Vietnam-issue Timex and shook her head.

"Why don't you have a diver's watch?"

"Because keeping time is the tender's job. You don't have to worry about that, though. Just put it in your pocket or something." He slipped the HeliOx-18B over his head. "One more thing," he said, lifting the mask off his face slightly. "Keep your shirt on. Some of these guys may have been at sea for a while."

She gave him a smile surprisingly like her mother's. Rodrigue readjusted the mask and stepped into the olive-brown water.

The rope wasn't polypropylene, it was nylon. A piece

of light hawser, two inches thick and long enough to be wrapped around *both* shafts, with considerable strain between. Rodrigue would've preferred polypropylene. With a little use, it became stiff and brittle. Sometimes he could work it loose because like wire rope it naturally wanted to straighten itself out. And the strands snapped apart if he had to saw through them. Nylon acted as though it had been melted into one glob, and it grabbed the serrations in the blade when it was cut. This one was a mess—a double mess, since both wheels had picked it up. Rodrigue went back up and clung to one of the truck-tire fenders, yelling for the skipper.

"Already?" the burly captain asked.

"Already, my ass! Why didn't you tell me you had both wheels fouled?"

"Well, what's the fuckin' difference, Rodrigue? One wheel or two?"

"Two hundred bucks."

"All right, asshole, two hundred. Now cut that shit out of them and let me get moving."

"No, no. The *difference* is two hundred. That's *three* hundred, total, and I ain't going under again until that little girl there has the other two hundred in her pocket."

"Get real, Rodrigue! I don't have another two hundred fuckin' bucks on me!"

Rodrigue took the mask off and rubbed his chin, squinting into the distance with his civilian eye as though wrestling mightily with his conscience. Finally he said: "Well, you want a lift back to the yacht basin?"

The crew-boat captain left a wake of profanity across the deck and stepped into the galley. Rodrigue looked over his shoulder and winked at Sarah, watching with her mouth open. He knew the man would get his money back from the boat company and the boat company would charge it to the drilling company, who would pass

84

it on to the oil company, who would pass it back to him when he bought fuel. But he loved to stick it to the "awl bidness." It was a game with him.

Immersed again in the warm yellow darkness, he stopped sawing at the rope for a moment and turned off the free-flow to listen to the low-frequency throb of a ship coming down the channel. Maybe she *was* attracted to Ferguson, with his four-eyed dignity and mocking sweatshirt. More likely she felt sorry for him. No, most likely still she simply wanted to see what it was like to roll around on all that fuzzy blubber, or to be pinioned under that pile-driving ass. Like tennis, she had said.

The metallic gasp of the HeliOx's regulator exploded in his ear. The rubbery smell of the cool air stirred memories that quickly resettled, like ancient silt on the bottom of the ocean. Dark and cuddling water was a great place to put topside affairs into perspective. Rodrigue had come too far and weathered far too much to kick a warm and willing body out of bed over a stupid matter like exclusivity. She was a gal who lived for the moment, and he would claim many of her moments yet.

Rodrigue sawed the line away from the propeller shafts, and he and Sarah were back at the yacht basin before the crew-boat skipper got his anchor up. He washed down the *Queen,* left the air hose on deck to dry, and replaced the rest of the diving equipment carefully in the locker.

"Think I could learn to dive like that?" Sarah asked as they cruised down Holiday Drive in his Blazer.

"Scuba dive you mean? Sure."

"Would you teach me?"

"No," Rodrigue said, pulling into the U-Tote-M for a beer. "You need a qualified instructor so you can be certified. They won't even fill a tank for you nowadays unless you're certified. I know some of those guys, though. I'll get you fixed up. Some of them are just about your caliber too. Young." He gave her a friendly little hug.

She got out behind him and stopped him outside the store with a hand on his arm. "Don't be mad at Sandy," she said, her eyes earnestly searching his.

"I'm not."

"You're different, you know."

"Yeah?"

"Yeah. She really likes you. It's just—I don't know, she's not a sex fiend or anything."

Rodrigue laughed in spite of himself.

"She's not! Really! It's just like she has to be free or something. Barney's not such a bad guy but I think he was too stifling."

Rodrigue took a fresh look at her. What had happened to the pouting little airhead? "It's no big deal," he said with a Third World shrug.

His spirits rose on the ride home. He was enjoying Sarah for the smart little spotted pup she was. He would enjoy Sandy later, in all sorts of ways. He was thankful to God for the chance to succeed where Barnett Culberson had failed.

Sandy's Triumph had taken the other place in the shade next to Ferguson's car so Rodrigue pulled around the side. He glanced up at the sun deck and saw the door open.

Half-open.

Rodrigue felt the cold wind of aftermath. He looked quickly into Sarah's eyes.

"Something's wrong. I want you to stay here and wait for me."

Her questioning smile lasted a fraction of a second. If the sound of his voice had not convinced her to obey, the look on his face would have. Her eyes went wide with fear, but she would do as she was told.

Climbing the stairs, he saw a bare foot sticking from the door, holding it open. He came up quickly and saw Ferguson lying in an awkward position, wearing only his pink cutoffs. One leg was bent beneath the weight of his body. His head was twisted sideways in a pool of blood, his left temple and eye swollen and blackened. His glasses were on the floor.

Rodrigue growled like an injured animal, leaped over Ferguson's body, and moved quickly to the bedroom in a low crouch. He found her on the bed, naked, lying back with her arms spread and one foot on the floor. She was staring blindly at the ceiling and there were two little purple spots on her face, one on her forehead and one high on her left cheek. The blood had puddled beneath her head and soaked into the spread, so it didn't show. But the lips drawn mirthlessly back from her teeth—the obscence earthly remains of her smile—left no doubt.

There was a quick rattle of hard-soled shoes on the stairs. He stumbled back out of the room, sick to his stomach.

"Sarah!" he croaked, his voice wet and angry.

But it wasn't Sarah.

CHAPTER 10

A black man in work clothes filled the door. He looked down at Ferguson's crumpled body and his jaw dropped. With a bitter curse, he hopped over the body into the room. He had a small automatic in his hand, and his gaze went past Rodrigue in flickering darts. Rodrigue knew what he must be but started for him anyway, an awful strength filling his hands. The black man poked the automatic in his face and sounded older and a lot calmer than he looked.

"Be cool, now, Rodrigue. FBI. Just be cool."

Rodrigue backed down. "I'm cool. Check it out."

With the automatic still ready, he looked into the bedroom, stood there for a while, then got down on his hands and knees and combed the bare floor between the wall and the sea-grass mat. He came up with two small brass cartridge cases.

"Twenty-two," he said flatly.

"Pro?"

He shrugged and went over to the door and bent

over, swaying slightly from the waist, like a human vacuum cleaner. "Lotsa people got twenty-twos," he said, mostly to himself.

"What about the girl? Somebody down there with her?"

"Yeah, she's okay," he said, looking at the body again. "What the hell was *he* doing here?"

Rodrigue laughed. It was a hollow sound that echoed in his ears. "Looks like he was fucking my girlfriend. You guys are the ones who've been tailing me I hope?"

The black FBI agent looked at him. "You about a cold motherfucker, ain't you?"

"That's right."

"You know that's supposed to be you, don't you?" He jabbed the little automatic at Ferguson's body.

"Yeah? Lotsa folks got twenty-twos."

"Right, man. That's right. You keep talking. I'm the best friend you got right now. Play it cute with me and look at the ride you take." He dragged the word out— "riiiiide"—and made it sound the way a snake crawls.

Numbness reached Rodrigue. "All I know is somebody's been following me and now everybody in my house is dead. That's all I know."

"Uh-huh. Yeah. You don't know nothing about no cocaine, do you?"

"No."

"You're lying, man."

"No."

He pointed the automatic at Rodrigue again and motioned with his head toward the door. "Let's go."

He could see Sarah through the windshield of a light blue Ford parked behind the Blazer. She was on the driver's side, sitting with the door open. She was looking down at someone crouched behind the door. Rodrigue could see a wing-tipped shoe and a hand resting on the door for support. The man was apparently questioning her. She lowered her head and shook it no.

The black man steered Rodrigue to a late-model Chevolet pickup parked next door. People from the yellow and blue houses were standing around watching. A sheriff's car came up fast and stopped next to the Ford in a cloud of fine sand. The agent hooked his thumb at the house and kept Rodrigue moving toward the pickup, taking him around to the passenger side as the onlookers shrank away. Rodrigue got in and the agent shut the door and leaned in through the open window.

"You not gonna do anything stupid, are you?" he asked in a whisper.

"No," said Rodrigue.

The agent went around, got in, and started the engine. A radio hissed under the seat. They sat there, not saying anything. More cars came up, some of them with emergency lights flashing. An ambulance. Someone was directing traffic on the road, hustling the rubberneckers by. People were everywhere, standing around. Rodrigue looked for Sarah, but she was gone.

Something on the radio caught the agent's attention. He reached for the mike and answered. It was jargon Rodrigue couldn't understand.

The black man stuck his head out the window and got a deputy to move the patrol car behind them. He did it quietly, with only a jerk of his head. The deputy gunned the car in reverse, making a reckless backward U-turn into the yard and scattering onlookers like startled chickens. Even then it seemed everything was in slow motion. They backed out, the deputy halting traffic on the side street for them. Through the windshield of a halted car, Rodrigue saw a face that caught his attention. It stared at him and yet there seemed to be no features. Square head and blank face and fingers patiently drumming a rock beat on the steering wheel. His radio was just loud enough for the bass to come throbbing across. As they passed, the man's stare followed and Rodrigue saw cruel slits, like a squint on a marble statue. Someone, undoubtedly, who didn't believe in the presumption of innocence.

The agent kept checking the rearview mirror as they drove toward town. He got another message, picked up the mike, and muttered something brief. The light blue Ford Sarah had been sitting in overtook them, moving fast. There was only a driver. It shot on past the entrance to the state park but Rodrigue and the agent turned in, winding around on a narrow road until they came to a gray car parked at a cove of the bay—a primer-gray Plymouth Duster with big wheels.

"Go with him," the black man said, pointing to the Duster with his chin.

A bronze-colored indio with a Charlie Chan mustache was at the wheel of the Duster. He put the car in reverse and spun it around on the oyster-shell road, leaving the pickup and the black agent in a cloud of gray dust.

"Much better," said Rodrigue, placing both hands on the dash for support.

The indio raised his eyebrows but kept his eyes scanning outside.

"Orange was too flashy for your line of work."

The indio looked at Rodrigue and laughed. "We gotta use what we can get, you know? Those DEA guys, they love it, man. Zooming around in street rods, man. I think they make a lot of their cases based on what kind of wheels they're gonna get from the guy."

"You FBI too?"

"Oh yes."

The sun was going down big and red over the marshy flats. They drove over the causeway and went north on Texas 3 instead of the Gulf Freeway. When they got to NASA 1, the indio spoke into the radio and turned right.

"Where're we going?"

"Gonna put you up someplace where you'll be safe for a while."

With the Duster in the turn, Rodrigue automatically grabbed the door handle for support. The FBI agent caught the movement and suddenly became all dark, shining eyes. "Hey, man, don't try nothing stupid, man. I'm the best friend you got in the world right now, man."

Rodrigue nodded and let his hand fall back into his lap. He had probably earned himself a pair of cuffs now.

They stopped across the road from the Johnson Space Center, at a motel grown slightly seedy since the glory days of Apollo. The indio parked in the back of the lot and talked briefly over the radio. Then they got out and Rodrigue noticed the blue Ford parked nearby. The agent knocked at a room on the ground floor and was answered immediately by a stocky, blondish fellow with a bulldog face and wearing a blue business suit.

"Any trouble?"

"Nah," the indio said. "Catch you later, man."

"Sit down, Mr. Rodrigue," the bulldog-looking fellow said. "Make yourself comfortable." Friendly words, but they didn't sound friendly.

"At last an FBI man who looks and sounds like an FBI man. You my best friend in the world too?"

"Special Agent Roy Wilson." He pulled out a small, tooled-leather wallet and flipped it open, displaying an official-looking ID. Rodrigue didn't look at it. He didn't know what an FBI agent's ID was supposed to look like.

"What's the FBI doing in something that's supposed to be a big drug deal? Where's the narcs?"

"When pillars of the community in three or four states suddenly start smuggling their own cocaine, we get interested."

"So who killed Sandy and Mike?"

"You tell me."

"I don't know. Nobody I know could do it. I might know people who might smuggle a little dope, but nobody I know could walk up and shoot people in the face like that."

"We're not talking about 'a little' dope. We're talk—"

There was a knock at the door.

Wilson moved quickly and opened it without taking his eyes off Rodrigue. It was the black agent, with a suitcase. He stepped in without a word and put the suitcase on the bed and took out a twelve-gauge riot gun in three pieces. He expertly snapped it together, stuffed the magazine full of shells from the suitcase, and leaned it against the door frame. The suitcase also contained shirts, toothbrushes, toothpaste, and deodorant, all still in packages from the K-Mart on the freeway.

"What's going on?" asked Rodrigue.

"I'm Special Agent Ed Gerrard," he said, offering his hand.

Rodrigue ignored it. "I know. My best friend in the whole fucking world. If I'm under arrest, you better look like charging me with something, mate."

"You're under protective custody," Wilson said.

Gerrard went to the desk and started leafing through the Yellow Pages. He stopped, bent to study an entry on the page, then wheeled abruptly to face the others.

"Rodrigue," he asked softly, "you do pepperoni?"

CHAPTER 11

Sarah was down, invisible beyond a parabola of hose that faded into deep blue water. She was calling on the radio. Suddenly it was a night dive and Rodrigue was alone on the deck of a barge swept with the cold orange glare of sodium lights. Sarah was calling, but he was afraid to pull her up. He knew he would be dead, grinning that hideous death-grin. But she was calling, so he hauled on the hose and then it was he who was being hauled to the surface by someone whose face looked blank through the shimmering ceiling of the water. It was a familiar blankness and Rodrigue was filled with dread.

It turned out to be Special Agent Wilson who was calling. He was standing at the foot of the bed, shaving with a cordless electric razor. It was still dark outside.

"Get up and get dressed, you've got a plane to catch."

Rodrigue sat up and rubbed his face. "I don't like flying. It's unnatural," he said tiredly. He felt the anger tensing his muscles but he tried not to give it away.

94

"Anyway, I'm beginning to believe I'm being denied due process."

Gerrard was in the bathroom, the shower running. The shotgun was in the corner.

"Let's go stand in front of a judge and let me call a lawyer and let's get on with the program," Rodrigue said, sliding his legs over the side of the bed.

"You may be crazy enough to try it but you're not fast enough to get away with it," Wilson said coldly, still shaving. "You're too fat. Fat and sloppy."

The taunts cooled Rodrigue. He was a captive but he didn't have to let them control his emotions.

"Aye," he rasped. "Aye, and worm-eaten and sour-bilged, but I got me civil rights, ain't I?"

"You've requested protection under the federal witness protection program," Wilson said, turning to knock the whiskers out of his razor into the sink. "Later this week a grand jury may or may not issue an indictment against you on charges of conspiracy to distribute a controlled substance. That depends on you."

Gerrard peeked out of the bathroom in a cloud of steam.

"But there's an attorney in Galveston who is prepared to swear under oath he advised you to sign up for the program and you agreed," Wilson continued. "We've got a copy of your signature off your fuel tab at the yacht basin that we can reproduce in any color of ink you want, complete with the skips a dry ballpoint makes."

Gerrard came out toweling his hair. "You've got no reason to protect anyone, Rodrigue," he said. He wasn't as hip in his speech around Wilson, Rodrigue noticed.

Wilson glared at Gerrard, then at Rodrigue. "You're a nobody, Rodrigue. A tramp. A bum. What happens if you're not back in a month, two months? They cut off your electricity and chain up your boat. Beyond that, nobody cares."

"Except *somebody's* trying to kill you," Gerrard said. "And amateurs can be a lot more dangerous than pros. You're a church-going man—they're liable to try to take you out right in the middle of the service. We're going to keep you alive, whether you want us to or not."

Yeah, Rodrigue thought bitterly, the absolute best friends in the world.

They stopped for doughnuts and then went to Ellington Field, where the Federal Bureau of Investigation tendered Rodrigue to a pair of peach-faced young air force noncoms with Air Police armbands. They marched him, hands nervously on the butts of their holstered pistols, through a gate in a rusty chain-link fence. Waiting on the vast runway, already shimmering in the heat, was a white executive-type jet with the NASA logo on its tail. The AP's stuffed him though the door, piled in behind him, and the jet was rolling before Rodrigue found a seat belt to strap around himself.

"NASA?" Rodrigue mouthed soundlessly. He was crestfallen. He could buck up to the FBI, the DEA, and the CIA—but *NASA?* That was like being spat upon by Will Rogers.

One of the AP's shrugged. "It was the only government bird available on short notice, I guess," he said.

The other AP frowned and unscrewed the lid on a Thermos. He poured three coffees in white plastic-foam cups and they contemplated the vibration ripples in the dark liquid as the aircraft strained for altitude in a wide arc over the Gulf.

Far below was a mottled strip of land—Bolivar Peninsula—with a metallic ribbon across it. Rollover Pass, it was called, named after the ancient practice of rolling hogsheads of contraband over the narrow stretch of beach from ships' boats to the fast, shallow-draft sailing vessels in the bay. Smuggling had been an honorable profession in those days. Rodrigue leaned forward against the restraining belt and looked back out over the Gulf, glittering with golden sunlight.

He thought of Mike Ferguson lying in a grisly pile like some huge discarded marionette. Poor Mike. Poor keep-in-their-faces Ferguson. If he wanted anything he wasn't begging for it.

Rodrigue's mind would not take him into the bedroom. She wouldn't have asked for anything anyway, it wasn't her style. Broad and shining, the Gulf of Mexico slid from view under the wing. Rodrigue wiped the thin stream from his right cheek and settled back in the seat to simply wait.

After a long while, the pitch of the engines changed and Rodrigue felt the plane descending. He looked down at a patchwork of furry olive-drab woods and red-ribbed fields. The jet banked steeply and the sun flashed a painful silver-white on the window. When he could see the ground again, it was much closer and full of bald red scars. The plane went into another steep bank and lost altitude so quickly it shuddered. Suddenly a gray, sterile-looking compound was shooting past the window.

A tall man with a thick mop of white-blond hair stood alone on the runway, wearing a loose-fitting Indian shirt of unbleached muslin, a pair of white cotton drawstring trousers, cheap Mexican huaraches, and a big gold Rolex. All the white glowed slightly in the harsh sunlight, so that the man looked faintly angelic, a gentile organisateur at that big Club Med in the sky.

The angel projected a broad smile as Rodrigue stumbled from the small swing-down step to the baking runway with his bagful of K-Mart clothes.

"You've been cooperating," he said. "That's terrific."

"Terrific. Like I had a choice. I'm a fucking prisoner and you out here all by yourself in your pajamas doesn't change that a bit."

"I read your record, John," he said. "I imagine you could've put up a fight."

Rodrigue had a sudden feeling this whole mess was a case of mistaken identity. The only kind of "record" he could have would be his service record, and that was, what—? Thirteen, fourteen years old? At least.

The angel clapped an arm around his shoulder and steered him toward a compound of low buildings behind a high, rusty chain-link fence almost exactly like the place he had left. They walked between white stucco buildings into a courtyard peopled with khaki-clad zombies— obviously prisoners—and stopped at a steel door into the main building, guarded by a man in a blue uniform of a type Rodrigue didn't recognize.

"By the way," the tall blond said, pausing just inside the door to grab Rodrigue's hand for an awkward handshake, "my name is Dr. Haas, Al Haas. I'm a special consultant to the FBI. I'll tell you right now I don't like the way the boys in Houston went out on a limb to get you here, but we've got to move on this. If we'd have given you the option to walk, you'd have taken it and you'd be a dead man by now."

"Uh-huh," Rodrigue said, throwing down the offered hand. "And as soon as you figure out I don't know what the fuck's going on, you'll give me the option to walk whether it kills me or not."

"But we think you do. You admitted as much to the reporter who was killed—"

"Is *that* where all this is coming from? That son of a bitch, God rest his soul, was about as reliable as—"

"Then there's the fact that you were out at sea that morning, the same time the small boat disappeared."

"I'm out at sea a lot."

"And you went to see the helicopter pilot who flew to that particular oil platform. You wanted to find out how much we knew, didn't you?"

"Look, the Coast Guard turned my boat inside-fucking-out . . ."

But this was no time to get defensive. They didn't have anything on him but strong suspicion—and he was getting more on *them* the longer they held him illegally.

But then he might have *too* much on them, eh?

Haas led Rodrigue down a linoleum-floored hall to a small room with a long wooden table. An old Sony reel-to-reel recorder was on the table, and there was a big old-fashioned desk mike on a heavy cast-iron stand. Haas motioned for Rodrigue to sit opposite the door, in front of the mike.

"Don't pay any attention to this recorder, it's not on," he said.

"No, this one's not. I can see that."

Haas sat at the end of the table, leaned both elbows on it, and said in an easy going, conversational manner, "You lost an eye in 'Nam. How'd that happen?"

"Nothing to it. Ran over a mine."

"Feel guilty about that?"

"You're starting to sound like a shrink."

"Good. Good. Better that than a cop, right?"

"I don't like cops, lawyers, *or* shrinks."

"I'm not interested in what you like or don't like," Haas said in a tone so suddenly hostile it startled Rodrigue. "What I am interested in is how you fit into a very complicated picture. We have other ways of doing that, but Special Agent Gerrard recommended they do it my way. I'm a psychiatrist, and my way is to go back and throw out some emotional garbage first, before we get down to cases. Now, you want to do it my way or do you want to do it their way?"

Rodrigue didn't know who *they* were exactly but he figured it wasn't the Red Cross. "Ask away," he said, sensibly.

"Good. Let's go back to the last one. Feel guilty about hitting the mine?"

"I don't know why I should, I was taking a piss off the stern at the time."

"You lost the boat and your whole crew."

Rodrigue shrugged. "It was a new crew. I hardly knew any of them."

"How much of an effort did you make to get to know them?"

He shrugged.

"You had been with the old crew quite some time, hadn't you?"

"Uh-huh."

"They had gotten pretty chopped up in that earlier action, hadn't they?"

He didn't answer.

"And you weren't even touched in *that* action, were you?"

Rodrigue shrugged again. "A few scratches. One of them almost got infected."

"And a Medal of Honor. You won a Medal of Honor for it. 'Under the leadership of Petty Officer Rodrigue, who demonstrated unusual professional skill and"—he was looking Rodrigue in his civilian eye and quoting from memory—"indominable courage throughout the two hour battle, the patrol accounted for the destruction or loss of thirty enemy boats and inflicted numerous casualties on the enemy personnel. You knew *that* crew, didn't you, John?"

"I knew 'em."

"Some of them died, didn't they, John? How many of them died?"

"Two." It came out a croak.

"I'm sorry?"

"Two. Two of them died."

"Has that been festering in you, John?"

100

Rodrigue laughed, the hollow laugh Gerrard had heard in the beach house—and *that*, he suddenly realized, was why he was being screened by a psychiatrist first. They thought he might be too crazy for sodium pentothal or bamboo shoots or whatever *they* had wanted to use.

"It's a lousy memory, all right," he said, "but it was a long goddamn time ago. Just *yesterday*, now, I found two good friends with little holes in their heads and I have had enough of this shit."

He grabbed the desk mike and slapped Haas across the face, hard. He jumped over the table, jerked the door open, and ran down the hall.

Two guards jumped out of a side corridor with shiny black batons held in a stiff-armed presentation, like kung-fu experts. An unseen third guard hit him with a body check from behind and went sprawling with him on the glossy waxed floor into the feet of the first two guards. Rodrigue elbowed the downed guard in the groin and aimed a kick at the groin of one of the others when he saw the end of a baton coming at his forehead.

CHAPTER 12

Rodrigue was suddenly aware of a face, blurry and disembodied. It shrank, and shadows swept across it like clouds over the moon. Rodrigue thought he saw an ear, and a shoulder. Then the face was large and near again. The eyes blinked. He heard his own voice say, dry and crumbly as toast:

"Where am I?"

"You're in the infirmary," the face said, floating away with the words. "They brought you over from the hospital this morning."

Images of other disembodied faces came back to him. They had come out of a stormy and drunken night, it seemed. There had been times when the face was a pest, not leaving him alone, nagging and prying. He remembered now keeping just this side of consciousness, like hiding behind a thin curtain. Now it seemed okay to come out.

"What hospital? What infirmary? Where the fuck *am* I, is what I'm asking you, you . . ."

The white-jacketed man looked up from a metal cart. He was a little old to be enlisted, but he had that lifer look. The cropped hair, dull eyes, and bored set of the mouth. He looked at Rodrigue with a mixture of impatience and curiosity. "Maxwell Prison Camp. Montgomery, Alabama. Where'd you think?"

"Hey," said Rodrigue, the spark returning, "free trip—you don't ask questions."

His skin felt like a wet roll of toilet paper, sodden and swollen. He reached up and felt a rough gauze bandage over the left side of his face.

"Where's my eye?"

The orderly snorted. "Locked up. With the rest of your personal effects."

"That goon really fucking laid into me."

"Yeah, well, you wasn't the only one in the hospital, champ," the orderly said without rancor. "Dr. Haas is there yet."

"Good, good," Rodrigue said, not really happy about it.

The room was bare except for two hospital beds, each with a gray metal nightstand. The one window was covered with heavy-gauge wire screen on the inside and shuttered tight with metal louvers on the outside. There was a bathroom through one door, and apparently a hall outside the other, the one they kept locked. Rodrigue could hear the clatter of feet fading for a long while when the orderlies left.

He could hear them coming too. He always sat up expectantly at the first faint sound of footfalls in the distance because it usually meant a tray of the cafeterialike food, or sometimes even a pot of coffee. Never a drink, though Rodrigue had tried to bribe the older of the three orderlies with promises.

Sandy was haunting him, continuing to grow in death the way they say hair and fingernails do. He kept seeing

103

that horrible lifeless grimace. She wanted something. Just like Diegleman.

Rodrigue had been in the infirmary two or three days, maybe a week, seeing no one but the orderlies, getting no news, no conversation beyond the smallest of small talk, when he heard what seemed like an explosion of feet far down the hall. A parade—tramp, tramp, tramp—but one with enough irregularities in the cadence to seem on the verge of turning into a stampede. As it grew louder, almost deafening, Rodrigue was amazed to discover that he was frightened.

The door swung open and two blue-uniformed guards stepped in. Others were visible at attention in the hallway.

"Let's go," barked one of the guards.

"Where?"

"The prisoner will shut up!" said the other guard.

Rodrigue almost launched into them with the desperation of a cornered animal, but he checked himself. He remembered a mock-POW exercise years before. Disassociate. Walk through it like a dream.

"Aye, aye," he said, smiling evilly.

There were eight guards altogether. They surrounded him and marched him down the hall in such a tight cluster he kept tripping on the heels of the man in front to keep from having his own heels stepped on. They led him to the same room he had bolted out of before—what was it, two weeks? a month?—and escorted him inside. Dr. Haas, with a bandage on his face, sat at the same table with the Sony recorder. No mike.

"Hope you don't mind all the company," he said, a weary gesture acknowledging the line of guards behind Rodrigue. The words came clipped through tightly clenched teeth. A puzzled look escaped onto Rodrigue's face, and Haas explained almost apologetically, "It's the jaw. Wired."

104

Rodrigue's face was blank again.

"Sit, sit," Haas said, obviously with some pain.

Rodrigue sat.

Haas breathed deeply. "Well!" He pushed back and tried to manage a smile. "Time is running out. I'm up against the wall." It came out "Aye-uh aginz de wah."

"You know," said Rodrigue cheerfully, "I can't understand about half of what you're saying. Does the goon squad come with a translator?"

"Me!" Haas said, rising suddenly. "I have to make you talk." He sat down again, shaking his head slowly. "I don't understand. They don't want you. Why don't you give them what they want?"

"Watch my mouth, asshole. I don't *know* anything!"

Haas stiffened, then sighed. "Why are you so hostile?"

"Oh, I don't know. Food's great and everything, but it's a bitch to get a drink around here."

"You know, Rodrigue, your smart mouth isn't going to help you get out of here. Listen, I'm not sure you understand what kind of trouble you're in here. You're a nonperson, do you know that? Do you know what that *means?*"

By the time he finished the speech, Haas's face was twisted with the effort. He rested a moment, then with a sweeping gesture of disgust, ordered the guards to take Rodrigue away.

The next eight hours in the infirmary, Rodrigue's spirits sank quickly. He owed Sandy, he owed Diegleman, he owed Mike, and he owed others. And he could never pay. Because he didn't know what they wanted. Her terrible blank mirthless smile appeared before his eyes in broad daylight. He sat still on the side of the bed in his too-small khakis with his elbows on his knees and his head in his hands and just waited. He heard the footsteps—more than one man, but not many more—long before they reached the door. He didn't look up until Bruce Phillips stepped inside, carrying an old Pan Am flight bag.

"A sight for a sore eye," said Rodrigue, almost blubbering.

"Hello, Rod. You all right?"

"I could use a drink."

The deputy sat on the opposite bed and winked. "Might be able to help you there." He lit a cigarette and hunted an ashtray, finding none.

"How'd you know I was here?"

"They can't hide you. You're a witness."

"Christ, don't *you* start! I don't know shit!"

Phillips's laugh turned into a cigarette cough. He pulled a bottle of Cruzan out of the flight bag. "Best I could do on short notice," he said, squinting through the smoke from the cigarette.

"Good enough," Rodrigue said happily. He grabbed a couple of used plastic-foam coffee cups from his nightstand and washed them out in the bathroom.

"Might take a little snort," said Phillips.

"Water?"

"Nah—yeah, better. Just a little."

"So what's the deal?" asked Rodrigue, the first healthy gulp warming his belly.

"Murder's still a state offense." Phillips flicked his cigarette ash into the cuff of his trousers.

Rodrigue pulled the cup from his lips and stared hard at his old friend. "There's this dope thing—but then there's something else."

Phillips sat listening.

"Sandy was married to a Barnett Culberson, and *he's* a telephone company executive from Atlanta. She was on the run from him—her and her daughter both. She told me he had her traced to Lauderdale where she—they—

106

were living with this airline pilot. Anyway, whoever it was who traced her, private eye or whatever, apparently beat the shit out of the pilot. Sandy told me she and Sarah— that's the kid—took off running and wound up in Galveston. So maybe her old man had her killed and Mike just happened to be in the wrong place at the wrong time."

"Or maybe he was mistaken for you."

Rodrigue glared at the deputy. "You too?"

"No, I mean maybe—if what you say is right—the private cop or whoever was out to punish Sandy's lover like he did the other one. My mind is open on the matter."

"Well, mine isn't. I know goddamn well you didn't get in here saying you were working on a murder investigation for goddamn Galveston County. You're just fucking humoring me. What are you doing here?" At that moment, Rodrigue felt he didn't have a friend in the world. And it didn't soften him any.

Phillips let a tiny smile escape. "Told them if they let me see you and see you're all right, I'd keep my mouth shut. But if they didn't, I'd start a fuss about Mike."

"Mike? What about Mike?"

"They're sitting on his killing. Right now he's just missing. Got a secret folder put around the ME's report and everything."

"Why?"

"Don't know exactly. Guess just so's there won't be too much light shed on their investigation while it's still so shaky. You *did* figure out that he was working with them, didn't you?"

"What?"

Phillips poured more rum into Rodrigue's cup. "Actually he was *trying* to work with them. He traded them your name for a few scraps of information about the task force. That's why they were on your tail so quick. Then when they figured he didn't know no more, they cut him off. He was probably hoping to get more out of you so they'd open the pipeline again."

"*You* working with 'em, Bruce?"

Phillips took a tiny sip of his watered-down Curzan. "It don't look that way. I'm working on Sandy's killing—or at least I'm supposed to *look* like I'm working on it. Kinda hard to investigate a murder when you've got to ignore the other body. At least what you've told me gives me something to do besides shine my shoes."

He poured more rum, watching Rodrigue closely. "But I'll tell you what, pal, I'll bet you a seafood platter it all comes to roost in this deal right here."

"What *is* this deal, Bruce?"

"Shit, Rod, you probably know more about that than me."

"C'mon, what the fuck's going on? You know I don't get mixed up in dope—and besides, this ain't a regular dope deal anyway. Drag me over in a fucking NASA plane and hold me *in*-fucking-communicado? Come *on!*" He poured himself another rum.

"Keep cool." Phillips leaned forward and spoke quietly, letting cigarette smoke seep out with the words. "I'll tell you what I found out, but don't you repeat none of it. These fuckin' federal boys are about one step away from the Gestapo. You know Leland Marchand?"

"Yeah, sure." Leland Marchand was a state senator from Houma, Louisiana, a city not far from where Rodrigue was reared.

"You knew he was running for governor over there?"

"So what?"

"So his nephew, kid about twenty, was over in Cartagena, Colombia, trying to scrape up a big score of coke. And the kid's a loudmouthed little bastard, apparently, 'cause he drags up a DEA informant right off the bat. This guy doesn't have the stroke to put 'em a deal together, but he pumps them for all they're worth. And evidently Marchand helped finance the trip. Evidently the trip is financed by *several* big wheels in several states. And this information is very interesting to the Justice Department."

"I see," said Rodrigue, helping himself to more rum.

"Naw, I don't think you do. Marchand's got a good chance of getting elected governor, by most reckoning. A damn good chance. That means he'll bump the first Republican governor Louisiana's had since Reconstruction. They know he's dirty—had him pegged for a coke-head for a long time—but he's got too much stroke to mess with on something like simple possession. But somebody at Justice thinks nailing Marchand with smuggling, big-time, would be quite a feather in his cap. Only they don't have enough to go on."

"Well, goddamn, if they had somebody undercover in Colombia—"

"Probably some punk working both sides. All they found out was that some wheels—including Marchand and God knows who else—are bringing coke in for their own use rather than risk buying it on the street where they might get stuff that's too potent, or not potent enough, or wind up buying it from a narcotics agent and so forth."

Rodrigue drained his cup.

"So they can't set up a buy, right?" Phillips continued. "Could've set up a *sale* if they had been ready to go in Cartagena, but they weren't."

He flicked an ash into his pants cuff. "They don't have time to set up a buy anyway—they don't know if this is a pipeline or a one-shot deal. They don't know where it's coming in, so they blockade a bunch of ports at random and hope for the best. And then when that boat shows up with nobody on it, and then the pumper for that rig disappears, the task force zooms in on Galveston. Then

109

Mike touts 'em onto you and they sit in your back pocket hoping you'll lead them to the local connection.

"They thought they hit pay-dirt when you went to see that chopper pilot, Chapman. Come to find out he and Marchand both served on the same aircraft carrier in Vietnam. Jet jockeys, both of them. But he's clean as a whistle. He don't have no money and he's not a user—that breaks the pattern—and *he* was the one who reported the abandoned boat at the rig.

"Here they've come up empty and suddenly somebody is trying to kill all the witnesses, so they grab you and they're going to squeeze you until you either talk or squish. *Now* do you understand?"

"Yeah," said Rodrigue, squinting into the empty rum bottle. "Let's go out and get a drink, y'want to?"

Phillips took another bottle of Cruzan from his bag and twisted the lid. "Sorry I didn't bring any limes," he said. "I forgot."

Rodrigue held out his cup with a lopsided grin. "Fuckin' Buck Greathouse is the local connection. Hell, I told that to Mike, but I guess the feds weren't taking his calls by then."

Phillips squinted through the smoke. "You sure?"

"Hell, yes! Look, the son of a bitch paid me two thousand bucks to sink the boat, the one abandoned at the One Seventy-four. Gave me a bunch of shit about it being for the insurance." He took a hard pull on the cup of rum. " 'Course I did it, all right. But I can pull it right back up too. What's left of it."

"Why in the hell are you protecting Buck *now?* If you'd have given him to them, you'd have saved yourself a hell of a ride."

"I wouldn't give these motherfuckers the sweat off my *dog's* balls, you unnerstan' me?" He wiped a rivulet of rum from his chin and glared at Phillips. "As soon as I figure out which one's pullin' the strings aroun' here, I'm

110

gonna kill him. Choke him to death. You can just kiss my ass good-bye when you leave this place, Bruce, ol' buddy."

"Hey, watch your mouth now. These guys will take you off in these red hills here and put you in a shallow grave. Believe it."

"I'm gonna kill at least one of 'em," Rodrigue said, stretching back on the bed.

"You really think Greathouse is getting the coke?"

"Buck Greathhouse," Rodrigue said, smiling at the ceiling. "Now *there's* a dead man. Think I'll fuckin' drown him. Tie sumpin to'm and then go down and watch'm drown, eh?"

"Rod, *think* now. Did Greathouse ever mention the coke deal? Did he ever talk about coke?"

"Whew! Think I'll zonk out for a minute, Bruce. Stick aroun'. Take that rack there."

"Naw, gotta go on back now, Rod. You take care of yourself." He started gathering up the bottles when Rodrigue suddenly sat up.

"Hey, lea' me tha' empty, there, Bruce," Rodrigue said with a flash of teeth. He snatched the bottle by the neck from Phillips's grasp and stretched back out with it tucked alongside his leg. "I'm gonna kill that motherfuckin' corpsman when he comes in here with those powdered *urp!* fuckin' eggs."

CHAPTER 13

Nausea hit Rodrigue so fast he barely had time to roll onto his stomach before throwing up. The sharp pricks in his hands and knees, the wet tickle on his face and neck, and the cool, heavy dampness—none of it seemed particularly out of place. He simply knew that he must be dying. Only later came the glimmer that he was outside somewhere in high grass.

It came as a relief—not that he was no longer locked up in the prison camp's infirmary, but that he had the whole world from which to suck air for his pounding head. He staggered to his feet and spun around slowly. A long line of blue lights trailed off into the distance. A cluster of buildings to one side had a white search beam rotating overhead. From somewhere beyond them came the sudden low throb of a helicopter warming up. An airport somewhere. Somewhere that smelled and felt familiar. Over to the left . . .

It hurt his eye to focus. His stomach was bucking

against his diaphragm and pain seeped through his temples and crawled along his flesh. Damn Cruzan—he felt he had been drinking gasoline. He walked a few steps and vomited again, violently.

He was covered with stickers—they dug into his hands and knees when he supported himself to vomit. And he discovered a new pain in his left breast. His navy eye was in his shirt pocket. He was bruised where he had lain on it.

He was wearing the clothes he had worn when Sandy and Mike were killed—khaki shorts and an Hawaiian shirt, both now freshly laundered and stiff from too much starch. He checked his wallet and pockets: he still had most of the two thousand dollars Greathouse had given him, plus the three hundred from the wheel job.

Rodrigue stumbled onto an old concrete runway with weeds growing in the cracks. He followed it away from the blue lights and found himself at a high chain-link fence. He scrambled up it and saw long streaks of light reflected in glassy water on the other side, and he knew he was home. That was Offatt's Bayou and the causeway beyond it. The federal government had dumped him at Scholes Field like a garbage bag full of fish heads.

Dawn had begun to separate sky from sea by the time Rodrigue cut across Broadway and picked his way into a neighborhood of narrow, oily streets lined with tiny frame houses and yards packed with rusting cars and trucks. Ahead in the dim light two men held a laughing conversation in the fast, drawling jive of Southern blacks. The intimacy of the place reminded him of Belize City and he felt both at home and homesick.

And just plain sick. He was gettin tired and the nausea flooded back in waves. Damn Cruzan . . .

"Say, Mistah *Rod?*" The voice was as soft as old velvet.

"Aye?" said Rodrigue, finding the shadowy figure on the small porch.

"Say, I *thought* that was you. What you doin' in here?" The man came down from the porch to the street.

"Jus' passin' through, matey." Rodrigue drew up and was surprised to find himself sweating profusely.

"Edgar Samuels. You don't remember me. You pulled me in from the north jetty last year. Old Falcon, remember? Sumpin' in the carburetor, it turned out. Say, you *hurt*, Mistah Rod?"

"Yes, I am, Mr. Samuels."

Like most southern whites his age, Rodrigue believed Negroes had traits inherent of their race. He was different in that he valued Negro traits. They were the warmest of humans in a cold, cold world.

"I have one helluva hangover," he said.

"Let me pour you some coffee, then, Mistah Rod."

"It'd just make me puke, Mr. Samuels."

"I knows what's gonna make you feel better, Mistah Rod, if you'll just listen to ol' Edgar."

"What'd that be, Mr. Samuels?"

"Tomato juice."

"Ah!"

"*Fresh* tomato juice, from fresh tomatoes I growed myself, right back there in that garden. It'll make you feel like a new man."

"Mr. Samuels," said Rodrigue, wrapping his arm around the old man's shoulders and squeezing, "I sincerely regret any evil I may have done you."

"You never done me no evil, Mistah Rod," Samuels said, grinning broadly. "You charged me a lot of money, but then that's what you do, ain't it?"

The tomato juice was no cure but it quenched the fire in Rodrigue's belly. Samuels gave him a ride in a rusty old GMC pickup. They stopped by the Kettle Restaurant for Rodrigue to pick up a newspaper—Volcker says the Fed will stick with tight money, recession or no recession.

114

It was the middle of July. He had been gone more than two weeks.

"Mr. Samuels, let me buy you a seafood platter," Rodrigue said, shoving a twenty-dollar bill in the old man's shirt pocket.

"Mistah Rod, you gonna insult me," Samuels said seriously, and he gently put the money back in Rodrigue's hand.

"Okay. But you got a free tow job coming, okay? You don't let 'em send nobody but me. You still running that same old cathedral hull?"

Samuels grinned and patted Rodrigue on the shoulder. "Oh, I'll be needin' you someday, don't you worry."

The oily fog from the *Queen*'s cold outboards did Rodrigue's stomach no good. On the stretch between the Pelican Island Bridge and the causeway, he had to put the engines in neutral and heave Mr. Samuels's fresh tomato juice over the side. The water was slick and the smooth high-speed run to the causeway, with his head out the window, made him feel a little better. In West Bay he had to slow to a crawl and pick his way through the shell reefs and spoil banks down the old Intracoastal Canal. He hadn't been back there in a long while.

The bait camp at Sea Isle was still closed. Rodrigue tied the *Queen* in one of the empty slips at the marina and hiked the mile or so across the island to his house on the beach.

The sun finally climbed above the ridge of clouds on the horizon and shed its brassy light on the cluster of beach houses. No one was stirring yet. Crossing the highway to the entrance to his street, Rodrigue suddenly flashed on the blank-faced young man who had so impassively watched him being hauled away. There had been something familiar about that face but he just

115

couldn't place it. Was he a neighbor? Could've been. Rodrigue, who spent so much time at the yacht basin, hadn't made many friends in the subdivision.

But even to his friends, Rodrigue remained something of a stranger. They joked with him, called him Rodrigue the Pirate, envied his mobility, and counted on his help in times of trouble, but there was always the flicker of something hard, like the glint of a blade in the moonlight, that kept them from getting too close. They had heard how he lived among blacks in Belize and spoke their jumbled dialect, and how he could walk into a Mexican cantina and drink with the locals. And yet he never quite fit in. He was the affable rogue, fun to hoist a glass with but never one to turn your back on.

He had cultivated their suspicions. If people didn't bother him it was because they were afraid of what he would do when molested. Well, now he had been molested big-time. Sandy, so determined to enjoy this life, had been swatted like a goddamned mosquito—shot in the face! The arrogance of it made rage boil over his grief.

He himself had been jerked around like a rag doll in the teeth of a mongrel. He wanted to stomp somebody, to strike out the way he had struck out at Haas. Poor Haas. He was just a puppet himself. A clever one, though. He had known the spot where even the gentlest nudge would be excruciating . . .

SN Eugene Diegleman was a smart rich kid from Worcester, Massachusetts, whose constant griping was the crew's anthem. He was small and witty and wisecracking and he looked amazingly like the product of a night of unprotected passion between Barbra Streisand and Woody Allen. Diegleman wasn't crazy about Vietnam and he hated the U.S. Navy.

They served together on a PBR, a thirty-one-foot,

116

totally unarmored fiberglass patrol craft with jet drives. Diegleman was the bow gunner and twenty-nine-year-old MM1 John Rodrigue was the skipper. They were in the Co Chien River, rafted up with another PBR. The other boat's engines were shut down and Rodrigue was slowly towing it to Hotel Canal, one of the many they would later call Purple Heart Alley, where the other boat would lay an ambush while Rodrigue stood by out in the river. Standing by didn't appeal to Rodrigue and he might have been a little harsh with Diegleman, whom he, like everyone else in the crew, loved like a brother. He told him to shut up and when he didn't Rodrigue shoved him, hard. Then everyone grew silent and sulked.

It was night and pouring rain. To the VC in the jungle alongside the canal, it would sound like a single PBR on a routine patrol. About a kilometer up the canal, at the place where Intelligence said medical supplies were being smuggled across after curfew, the chief who was skippering the other boat silently ordered his crew to throw off the lines. The boat drifted into the jungle while Rodrigue rumbled on down the canal. When he came back an hour later he could barely pick up the hard outline of its stern in the starlight scope. He went back into the river and waited. If help was needed, the chief would simply key his mike one time.

Instead a storm of automatic-weapons fire erupted up the canal, and then the other boat's bow-gunner came on the radio begging for help. Instead of medicine smugglers they had stumbled onto a troop crossing—a hundred or more heavily armed VC being ferried across the canal not fifty feet from the hidden PBR. Somehow the chief had been discovered and his boat was being chewed to pieces.

Diegleman was a malcontent but he was no coward. Even as Rodrigue reached for the throttles, he scrambled forward into his gun pit . . .

117

* * *

Home at last, Rodrigue climbed the stairs haltingly, struggling to blot out the vision of Mike's leg jutting from the open door. Gradually he realized there were voices coming from inside. He heard arguing. He climbed faster, numbed by a sense of unreality. He found the door closed but unlocked. He opened it quietly and stepped quietly into an empty room. The voices were coming from the TV, tuned to an early-morning melodrama.

From the kitchen came the distinctive smell of comino. That was real enough. Somebody else was living here.

A hideous face suddenly appeared over the top of the couch and screamed at him. He yelled back in surprise. The face screamed again and fell away with eyes rolled back.

Rodrigue felt faint and staggered against the dining table. The face appeared again, cautiously, like a rising moon—it was Rosa. Bronze Aztec queen that she was, she was pale to the point of being blue around her lips and nostrils.

"Jesus, you scared the shit out of me," he said. "Pardon my French."

" 'S'okay, you scared the shit outta me too," she said.

"What're you doing here anyway?"

"Señor Phillips, he told me to come out and clean up. He helped too. With the blood, you know?"

"What's that cooking?"

"Menudo. Señor Phillips . . ."

Menudo, a beef tripe chili, was the Mexican cure for a hangover.

So Phillips had been his interrogator.

Sure. Drugs hadn't worked, the shrink hadn't worked, so they brought in an expert who did the trick with a bottle of rum. A couple of bottles. God*damned* Cruzan—*whew!*

118

He had been tricked into fingering Greathouse.

That was all they wanted—to bust the cocaine ring to stop Leland Marchand from becoming governor of Louisiana. They didn't care who killed Sandy and Mike. Maybe Bruce Phillips did, but Phillips was a survivor. He wouldn't throw himself off a cliff over it.

Rodrigue was a small fish and they had simply thrown him back, expecting him to dart away gratefully, to just go back to whatever he had been doing. They couldn't very well ask him to testify against Greathouse, not after abducting him and holding him illegally. The federal government hadn't been all that impressed with Rodrigue the Pirate, anyway. He was just—what had Wilson said? A bum? A nobody. He had come home and interrupted the soaps.

He showered and changed and tried the eye, but the socket was still too sore. He found his old black patent leather eyepatch, the one he had used to impress jaded ladies in waterfront dives. He ate some of the menudo. Phillips had already paid Rosa but he paid her more and put her to ironing until Felipe, her youngest son, came by to pick her up.

Up to coffee now, Rodrigue started a pot dripping while he dialed Phillips's home number in the off chance the deputy might be there. Nobody answered. He needed to find out it Sarah was okay, but he didn't want to call the sheriff's office or even leave word at the yacht basin, at least not until he was sure of his own status. Phillips had a very political job.

When the coffee was finished Rodrigue poured a cup, took it out on the deck, and went through the *Post* he had picked up in town. Nolan Ryan was nursing a sore shoulder. In place of Mike's column there was a commentary off the wire contrasting Britain's "spendid little war" in the Falklands with U.S. covert actions in Central America. Mike would've loved it. But there was not a word in the paper to indicate there had ever been a Mike Ferguson.

A young woman herding kids on the beach kept glancing nervously Rodrigue's way. That was good; the legend grows.

But that night his eye would not close. Who killed Sandy and Mike and *why?* An outraged husband? No. Too cool and professional. Okay, a goon hired by the husband. No. Had they been beaten to death, maybe. The pilot had been beaten. Maybe Barney had hired new talent, who knows? Maybe . . .

There was no escaping the possibility that Greathouse had done it, or had had it done, because he thought Mike was about to incriminate him. Ferguson had done everything but draw a map to Sea Isle for anyone who might be looking for him. Or Greathouse could've been out to kill Rodrigue, knowing that he was the source of Ferguson's information. It was hard to believe, but Greathouse had certainly gotten himself in deep trouble.

And yet Greathouse, rich as he was, was just another small fish.

Sure. They were after Leland Marchand. Greathouse might be tossing and turning on a bunk at Maxwell that very moment—if they had been able to find him. Maybe some DEA goon had him pinned down on Grand Cayman.

No, they wouldn't be so cavalier with the likes of Buck Greathouse. Besides, they might need his testimony. But how in the hell had he gotten mixed up with Leland *Marchand?* It wasn't on some aircraft carrier, that was for sure.

Well, forget about it.

Leland Marchand. The big fish.

Forget about it.

Greathouse would wind up an "unindicted coconspirator," that's what would happen.

Forget about it.

Probably wouldn't even question him about Sandy and Mike. Wouldn't want to know. Already swept Mike's murder under the rug.

Forget about it.

Forget about it, he thought desperately.

But Sandy wouldn't let him.

CHAPTER 14

"The best thing for you to do," said Charlie Hagan seriously, "is just forget about it."

"Fine. I just don't want Greathouse to forget about it."

Rodrigue had just told the Coast Guard investigator all about sinking the boat for Buck Greathouse.

Now Hagan paced nervously in front of his desk, pipe in hand. Normally he presided over every situation with calm detachment, like a college professor watching students take an exam.

"If you just need to confess, go see a priest," he said, "because I can tell you right now the FBI's not interested."

"I don't want anything to do with . . . What the hell do you *mean* they're not interested?"

Hagan sat on his desk finally, talking around his pipe stem. "Those fellows on that little fishing boat are lost at sea. Period. And that task force investigation has had a lid clamped on it. It never happened."

"What?"

Hagan shrugged and relit his pipe. "I don't like it, but there you have it. It's politics. High-level, *dangerous* politics." He glanced meaningfully at Rodrigue. "What happened to your eye?"

"Bumped it. Do you know what it's all about?"

Hagan glanced down the empty hallway. "All I know is the same day the PHI pilot reported that boat abandoned at the Galveston Block One Seventy-four production platform, we relayed a mayday from a Grand Banks 42 that was taking on water in heavy seas about a hundred miles out. I think one of the birds at Ellington was down for maintenance and another engaged in some operation, I don't know. Anyway, we relayed the call to Coast Guard New Orleans and they flew four men off the yacht. From what they said, a hose on some through-hull fitting had either ruptured or worked loose—something an experienced boatman could've dealt with easily. But these guys were no boatmen and by the time the chopper got there it was too late for a handy billy and they had to be lifted off her as she sank."

A handy billy was a portable gasoline-powered pump that could be lowered or dropped to a sinking vessel.

"Flying them back in," Hagan said, "the chopper crew said one of the men—a kid, really—became delirious from fear or fatigue or what have you. He told them he had just killed two men in a small boat at a platform off Galveston. The other three people said he was hallucinating and the crew tended to believe that. Of course they didn't know there really was an abandoned boat until it was too late."

"Too late?"

"The people were released."

"So what? You guys don't just release people. You count scars and take blood first. Couldn't you have just picked them up again?"

Hagan studied the ashes in the bowl of his pipe. "I told you there's political influence involved here," he said finally. "What I got, I got from the chopper crew, not official channels. Officially, the rescue never happened."

"Okay, then, what's your guess?" asked Rodrigue. Hagan was a puzzle-solver by nature as well as profession. He would have picked up all the pieces he could find.

"Just what chit do you think you're cashing in here?" the investigator asked coldly.

Rodrigue eyed him evenly. "Don't do *me* any favors. You know what's right and what's not."

Hagan scratched his pipe stem around in his beard thoughtfully. Rodrigue was a thug with a strange sense of honor. And resourceful—very resourceful. He might actually get to the bottom of this.

"The Grand Banks was an inspected vessel belonging to a developer in West Palm Beach," Hagan said warily. "A very *prominent* developer who also happens to be a wheel in the state's Republican party. And the kid who was babbling about—"

"Oh, bullshit, Charlie! I can't believe this is just about the ins versus the fucking outs!"

"Listen up," said Hagan, impatient at being interrupted. "The kid who said he killed the two fisherman is the son of the developer who owned the Grand Banks. *Republican*, okay? But two of the others were nephews of some high-powered Louisiana politician. A *Democrat*. And that's whose coattails they evidently got away on in New Orleans."

"Leland Marchand," Rodrigue said to himself.

"That's the guy. So you're right, it *isn't* your normal political backstabbing. But it's definitely *political*. You don't shut down a Coast Guard investigation—Jesus, let alone an FBI task force—without *somebody* pulling some strings *way* up the line. And what all this has to do with the vanished Buck Greathouse, who as far as I can figure out is pretty much apolitical, is beyond me."

"Two of Marchand's nephews and the son of a Florida developer . . . Who was the fourth one on the boat?"

Hagan shrugged. "They think he's from here but he was never positively identified. The crew got the idea he might've been the skipper. Maybe just a hired hand, who knows?"

Rodrigue shook his head. "It just doesn't make any sense."

"It's cocaine," Hagan said, lighting his pipe.

Rodrigue took it slow on the crumbling back street. The safety chain clanked mournfully against the tongue of the trailer. All he had to do was put his boat back in its slings and he was back where he started when Greathouse called. He had swung by to see Charlie Hagan on impulse, but he really intended to put it behind him, to get his life on an even keel again. Sure he did.

But he had to find out about Sarah first. Was she still in danger? He was thinking maybe he ought to fly to Atlanta, but then what? He could snatch Barnett Culberson off the street and stomp him until he came up with some answers, but then what if Culberson had had nothing to do with it? Or what if he *did,* but did it in some kind of Daddies From Hell effort to take his little girl away from all the dens of iniquity once and for all. Could you fault him for that?

Rodrigue trusted his instincts more than his power of reason, and Atlanta simply didn't feel right. Greathouse didn't either, really—Rodrigue had expected him to send some goon to put sugar in his gas tank or buy the yacht basin and have him evicted, not to make little blue holes in people's faces. But Greathouse was involved some- how, there was no question about that. The skinny redhead from the rig was hiding out on his boat. And

Greathouse was the one who had gotten Rodrigue into this mess in the first place. Maybe *that* was why he felt the urge to find the *Wahoo Too*, to settle that simple score.

No, with the *Wahoo Too* were the answers that would lead him to Sandy's killer—to Greathouse or beyond. Probably beyond. It didn't matter. He wouldn't rest until he found him and killed him. He owed her that much.

Rodrigue swung by the back parking lot at the yacht basin, looking for Phillips's car. It wasn't there. He went to the public lot and was unloading the *Haulover Queen* at the bait camp ramps when Taylor, who was stacking sacks of ice in the bed of his pickup, spotted him and walked over. "What the hell happened to your eye?" he asked.

"Lost it in Vietnam," Rodrigue replied gruffly.

"I mean the glass eye. Why're you wearing an eye patch?"

"I like it. Any word from *Wahoo Too?*"

"Yes, there is," said Taylor, stung by Rodrigue's preoccupation. "Jack English saw Mickey comin' into the municipal marina on Cozumel. The one way up the road from town, y'know?"

"Uh-huh. Seen English lately?"

"Yeah, he was on the *Black Key* a little while ago. They just got in yester— Hey, where'ya goin'?"

Rodrigue was already pulling the Blazer off the ramp.

"Where ya been, anyway?" Taylor called. "Hey, what happened out at your house the other day?"

Rodrigue parked and walked back. "What'd you hear?"

Taylor shrugged. "Some kind of accident. You know how fuckin' closed-mouth Bruce is. There was an ambulance—wasn't you there?"

"Uh-uh. I've been traveling quite a bit." They were words, as best he remembered them, from a Jimmy

126

Buffett song. It was a code that meant he didn't want to talk about it, but it was a little too subtle for Taylor.

"Hey, didn't you hear about Mike, then?"

"What about Mike?" He tried not to sound interested.

"He's fuckin' disappeared. It was in the paper and on TV and everything. Found a note from him said he was going to Central America and fight for the commies. Remember he talked about that?"

Rodrigue laughed and shook his head. "I guess the son of a bitch'll be mooching beer off me this winter."

He took the *Haulover Queen* around to his slip, put her in the slings, hosed her off good, and checked the batteries.

The *Black Key* was a sixty-three-foot Monterey with a tower, outriggers, and more electronics than the Space Shuttle. It was owned by a consortium of dentists and physicians and campaigned on the billfish circuit from Chub Cay to Tobago. Her skipper, Jack English, was a tough little man with a posture like a pool cue, a big handlebars mustache, and a wide, toothy grin. Rodrigue found him at the end of B Row, flushing the freshwater tank with a garden hose.

"Good trip?" he said when English looked up.

"Yeah, okay. What happened to your eye?"

"Ain't got no eyeball in it. Just a hole. Looks ugly as hell."

"I know that," English said with a habitual twitch of his mustache. "I mean why aren't you wearing your glass eye? Trying to look like the pirate you are?"

"It's a long story. Say, heard you ran into Mickey Aimes down in Mexico. Still down there, you suppose?"

"I guess. I got the idea Buck would be doing some fishing down there. Sails are hanging in real good, but that's about it. 'Course that's always 'about it' for Cozumel."

"You talk to Mickey?"

127

"On the VHF, as I was pulling out of the marina and he was pulling in. That was, what, six, seven days ago?"

"What'd he say?"

"Nothing much. What's up, Rod?"

"Might fly down there, if I can bum a place to stay. Like on *Wahoo Too*. Jerry Taylor said it was the municipal marina? The one north of town?"

"Yep. Hey, if you go, wanna carry something down there for me?"

"Depends what it is. I'm not carrying any goddamn outboard motor or anything. Not without a fat fee, anyway."

English laughed. "A little ol' depth-flasher unit. Fits in a gym bag and weighs hardly nothing. One of my owners stayed down there to spend the whole month scuba diving. He's hired a little boat but he wants something to tell him what his depths are so he can keep out of trouble. I guess you know all about that, don't you?"

"Well," said Rodrigue, rubbing his chin thoughtfully. "Okay, I'll take it. But maybe you ought to go get me a beer out of the box, just so I can keep my standing in the fraternity of professional pirates, eh?"

CHAPTER 15

The low, thick scrub of the northern Yucatan flew by the window. As the tires screeched on the runway, Rodrigue balanced the rum and soda he had hidden from the stewardesses on their final sweep of unbuckled belts and lowered seat backs. The Aeromexico Boeing 737 roared and shuttered and coasted toward the terminal. Rodrigue gulped the last of his drink and stuffed the plastic glass into the elastic pocket on the seat in front of him. In halting English on the scratchy PA system, a stewardess was welcoming the passengers to Cozumel.

"It looks like they haven't had rain in weeks," said his newfound friend, the woman who had taken his window seat. She smiled weakly and gazed out hopefully at the blinding runway apron.

She no longer looked like an old-maid schoolteacher, Rodrigue thought, although she was certainly out of place on this flight. She was traveling with a large straw bag, a thin sweater, and a well-thumbed copy of *Fodor's* that she had tucked away when she learned her seatmate was a seasoned visitor to the Caribbean island.

"Not since yesterday afternoon, anyway," he replied. "The limestone just soaks it right up."

He was grateful for her. Far worse would've been to wind up next to some macho clod with a Gilbert Roland cigarillo—like most terminating flights to Cozumel, this one was full of vacationing scuba divers. Also she had kept his mind off the fact that behind that flimsy door up there humans were trying to make a mechanical elephant fly.

Rodrigue didn't drink more than usual on the flight. That was impossible in coach. He started with two drinks and then had to chase the drink wagon down the aisle for two more.

"Would you like to trade places?" asked the woman, then in the aisle seat.

"If you would like," said Rodrigue, standing and balancing the drinks. "But I promise this is the last time. Four's my limit."

"If you don't mind, actually. I like to look out."

"In that case, ma'am, it is an order."

Her eyes, Rodrigue was noticing, were an almost startling blue. They were crowned with pale lashes that gave her the wide-eyed look of a child, yet there was also an intelligent sort of mischievous twinkle. She turned out to be younger than he had thought. She was pale, with dry skin and no makeup. Faint yellow freckles were sprinkled liberally over her nose and cheeks. Her hair was the red of an Irish setter and was rolled into a rope down her back, like a Mayan campesina. When she smiled, her skin crinkled like parchment over her high cheekbones and her thin, dry lips drew back over delicate white teeth, perfect except for one crooked canine. Rodrigue found to his confusion that he was enjoying her company.

And despite his boorish display with the liquor, she seemed to be enjoying his. Instead of gazing out the window she turned her attention to him. Well, why not? A tall dark stranger in a black eye patch and formal white guayabera, speaking with a faintly French accent and wearing well-broken-in boat shoes with no socks. Not that bad-looking either, Rodrigue imagined. For a moment he wished *he* were on vacation, dissolving the ugly memories in rum and sunshine.

"Do you dive?" she asked, still making small talk as the plane lumbered toward the terminal. It was almost like asking someone on a December junket to Vail if he skied.

"Uh-huh. You?"

"No, I never learned," she said without regret.

Even before the plane came to a halt the vacationers pushed into the aisle to fetch their net dive bags and Hawaiian Punch hats from the overhead compartments. Rodrigue didn't budge. No point in getting in a hurry. The ground crew wasn't in a hurry. The cabin attendants weren't in a hurry. Nobody on Cozumel got in a hurry in the middle of a July day except tourists. Their smothered impatience made tourists stand out like a tap dancer at a funeral.

"Are you here with a group?" she asked, content to wait with him.

"No. On business, I'm afraid."

"Oh." A curious trace of dejection passed through her downward glance. The aisle cleared beside them. The woman craned to see the crush of passengers receding toward the front of the aircraft. She gathered her bag and sweater.

"I've enjoyed it," Rodrigue said, and he rose to clear the way for her.

"So have I," she replied with a new nervousness. Rodrigue handed down her travel bag and then

131

collected his duffle containing four changes of clothing rolled navy-style, a pair of old canvas boat shoes, shaving kit, a new can of Cutter Insect Repellent Spray, and the Humminbird Super Sixty depth-flasher complete with transducer and mounting brackets that Jack English had given him to bring to a Dr. Merkel at El Presidente.

Strangers again, they shuffled in silence toward the exit, where two stewardesses and the copilot stood muttering pleasantries to every third passenger. He watched her return a crinkly smile and stride puposefully down the ramp and across the blistering apron. A freak gust lifted her dress and revealed very white but very long and shapely legs. Rodrigue was ashamed of himself.

He waded through the sluggish immigration and customs checks with growing impatience—not the smothered kind of the tourists but the more explosive Latin version. Back out in the glaring sunlight, he commandeered a waiting taxi, tossing his duffle into the backseat ahead of him and barking *"¡Andale!"* In his guttural South American Spanish, he directed the driver to the small marina where Greathouse's *Wahoo Too* was supposed to be berthed.

Rodrigue had the driver park on the far side of the low concrete block building that housed the marina office and he walked around to where the larger boats were usually tied along bulkheads fringed with lofty coconut palms. The Hatteras wasn't there. In the shade, in three piles like collapsed tents, were black rubberized auxiliary fuel tanks. Rodrigue stretched one out—it said *Wahoo Too* in faded white stenciling.

The space adjacent to the discarded bladder tanks was vacant. In the next slot seaward, a crew of young locals bathed a venerable old Ocean in tired, dirty suds. "Where is the boat that belongs here?" he called in Spanish to the youngster working on the saloon windows from the rail.

"Who knows?" replied the boy with an unenthusiastic shrug. "Is it not a fishing boat? Maybe fishing."

He could have checked with the marina officials and found out for sure, but he didn't want to draw attention to himself. Besides, it was the logical explanation: Buck was down here fishing. If he were on the run, he wouldn't have left the bladder tanks. And if he had been snatched up by the DEA or somebody, Mickey wouldn't be out tooling around on his own. It was just like Hagan said, life goes on.

Until the boat comes back at sundown, he thought.

"Where now?" asked the driver, delighted to have lucked onto a live one.

"Mayan Plaza!" Rodrigue said impulsively. Instinctively. He recognized the instinct and settled back in the worn backseat of the five-year-old LTD with the gritty relief of having met your own worst self.

The Mayan Plaza was a new, expensive seaside hotel a couple of miles north of town. It was the kind of place you treated yourself to. At the desk in the cavernous open-air lobby he leafed through a brochure advertising a remote fishing camp on the mainland. Bonefish and permit and tarpon. Fly you right over from Cozumel. *God*, he thought, when was the last time he had just gone fishing?

Not having a reservation was no problem in the middle of July. The room wasn't much, just a white-walled cubicle near the elevators on the tenth floor, and they charged him winter rates. Rodrigue sat at the foot of the bed and wondered what he would do when the *Wahoo Too* came in. There was no use in making plans— just a design for futility. You became locked in, lost flexibility. Better to go with the flow, Rodrigue heartily believed.

He decided to have a few rums at the bar while he was waiting to find out where the flow was going. He shaved

133

and brushed his teeth and tried the eye but still found it uncomfortable. He combed his hair, adjusted the black patch, and rode the small, slow elevator to the ground floor.

The redheaded woman was there, alone at the table, absently studying the lush garden, a drink in a green coconut sitting before her.

"May I join you?" he asked, feeling an unaccustomed tingle as the blood rushed into his face.

"Why not?" she said coolly in Spanish after recovering from a flicker of surprise.

He sat and snapped his fingers at the waiter.

"I am called John Rodrigue," he said, also in Spanish, extending a big suntanned hand.

She took it in her own, soft and cool and white. "My name is Ann Eller. From Houston," she said in English.

"I always wanted one of these," she said, resuming their small talk with a nod toward her coconut drink.

"They're pretty lethal."

"And a little, well . . . *touristy,* don't you think? Are you staying here?"

"Uh-huh. I missed my contact, unfortunately, so now I have time on my hands. I'm delighted to run into you. Would you consider having dinner with me?"

Run into her, his ass. It was chancy, of course, but if you had one shot at "running into" a particular class of tourist on Cozumel, your best shot was at the Mayan Plaza.

"That would be lovely," she said, blushing radiantly.

The waiter came. Rodrigue ordered rum and soda. "Can I get you another?" he asked her. "Or would you prefer something different?"

"Another coco loco would be lovely," she said with sparkling eyes.

They made more small talk, about the humidity, about the flower arrangement though which she had to sip her

134

sweet rum drink. Then she leaned forward and said earnestly, "I'm dying to know something about you but I really don't now how to ask."

"Lost it in Vietnam," he said flatly.

She sat back giggling with her hand over her mouth. "I didn't mean the eye, necessarily. I meant who *are* you, what do you do? That's what we're all concerned with in the end, isn't it? What a person *does*? Sorry, I'm new at this."

"I was a commercial diver for ten years. Made a lot of money and didn't spend it all. A couple of years ago I got the bends—decompression sickness—and I decided to retire. So, I'm retired. Now tell me about you."

"Well, in the first place I'll be thirty years old next week. And right now that's where I'm at, so to speak. If you know what I mean."

"You better switch to Seven-Up."

"Why? If a person can't get snookered when she's thirty years old, there's no excuse under the sun."

"That's *snockered*. I'm being perfectly honest with you."

"Oh, yes. 'Snookered' would be, what—? Used? Abused?"

"Here, don't drink anymore of that." He slid the coco loco away from her. "Go get your suit and let's take a little dip in the pool. It'll clear your head and make you hungry. Then we'll go have some conch ceviche and broiled lobster."

"Suit," she said, trying the word.

"Swimming suit."

"I know, but I honestly didn't think to bring one. I usually stay on the more cultural route through San Miguel de Allende and so forth."

"Come to think of it, I don't have one either," he said, slapping his forehead. "Shall we hit the boutique?"

Taking his drink along—quieting the waiter with a

135

couple of hundred-peso notes—he steered her into a glass-walled room lined with gleaming gold trinkets and dull gray replicas of pre-Columbian artifacts. He talked her into a chic black one-piece with no back and French-cut legs that would come to her waist. He would've loved to buy it for her but was afraid to offer, afraid it would seem too wolfish. She solved the dilemma for him by stepping up and paying with her American Express while he was still in the corner holding a tropical-print boxer up to his waist and looking at his reflection in the glass wall. They made a date to meet at the pool bar in ten minutes.

After half an hour Rodrigue decided she had chickened out, but then there she was, suddenly, sliding onto the submerged, tile-covered barstool beside him, trim and firm, with surprisingly full breasts that had been hidden by her bloused cotton dress.

She tugged self-consciously at the bodice of the sheer black swimsuit. "Sorry I'm so late. It's not like me, it really isn't. Coco loco," she said resolutely to the bartender's politely arched eyebrows.

"I was scouring the shop for a commodity called 'bikini wax.'" She took a pull on the coco loco as soon as it arrived. "I wasn't quite prepared for such a high cut in the legs."

The image of this delicate creature with her legs spread rubbing cream into an auburn groin flooded Rodrigue with lechery that clotted into something pretty close to guilt.

"I hope you also thought of sunscreen," he said. "You can burn even in the shade around here."

"Oh, yes. Waterproof."

"Good, then I'll race you to the deep end."

"Can you get that wet?" She flicked a slim finger at the leather patch.

"Sure. I used to wear it diving to impress the native tenders."

Rodrigue never swam when he could sit and drink, but he wanted to get her away from the coco locos. He knew he should leave her alone to find a suitable partner to share her vacation. He often did things he knew better than to do—but he shouldn't be using a sweet, shy young woman to exorcise Sandy. If he had done what he knew he should have done and left that goddamned boat where it sat under that goddamned platform, Sandy would still be alive. Typically of him, he had simply shoved it out of his head and kept on. Kept on keeping on. That was Rodrigue. Follow Rodrigue, get your ass killed.

It was a race indeed. Ann swam smoothly, burying her face in the water like an Olympic free-styler and then getting all the air she needed with a dainty sniff as she spun to face him.

"You need some exercise, Mr. Rodriguez," she said happily.

"It's Rodrigue," he said, puffing. "The French version."

"Oh, and do you also speak French?" she asked, switching to the stiff-cheeked Parisian form of the language.

"*Mais,* yeah," Rodrigue answered in Cajun. "But it is not the same French, you know?"

"Ah, yes, the French of Louisiana. I hear it sometimes."

"Where? Houston?"

"Yes, Houston. God, I'm having fun," she said, resting one dripping white arm on the cement rim of the pool. "I don't think I expected to."

"Aw, *avec moi?*"

"No, I mean just down here. This hedonists' paradise. I guess I've always sort of looked down on the fun-in-the-sun scene."

As if she had hurt the passionate Mexican sun's

137

feelings, suddenly it was pouring rain, drumming loudly on the broad green leaves and raising the acrid smell of simmering concrete. She saw it as an opportunity to shield her unaccustomed nakedness and make a dignified exit.

"Call for me when you're ready, okay?" she said, laying cool fingers on his beefy arm for one delicious instant. Then she was out and running in half-steps across the slippery patio, an exciting vision of long white thighs and hard white buttocks.

When he rang her room three hours later, she answered, *"¿Bueno?"* in the Mexican fashion.

"It would be with great pleasure for me to call for you if you are ready," Rodrigue said formally in Spanish.

"Almost," she said—a little warily, he imagined. "Shall I meet you in the lobby?"

"Five minutes?"

"Five minutes."

She wore her thick red hair up. She had a long slender neck and sexy little pinkish ears with a single pearl in each lobe. A black lace shawl added an untouchable touch to a come-hither outfit, a black-and-white print sundress with toucans and palm leaves. Through the shawl, Rodrigue could see by the glow of her shoulders that the sunscreen hadn't been entirely waterproof. Or maybe it had been ineffectively applied. She *had* gotten a little snockered.

In a taxi they went to the Cabañas del Caribe, one of the oldest hostels on the island, with thatch-roof cottages scattered in a palm grove and an intimate restaurant at the water's edge. They started out on the balcony, where they could watch small tarpon playing in the lights, and Rodrigue ordered his usual rum and soda with lime. Ann, sensibly, had a Coke.

"I come to Mexico every summer," she said, "and I

had never had a coco loco until today. And I'll tell you what"—she leaned forward conspiringly—"I had *always* wanted one."

"Well . . ."

"I'm a librarian for Mobil," she injected, determined to spill it. "All of my friends are academics, sort of. Teachers and librarians. 'All of my friends'—I have three good friends. We usually vacation together. Two years ago we went to Europe, but the rest of the time it's been Mexico. It's inexpensive and—well, you know. I make quite a bit of money, actually, but the others don't."

"Mobil *Oil* Company?"

"Yes. You didn't know oil companies have librarians? Of course they do. We catalog all sorts of interesting information. Geophysical reports. Tanker status and distribution."

Rodrigue listened with genuine interest.

"We don't normally go to the tourist places," she said, almost apologetically. "And this year . . . I don't really know how to explain it. Maybe I just needed to be alone. I mean my values haven't changed, I just—"

"I tell you wot, you're lovelier and downright sexier than any twenty-year-old I know," he said.

"Yes, that's it, isn't it? Thirty years old. Life is passing me by," she said with a melodramatic forearm to the brow.

"Hey, the caboose is still *way* back there."

"I'm reluctant to ask you about you. I don't know why."

"Maybe you're afraid the truth will fall short of the image," said Rodrigue. "'Plat san an' stone breeze.'"

"I beg your pardon?"

"It's a Creole saying. Plot or cultivate sand and tear up the wind with rocks. Can't be done, at least not by the average person. It means basically to live a mysterious

139

life. I think it must have something to do with voodoo. Anyway, keeping up a mysterious image is a very real means to power in some parts of the world."

"So how many languages *do* you speak?"

"English, sort of," he said, ticking them off. "French, of course, which I grew up speaking. Then we lived in Venezuela for a while when I was a kid, so I learned Spanish. I can say some pretty nasty things in Vietnamese. Then there's Creole, which really isn't a language but might as well be."

"Creole . . ." she said thoughtfully. "We're speaking about black Caribbean, I guess?"

"Uh-huh." It was what Creole meant nowadays. Historically, it had served to distinguish whites born in the New World from those born in Europe. And in Louisiana, to distinguish the descendants of the original French settlers of New Orleans from the broader population of Cajuns from what's now Nova Scotia. Rodrigue's own ancestry was a wild jumble. There had been a Spaniard, certainly, but there probably had been women of African origin too. Maybe genetics was involved in Rodrigue's ability to master the difficult pidgin of the Caribbean.

"Have you lived in the Caribbean then?" she asked.

"Off and on for years. Still do. And you? You don't strike me as a native Houstonian."

"Why not?"

He shrugged. He had a dim view of Houstonians as a crowd although he liked them individually well enough. It was more to do with the image of the place as the mecca of the Fossil Fuel Age, but he wasn't about to let himself be backed into a corner over it.

"Well, you're right," she said. "Cleveland, Ohio. But I've lived in Houston for, gosh, seven years now. Moved right out of college. Where in the Caribbean?"

"Where what?"

"Where do you live?"

"Oh, in Belize. Just in the winter. In the summer I stay in Galveston."

"Goodness, that sounds wonderful."

"It has its drawbacks," he said, forcing his civilian eye to turn melancholy.

"I suppose you can live anywhere you choose. That's wonderful. I don't believe I would pick Galveston myself."

"I doubt you'd pick Belize City either. Nor would I, probably, if had been a matter of picking. It was more like shuffleboard—where you run out of momentum is where you are. Now I have friends in both places and they're both home."

"It still sounds awfully exotic to me. A mysterious stranger in an eye patch, coming to a lush tropical island on a mysterious mission. Is what you do dangerous?"

"Nah. If it's more than five atmospheres, I don't mess with it."

She looked puzzled. "Atmospheres—you mean like *locales?*"

He laughed. "No, I was talking about diving depths. I just do shallow work nowadays."

"Oh!" She giggled. "No, I . . . I don't mean to pry. I'm really being too nosy."

"Oh, you mean *here?* No, this is kind of like personal business. I'm not trying to say it's none of *your* business—it's just that it's not what I normally do. A friend of mine passed on recently and I, uh, need to do something for her."

"Oh, I'm sorry."

Rodrigue shook his head, smiling. "Don't be. This wouldn't have been a very enjoyable trip if it hadn't been for you."

"Why, thank you, kind sir."

"Shall we dine?"

141

That's what they had come for. They would eat, he would see her safely to the hotel—to her door if it seemed appropriate but conducting himself like a gentleman in any case—and then he would go beat the truth out of Buck Greathouse. He ought to be doing that right now, but . . . But what? A man's gotta eat? No, he thought bitterly, a man's gotta stroke his ego. He was making this girl like him just because he could and then he was going to walk away from her. He had to. There wasn't room for her.

"But of course," she answered, happy and expectant.

Inside, back along one wall, where a row of small tables was cordoned off by a bamboo railing for even more intimacy in the small, thatch-domed dining room, Greathouse sat with a busty blonde, quietly gouging at a platter of seafood. Rodrigue tended Ann's chair, then he leaned over and whispered in her ear.

"Would you excuse me for a moment? I see an old and dear friend," he said, smiling the even, evil shark-smile.

CHAPTER 16

The red-faced millionaire looked up at Rodrigue with a mixture of surprise and annoyance—but no fear, which surprised and annoyed Rodrigue. He would take care of that in due time.

"Hiya, Buck," he said. "Come here often?"

"Hullo, Rod." Greathouse glanced back at his plate as though the sea life on it might scurry away if left unguarded. "What happened to the eye?"

"Long story." He sat down and extended his hand to the blonde. "John Rodrigue."

She looked about twenty-five, tanned and fit. From the pale fuzz that grew on her temples Rodrigue could tell she was a natural blonde. He noticed such a thing, even at such a time, because natural blondes held a strong prurient attraction for him. Her features were a little too pronounced for his taste—teeth too big and square, jaw too strong—but there was definitely a world-class body spilling out of the white sundress. She slapped

Greathouse on the arm and said, "Bucky!" in righteous indignation.

"Sorry. Nancy, Rod. Rod, Nancy. My wife."

He said it with more awe than pride, Rodrigue imagined. Greathouse had had a spectacularly expensive divorce. The new Mrs. Greathouse beamed.

"Congratulations," Rodrigue said to the woman. "Listen, you see that redhead alone over there? Would you go over and help her order? Order for me too, will you? I'll have the grilled lobster."

If there was going to be a fight, it would start now. But Greathouse was subdued, still toying with the food on his plate. Finally he nodded at the woman and said, "Stay over there until I call for you." The blonde made a face, a combination of a pout and a quizzical look, but she left obediently.

"Good, good," Rodrigue said through gritted teeth. "I'd hate to have to kill you in front of your new wife."

The old fire flashed briefly in Greathouse's eyes and his arms tensed.

"Don't move a muscle, Buck," Rodrigue warned. "Just your mouth. Who killed the people at my house?"

"*What?* I don't know anything about anybody getting killed at your house!"

Rodrigue didn't give Greathouse credit for being a skillful liar. It's the hungry who lie well, and Greathouse hadn't been hungry in a long while. The astonishment had to be genuine. Hatred rose off Rodrigue like steam from a pot. But he kept up the act.

"Yeah," he said, "and I guess you didn't know that boat you hired me to sink was up to its gunnels in a dope deal, did you?"

"Oh, Jesus Christ! I swear, Rod, I didn't even put it together." He was shaking his jowls like a bulldog ripping up a rabbit. But his focus was inward, more like he was

144

grappling with his own stupidity than trying to convince Rodrigue of it.

"Well, I want to hear the whole fucking story right now, and don't leave anything out."

"Oh, shit! It all makes sense now. That goddamned McWherter! Oh, man, they killed Mickey, Rod!" He looked up with pain in his eyes. "Killed Mickey and stole *Wahoo Too!*"

"Mickey Aimes? Dead?"

Greathouse nodded vigorously, running his fork around in his plate again. "Dumped him in the brush on the road from town. Fuckin' meskins are keeping it quiet because they don't want to scare the tourists."

"Start all over. Who in the hell's this McWherter? He the tall skinny guy who came over with Mickey?"

Greathouse nodded again. "Mickey wanted to get the hell out. Shit, you know what fishing's been like. When that front came through, I told him to get going. McWherter heard about it and wanted to go along."

"How'd you know this McWherter?"

"Aw, the sonofabitch sold me coke. I mean, all I wanted too. Met him through this cunt I was fucking. He worked out on the One Seventy-four, but I never linked that up with the goddamned dope! So fuckin' stupid!" He shook his head again.

"Why'd you have me sink the boat, then?"

"*McWherter!* Like a stupid shit, I actually thought he wanted it done so a friend could collect the insurance! He came over and wanted me to send Mickey out to do it. Shit, I should'a known there was something wrong. He was about to piss in his pants. But, shit, he was *always* about to piss in his pants! Jesus, how bad does this get?"

"Bad enough. Counting Mickey"—Rodrigue's voice broke as the quiet, efficient skipper smiled in his memory—"there's been at least five murders."

145

"Jesus Christ!"

"I don't know why, Buck, but I'm a little surprised to see you mixed up that strong with cocaine."

"*I'm* not mixed up with cocaine! Oh, I've used a little of it, but shit, gimme my Jack and I'm happy. The coke is for the fuckin' cunts. Man, the prettiest little college coed would rim the blackest nigger on Scott Street for a sniff of that shit. I just kept it around to keep myself in pussy."

"Yeah?" Rodrigue looked at the blonde with Ann Eller. "So who's that young lady?"

"I told you, my wife," said Greathouse with a sarcastic flourish of his hand. "She could suck the chrome off a two-inch trailer ball." There was no joy in the statement, but there was pride.

"Frankly, Buck, I expected to have to come down here and cut your throat for murdering some friends of mine. Instead I find you on your honeymoon. Something's missing somewhere."

"We were going on to Cayman next week if the weather held out." He picked up his fork and put it back down.

"I don't think anything of it, you know?" Greathouse's eyes asked for understanding. "Then all of a sudden I'm reading in the paper all about this big cocaine investigation and it scares me—not because I figure it had anything to do with *me*, you know, but just because I can see that kind of thing comin', and I figure I better get out of it before I did wind up getting involved in something like that. So I go to Nancy. She's getting a little too fuckin' old for the high life anyway, I can see that. But God! what a piece of ass she is! I tell her no more cocaine. We'll just sign a fuckin' contract—and that's what it is too, make no mistake about it: she fucks me and sucks me when I want it, and shows it off when I want her to, but behaves herself like a real Mrs. Greathouse. I treat her decent and

146

give her a prorated period of the pie that gets bigger the longer she behaves herself."

He gazed contentedly at the blonde, who was talking animatedly to a puzzled Ann. "Now I'm getting where I like the little cunt," he said, smiling for the first time in Rodrigue's recollection. "Besides, she's saving me about two hundred grand a year I was spending on coke."

"Two hundred *thousand* dollars? Christ, man, you *are* the connection the feds were looking for and you didn't even know it!"

Greathouse shot him a panicky look.

"Relax, the investigation's been called off because of political pressure. That wouldn't be coming from you, would it?"

Greathouse's face turned blank.

"Nah, I didn't think so."

Rodrigue was aware that the malaise had been eased somewhat. He guessed that he must harbor some weird affection for Greathouse and was relieved to find out the hedonistic millionaire was innocent, in his own grimy way. Now he was thinking again. "What's the story with your boat?"

"Mickey and McWherter brought her in—came in, oh, a week ago. They said down at the marina that four strangers came aboard, evidently friends of McWherter's, and then the next day she was gone and poor fuckin' Mickey. . . . God, what a captain that fucker was, huh?"

"So who's looking for her?"

"Aw, the meskins, but fuck—"

"Yeah." Rodrigue's mind was whirling. Four strangers—the same four who were rescued by the Coast Guard off the sinking Grand Banks? As soon as they were released they had phoned McWherter, who was the real Galveston connection though Greathouse blindly supplied the money. McWherter panicked and skipped out, and then somehow let the others know where he was. So they came over and killed Mickey and stole the *Wahoo Too* and are on the run. But to where?

"How long's the boat been gone?"

"Four days."

"No contact at all since she left?"

"None."

"No sightings reported?"

"Nope."

"What about fuel, did they fuel up before they left?"

"Not on my ticket, they didn't. And they left the bladder tanks on the landing where Mickey had dragged them to get them out of the way while he washed down the boat." A sadness entered his face.

Leaving the bladder tanks probably meant they had panicked. Maybe Mickey got hard to handle and had to be killed before they had planned. It was a big mistake. If they were short of fuel, their options were significantly reduced.

"You want me to try to get her back for you?"

"Shit, yes! Can you?"

"I said I could try. Cost you ten thousand dollars."

"Forget it. I got insurance."

"The insurance company ain't gonna kill whoever killed Mickey. *I'm* gonna do that."

"Five thousand."

"Fifteen, and I keep my mouth shut to boot."

"All right, you fuckin' pirate," Greathouse said with another rare flicker of a grin. "I know what your game is and I want some of it. Ten thou—"

"In advance. Which means tomorrow."

"Tomorrow's Sunday."

"Okay, asshole, tonight then."

"No problem, no problem. But look: I got fucked over by some bad people and I sicced you on them. That's how I want the word to get out. You don't fuck with

Buck Greathouse, same as you don't fuck with John Rodrigue."

"Fine. Just send it to my table."

"Fine. Send Mrs. Greathouse back here."

After the blonde had departed, Ann rolled her eyes and said, "Wow."

"Bad girl makes good."

"How do you mean?"

Rodrigue explained. Sort of.

"Hmmmm. There's a moral in this someplace."

"Curious choice of words," he said, leaning forward and venturing to touch her hand. "Looks like I'm going to have to come out of retirement for a while."

She looked down at his hand on hers as though they were objects of an exotic native art. "I . . . I wanted to meet somebody interesting. *Different*, you know? I'm kind of in a rut. I wasn't exactly looking for . . . you know, I really didn't let myself think too much about what I was expecting or wanted or whatever. The grilled lobster okay? That's what I ordered for us."

"Great. Probably the only grilled lobster in Cozumel you can chew without getting muscle cramps."

Greathouse was serious about showboating; the money arrived in less than an hour (from the hotel cashier? No, probably from an obliging banker who reopened the shop for a slight commission) in five rubber-band-wrapped stacks of U.S. twenties placed on the table with ceremony by the restaurant's hostess. Ann's eyes widened and her jaw dropped.

"Operating capital," Rodrigue explained.

"Pound sand and—what?"

"*Plot* sand and stone breeze. How's the flan?"

"Lovely."

As they walked from the restaurant their hands came together. All they had to do was make it through the palm grove out to the drive and into a sweat-smelling taxi. But the sea loomed near, like a wall of polished black marble. Moonlight flickered through clouds racing high overhead. The palms rustled softly in the warm, steady breeze. They stopped.

He would remember the smell of her, the hardness of her breast, the shy lowering of her eyelids, the softness of her lips, and the sudden urgency of her kiss. But they said good-bye quite properly with a peck in the huge, hollow lobby, and then he went alone to arrange for the flight.

CHAPTER 17

Rodrigue tried his navy eye again and found he could wear it comfortably, so he stowed the eye patch in his shaving kit. He stared at the haggard, weather-beaten face in the mirror. Ruggedly handsome, he decided. But not *that* handsome. It had been the exotic surroundings. And the aura of mystery around him. She wouldn't have given him a second look on the bench outside the yacht basin bait camp. Not that it mattered, but it would've been nice to let the infatuation run its course.

Abruptly he twisted on the cold water and doused his face with double handfuls. There was work to be done. He hurried through a shower and shave and crammed his dirty clothes into his duffel. Too late he realized he had forgotten to deliver the portable depth-sounder to the scuba-diving physician at El Presidente. He hurried down to the desk, checked out, and squeezed into a cab with three fishermen from Dallas and enough fly-fishing tackle to start an Abercrombie & Fitch.

The six-passenger plane touched down on a bald limestone strip that shone like an ivory gash in the black jungle. Flickering in two rows were kerosene smudge pots. The plane came to a bumpy halt and the fishermen clambered out into the moist, humming darkness. Beyond the invisible screen of brush, nestled in a palm grove on the beach, was the fishing lodge Rodrigue had read about at the hotel. The excited murmurs of the departing fishermen were quickly swallowed by the damp vegetation. The pilot slammed shut the luggage compartments, climbed in, and started the engines again.

Rodrigue had chartered the plane to fly him on down to Belize City, another 160 miles from the lodge. Flying low along the wilderness of the eastern Yucatan, Bahia de Chetumal, and Ambergris Cay, they sighted the lagoon, glowing in the false dawn. They had to land at Belize International upriver first, to clear customs, then Rodrigue talked the Mexican pilot into hopping him down to the municipal strip at the water's edge in Belize City. Without as much as a glance at his surroundings, the pilot spun the plane and lifted it slowly into the dying land breeze. Rodrigue shouldered his duffel and hurried through the still-sleeping town, windows shuttered against the night insects, to make the early Mass at Holy Redeemer.

The Second Reading was from Luke. Part of it broke through the rustle of words that until then had been as soothing and unintelligible as the soft roar of the surf: *. . . and fell among robbers, who both stripped him and inflicted blows, and went off, leaving him half-dead. Now, by coincidence, a certain . . .*

Rodrigue stood in the half-empty church lit by the dim winking of candles in dark mahogany, feeling the anger returning. No-see-ums made his ankles sting and he wanted a drink. What about the robbers? he thought.

Everyone sat and Father Lynch waited for the stirring to subside. His sad blue eyes lingered on Rodrigue long enough to reflect acknowledgment. Rodrigue dreaded what would come next. Father Lynch was a burr in the otherwise comfortable relationship Rodrigue had with the Creator. An Irishman exiled to an uneasy coexistence with the British, Lynch was in sympathy with Rodrigue's love of strong drink. And living in a steamy Caribbean city that throbbed with African passion, he could overlook Rodrigue's womanizing. What troubled Father Lynch was Rodrigue's lack of contrition.

Rodrigue thought live and let live was all there was to it, which was why he was dreading the priest's words at that moment—Rodrigue was no longer willing to let live. But it was the usual homily about the Good Samaritan. He let it waft around him like a soft warm breeze while he sought his own peace.

Vengenace belongs to God.

And God will have His vengeance. Soon.

Whose vengeance? Whose blood-lust? It was Rodrigue's. And when Rodrigue got vengeful, sometimes the wrong people died.

He would go alone. And it wasn't blood-lust. If robbers weren't punished until they touched the face of God, there would be far too many robbers.

It was *deterrence*, that's what it was—deterrence through swift and sure punishment. Like Ferguson said, you had to keep in their faces. Okay, and if you happened to enjoy it a little, then administering punishment could be considered vengeance—okay. Deterrence through vengeance equals justice.

Rodrigue had to work it out before Communion. He couldn't go to Communion with a cloudy conscience. But he couldn't *not* go to Communion, either. His faith was sometimes tenuous, but he had been taught not to give up on it.

After the homily it took about thirty minutes, on the average, for the back pews to join the Communion procession. Dealing with that time frame week after week, Rodrigue had developed a means of dumping moral dilemmas like the flushing of a toilet. He would simply do what he thought was right—and if it turned out to be wrong, God would either stop him or forgive him. He winked his good eye as Father Lynch shoved the Host toward his tongue, and the priest smiled the begrudging half-smile he used on souls he couldn't hope to save.

Rodrigue stepped out while the choir of exuberant Creole women sang the recessional hymn. He stopped for a moment to gaze at the faded red tin roofs, whitewashed cisterns, louvered French shutters, and lush tropical vegetation. The scene was coppery in the morning light. It was good to be home. He crossed Haulover Creek, now dark and swollen, and went to Mom's, an airy café at the cluttered crossroads of downtown.

"Marnin', John, kin ah ketch you sumpin'?" said a tall young black in lilting Creole. He was just a customer, a nodding acquaintance of Rodrigue's, a friendly fellow who might've pitched in and helped wait tables even if he weren't dying to know what Rodrigue was doing back there in the rainy season.

"One-one black caffee and battle Caribbean."

"Fu true? Battle Caribbean wit de caffee?"

"Yes, maan. Fu de tu'muck's sake, eh?"

The teenager shrugged and conferred with the old woman rustling ham and eggs for the scattering of street hustlers, fishermen, and merchants from the waterfront markets. A girl of about ten ran out, jangling keys, and returned with a sealed bottle of the local rum. The teenager carried it on a tray with a steaming steel pitcher of coffee and a heavy navy-style ceramic mug. Rodrigue paid with one of Greathouse's crisp twenties.

"You gwine ketch me one Nicky Fuentes an' you tek the res', eh?"

"Nicky? Tenks, maan. Ah gat am."

Rodrigue poured coffee into the mug and sloshed some of the amber Caribbean on top. He sipped and added more rum.

Fuentes was a San Pedrano, a native of the village of San Pedro on Ambergris Cay, which had closer ties to the main population of Yucatan than did the essentially British Belize City. He was the color of old brass, with a broad face and shoulders and long, coarse auburn hair. Rodrigue assumed he was mostly Maya, but nobody in Belize was much of any one thing. He came, in blue-jean cutoffs and a T-shirt from some scuba club, before Rodrigue finished his second cup.

Fuentes greeted Rodrigue happily in Creole, but Rodrigue replied in Spanish to discourage eavesdropping. "Have you a boat I can rent that's suitable to go to sea?"

"Why not? But why are you without a boat? Is your boat damaged?"

"I came by airplane. What boat have you that is suitable?"

"The big Mexican skiff. What is that, anyway? Rum? Rum and coffee?"

"Here, try it." He offered his mug.

Fuentes sipped. "Ech!" he said, grimacing.

"Good, eh? Here, let me get you a mug." He snapped his fingers and pointed at the mug. "One-one fu mi fren," he shouted.

Rodrigue knew the skiff Fuentes was talking about. It was a twenty-three-foot open boat of heavy fiberglass with a wide, sweeping bow and thick gunwales that formed one encircling flotation chamber. The type was known as a Yamaha skiff in Mexico because the well-known Japanese company had imported the first ones

155

before Mexican boatwrights scattered all over the country learned to reproduce them. This one was powered by a forty-eight-horse Yamaha outboard, a reliable workhorse exported to developing countries. Fuentes used the skiff to carry fishermen down to the Southern Lagoon for tarpon and snook. It would suit Rodrigue's purpose admirably as long as he stayed in the Inner Channel, inside the reef. And no tropical weather blew up.

He was fairly certain he would find the *Wahoo Too* somewhere in the maze of mangrove cays inside the great reef stretching from Ambergris down to the Gulf of Honduras. Where else? They had committed a crime in Mexico, so they would avoid a Mexican anchorage. They would avoid Cuba too, if they had any sense. Having given the Coast Guard the slip in New Orleans, they probably wouldn't head for Florida, where the coasties patroled heavily. That left either a long westerly passage during hurricane season, for which they probably didn't have the fuel—or the much shorter and safer run southward to the cays of Belize and Honduras. There were thousands of these mangrove and sand cays stretched over a hundred miles. But a big fine boat like *Wahoo Too* wouldn't go unnoticed.

"Have you heard of a big North American yacht in the area?" he asked Fuentes. "A fifty-foot Hatteras equipped for the catching of marlin? It is called the *Wahoo Too*. Probably headed south."

Fuentes shrugged. "It should be called *Marlin II*. But no, I have not been told of such a boat. If she fueled, it would have to be at San Pedro, Cay Chapel, or Stann Creek or Punta Gorda on the mainland. Or here, of course, but no such boat has fueled here. I would have heard."

Rodrigue rubbed his chin and squinted at the ceiling with his good eye. Okay, it was something over 300 miles from Cozumel to the coast of Honduras. Assuming they hadn't topped off the *Wahoo Too*'s tanks at Cozumel, they would have to get fuel somewhere in Belize. And diesel at the dock was only available at the places Nicky had mentioned. He would check each source one by one. He'd pick up her trail.

"Nicky," he said, leaning forward and grasping Fuentes's forearm. "I need to rent the boat and buy some provisions, including some fishermen's clothes. Old but clean, eh? Extra fuel tanks and plenty of two-cycle oil. A tarp. Some food. Limes—plenty of limes. Four bottles of Caribbean. Water, of course. And a twelve-gauge shotgun with the shot for killing deer."

Fuentes's eyes shone darkly, "I go with you."

"No. Listen, this is just a hunting trip. A little vacation for me. I need to go alone."

"They say you are a brujo, you know," Fuentes said appraisingly. He was thinking Rodrigue was planning to kill the people on the Hatteras and steal it, but that he probably had a good reason. He wouldn't ask about it.

"My station in life improves in Belize," Rodrigue said with a cold-eyed smile. "Up north they call me a pirate."

"Hah," said Fuentes, dismissing it with a wave of his yellow-brown hand. "Here, all are pirates."

"Will you also call San Pedro for me?" Rodrigue added. With his lingering contacts on Ambergris, Fuentes could save an extra thirty-five miles out to the northernmost fueling stop in the country.

"Why not?"

Rodrigue had an inspiration: "Also, add a twelve-volt battery, some electricians' tape, and a new broom to that list you have in your head."

Fuentes shook his head wonderingly. "I cannot begin to guess what it is you want with a broom, but you do not need the battery. The motor starts with a pull-rope."

"I know that, cabron. I want the battery to operate a little fathometer I have. There is a trick I have with fathometers that might be useful."

Fuentes's boat was flat-bottomed and narrow for its length. The forty-eight-horsepower motor would plane it at twenty-five or thirty knots. And because it had almost no draught at planing speed, he could travel at night. A boat like *Wahoo Too*, being operated inside the reef, would need sunlight for the skipper to read the color of the water, to stay in the depths and avoid the many coral heads. And they would have to take it slowly. If he could get on their trail, he could overtake them.

It looked shipshape, rocking with the boat wakes in Haulover Creek. Fuentes had thought to lay in some pimento stalks—a tough, canelike wood—and some twine he could use to fashion an awning with the tarp. Rodrigue hadn't thought of pimento or he wouldn't have asked for the broom. No matter. It would add to his brujo image. A broom . . . like he might straddle it and fly back to town if he ran out of rum.

Fuentes had also included matches, waterproofed in an olive jar, and pine fat wood to help him build a fire if necessary. The food was mostly canned, with the requisite can opener and even a spoon and a butcher knife.

"But ah cud'dn gat one so-so muma, John," Fuentes said sadly. "No-mo no-mo counta da cus'tam mek dehn wut too much. Ah gat one warry-saama nuf."

Rodrigue took the sharp new machete. It was a poor substitute for a shotgun, which Fuentes had said was impossible to get because duty on them had made even an old single-shot Savage too precious to loan or rent and illegal to sell without the proper papers. The machete would have to do. He slid it carefully back into the makeshift sheath of folded and taped cardboard and put it in the skiff.

158

"And San Pedro?"

"Yes, maan. Da boat garn by yes'sideh marnin' outsad da ref. Hook-'em-up too. Garn souf, dey say."

"Hook-'em-up?"

"Yes, maan."

That was good news. If the skipper was pushing her hard this far south and hadn't stopped for fuel at San Pedro, he would almost certainly have to stop somewhere before he passed Punta Gorda—if he intended to pass Punta Gorda at all. Belize, with its numerous uninhabited cays and no navy or coast guard, was as perfect a hideout for modern-day pirates as could be found.

The afternoon was wearing on and Rodrigue was anxious to get started. Dressed in a gray shirt, tan trousers, worn leather shoes, and a thick straw sombrero, he stepped down into the skiff. In the tin cup Nicky had provided, he mixed himself a stout grog-and-lime to see him through the Drowned Cays. He puttered down Haulover, rounded the point, and goosed the big skiff on step for Cay Chapel.

CHAPTER 18

The rain advanced in a solid wall. The wind rose in quirky gusts and put an uncomfortable chop on the shallow water. Rodrigue slowed the boat. With the wind pushing it, the rain stung at first. Then it fell in a gentle, whispering deluge, flattening the seas again and circling the boat with a gray curtain.

At the slow speed, Rodrigue found he could leave the tiller and the boat would plow steadily forward more or less on course. He got up to see what he could do about getting the rainwater out of the bilge. Nothing, he decided. If she swamped, she swamped.

It was a grand feeling, cruising majestically along in a gray nothing world, hidden in the warm rain, like old Dominique in his heyday, a citizen of the sea. No FBI, no DEA, IRS. A free man.

"Arrr," he said, scanning the invisible horizon in a one-eyed squint.

He clambered back over his provisions to his cup of

rum, now seriously diluted with rainwater. "Bah!" he said, flicking the contents into the downpour. He took the bottle instead, and his new machete, and stepped precariously back to the bow, where he stood with one foot on the gunwale, swigging rum, waving the machete, and bellowing commands out of the Hornblower books. He had just ordered the yards braced when the boat came to an abrupt halt and he went cartwheeling through space, hitting damp sand with a *thunk!* that knocked the wind out of him.

"Aye," he said painfully. He stabbed his machete into the sand and used it to pull himself to his feet. He eyed the bottle still in his hand—it was sandy but unbroken—then he looked around him. The boat was beached and silent, the outboard having stalled when the prop bogged down in the sandy bottom. Inland, the rain drummed noisily on dark, towering vegetation. And up the beach to the north, Rodrigue heard the unmistakable rattle-pop of a gasoline-powered high-pressure air compressor. He limped toward it, favoring his bad knee.

The unexpected sight of a burly, dark-visaged man with a straw sombrero on his head, a machete in one hand, and a bottle of rum in the other caused Brad Potts to drop his Craftsman ten-inch adjustable wrench and then hastily pick it up again. Potts, proprietor of St. George's Lodge, was under the thatched roof out back, refilling tanks from the day's dive. He prided himself on being imperturbable but he hadn't expected to be accosted by a drunken, machete-wielding Creole. Then he thought he recognized the face.

"John?" he called hopefully. "John Rodrigue?"

"Aye, sez I," said Rodrigue in his gravelly pirate voice.

"What the Sam Hill are you doing out here?"

"On the trail of some scurvy blighters, Potts." He looked around as though it were the first time he had seen the dive resort on St. George's Cay. "Missed me landfall, though. I was bound for Cay Chapel."

Potts laughed. He didn't know what the joke was but he laughed anyway. He knew better than to take Rodrigue for the buffoon he sometimes appeared to be. Rodrigue was a competitor, technically, but since he was based in the city and only took walk-on trade and referrals from Mom's and didn't do any advertising and sometimes even sent business out to the lodge, Potts was favorably inclined toward him.

"Say, matey," Rodrigue said, rubbing his chin and glaring at Potts in his one-eyed squint, "ye wouldn't be having an extra tank I could rent from ye, would ye? Tank and regulator, weight belt, and mask and fins? Don't have to be fit for deep water, now."

This was lobster season, Rodrigue remembered, and in his drunken condition he had decided he would stop and dive for lobsters somewhere to the south, so he could more realistically pose as a fisherman once he found the *Wahoo Too*.

"Sure, John. I just have two guests on board, a boss and secretary from Toronto, so equipment's no problem."

"Never know when a little scuba gear might come in handy, eh?"

"Sure, John. Where's the *Queen?*" He looked though the slackening rain at the dock on the back side of the island.

"Ah, yes, well, I'm in another boat, you see, matey. You just load me up and I'll see to 'er."

"No problem. You'll stay for dinner of course? Lots of lobster coming in now."

"Can't. Got to get around to Cay Chapel. How 'bout some gas? Can I top off me tank?"

"Sure, but what's at Cay Chapel? You serious about chasing someone down?"

"Aye, a Hatteras, a fifty-footer called the *Wahoo Too*. Stolen from Cozumel four or five days ago. Should've been needing fuel 'bout the time she hit our coast. I'm gonna kill 'em all and recover the boat." Rodrigue said it seriously, Potts thought, but then he broke into his cold-eyed grin. With Rodrigue, one never knew.

"Tell you what, c'mon in and let me radio the marina there. Save you a trip."

Rodrigue brightened. "Capital idea, mate!" He toasted with the sand-caked rum bottle and took a long drink.

St. George's Cay, where Rodrigue had landed, was ten miles south of Cay Chapel. Once the capital of British Honduras, it was a tiny strip of land with a sugary beach facing the sea, a row of Caribbean-style houses nestled in airy palm groves, and a dense mangrove swamp along the inland side. The lodge occupied the southernmost end, and Potts had filled and cleared the mangroves behind it to create the sandy beach where Rodrigue had come ashore. The grounds were a neat and orderly reflection of Potts's engineering background. In contrast was Fishing Town at the other end of the island, a collection of fishermen's shanties that over generations had grown as disarranged as the tropical vegetation that enveloped them.

The lodge was palatial by Belize standards, tall ceilings, big French windows, the kind of place that made a good retreat from either the blazing tropical heat or the drumming monsoons. To operate it, Potts had the help of his wife and a never-ending flow of adventurous young dive bums from the States. Inside, Phyllis Potts was all tanned face, white teeth, and damp blond hair still showing the grooves from the comb. In her flowing cotton muu-muu she was the quintessential California girl-matron. Rodrigue and Mrs. Potts didn't like each other, for no good reason.

She was serving a tall gin-and-something to a tanned, trim man in Banana Republic khakis at the bar. They both looked startled when Potts and Rodrigue entered. The man, who had a young-looking face and gray hair, took longer to recover.

"I'd offer you a drink, John, but I see you brought your own," Mrs. Potts said icily.

"Aye, darlin'," Rodrigue replied, removing his sombrero with a courtly flourish. "Let it be said John Rodrigue always brings his own."

"Make the introductions, Phyl," Potts said with a hint of reproach in his voice. "I'm going to try to get Cay Chapel on the wireless." (The Pottses savored the residual English flavor of Belize.)

A brunette with sharply etched eyebrows and high cheekbones glided into the room. She too had that just-out-of-the-shower look that was the après-dive fashion. She was wearing a sheer white East Indian outfit that was beholden to her body for any shape at all, and she was using her joyous expectation of a tall gin-and-something to ignore the dirty, hulking peon with the sword.

"Rene and Eric, may I present Captain John Rodrigue." Phyllis said sarcastically. They turned nervous grins toward him and murmured.

"Enchanté," said Rodrigue, bowing deeply.

Phyllis shook her head and smiled in resignation. A firm believer in psychocybernetics, she knew how to trim her own attitude for smoother sailing. "May I freshen your drink, Captain?"

"Aye, milady," said Rodrigue, moving to the bar with a spatter of rainwater on the polished mahogany floor. "If ye would just provide me with a tankard so's I might drink fittingly with civilized persons."

"Aye, aye, Captain," she said, flashing a reassuring smile at her guests, who were staring with frozen grins.

She dropped precious ice cubes into a beer mug. "John, here, is the descendant of one of Jean Lafitte's pirate chieftains," she said by way of explanation.

"Really!" said the secretary.

"Hmmm," said her boss.

"Aye, an' a throwback as well," said Rodrigue, helping himself to a slice of lime from the dish on the bar.

Phyllis was explaining that many people in Belize were descendants of pirates when Potts came down from the loft. "John, are you sure that boat was stolen?" he said, interrupting his wife.

"Sure's I'm standing here. Is she there?"

"Yeah, *was* there, all right. Took on fuel and drinking water and left yesterday afternoon. Gwen said they seemed like normal rich Americans on a lark. Loud but friendly, you know."

"Aye," Rodrigue said, darkly. "I'll be wanting that tank now, if you please. And some gas."

"Well, very nice to meet you," said the secretary.

"The pleasure was all mine," he said with the sleepy-eyed smile. He longed to see her and her flimsy outfit in the draft from the ceiling fan once more, but duty called.

Potts laughed in spite of himself when he saw Nicky's Mexican skiff. "*This* is what you're going after them in?"

"Sure. I'm a local fisherman. I'll go aboard to sell 'em some lobster."

Potts stared at him. One simply never knew about Rodrigue. He shrugged and waded out to help stow the scuba tank under the tarp, where it would be sheltered from tomorrow's glaring sun.

The sun dipped below the clouds over the mainland and bathed the world in a cool mauve light as Rodrigue and Potts shoved the skiff out into water deep enough for Rodrigue to lower the outboard and jerk-start it.

A yellow plastic jug that had once contained cooking

oil bobbed in the water ahead. Rodrigue scanned for others. In the dimming light he made out a line of them stretching not the big lagoon. Sneaking a glance back over his shoulder, he stopped at the second one and hauled the cagelike lobster trap to the surface. It was empty. The next one had one lobster and the one after that had two. That was plenty. He rolled one of Greathouse's crisp twenties, stuffed it into the empty rum bottle, twisted on the lid, stuffed the bottle into the trap, and threw it back overboard. It was a good trade. Twenty dollars U.S. for three lobsters was a damn good price for the fisherman, and Rodrigue hadn't been that anxious to go swimming.

CHAPTER 19

Dawn was a relief. The low clouds over the Caribbean glowed dimly with sunlight and the vast passage inside the broken reef became a warm avenue of purple water. Rodrigue imagined he had just awakened from a long, deep sleep.

But the night had been holy hell. He had stopped for a couple of hours, anchored in the lee of a sand cay south of the big flat off Belize Harbor, but he couldn't stay asleep. Sandy appeared, close and smiling, then turned into a grinning skull as she floated away into the darkness. And there was Diegleman, and he wanted something. He was begging with outstretched arms, but Rodrigue couldn't figure out what he wanted. Mike Ferguson came and droned something urgent in his ears and made him shake away sleep to hear the rustle of the wind across his canvas tarp.

Rodrigue might've taken these visitations as actual ghosts except that Sarah came too, haunting him most horribly of all by inviting him with heaving belly and parted legs, then becoming a wimpering child.

The rum had changed from elixir to poison, and he yearned for someone to talk to. He could've turned around and beat it back to St. George's for a clean bed and a breeze to keep down the bugs. Or better yet, he could buy someone's seat to Miami, turn right around, and be back on Cozumel by afternoon. Instead he had jerked the Yamaha's starter rope and shoved the tiller around, pointing the skiff's wide, swooping bow southward again.

The years of working with air and light at the far end of a long tether had given Rodrigue a great imagination when it came to escape. But like any good diver—and he had been one of the best in his time—his synapses had a fail-safe to keep the thought from becoming action. Once committed to a job, he might not have been able to bail out to save his life.

Now the majesty of dawn over the Caribbean lifted his spirits and he was glad he had pushed on through the night. The *Wahoo Too* might have too, although it would've been a little risky, even outside the reef, navigating without reliable loran and the lighted aids taken for granted in U.S. waters. Probably they had gone on anyway, he decided. Smuggling cocaine, stealing yachts, and murdering people were risky undertakings.

The sky became light blue and the water became pink, and a cluster of palms in the distance shone brassily above a dark smear of mangroves. The air was still and musky with the smell of sea plants. Rodrigue had traveled in the shallows inshore of the reef, circling the larger mangrove cays, keeping the outboard down to a quiet purr. He didn't have a chart—would've had to wait a day to get one since no one he knew ventured into the southern cays.

He didn't know what kind of speed the skiff had been

making, but without a chart that was useless information anyway. He had been ten hours from St. George's, less the two wasted at anchor. Assuming ten miles an hour, that would be eighty miles. But they were zigzagging, loop-the-loop miles as he wandered from cay to cay searching for the Hatteras. He was probably somewhere below Stann Creek, at least.

Although diesel fuel was available at Stann Creek, it was just fifty miles from where they had taken on fuel at Cay Chapel. If *he* were on the run, Rodrigue mused, he would head for the remote Sapodilla Cays—a hook-shaped chain at the tail end of the barrier reef, almost in the Gulf of Honduras—and use Indian villages on the Monkey River for resupply. Parts for the boat and other necessities from the civilized world could be had through Placentia or Punta Gorda, both of which were connected by an all-weather road to Belize City. Of course that would be dangerous, but if local officials could be bribed . . .

Rodrigue realized he was customizing the scenario to suit himself, putting himself in their place and not altogether unhappily. So what would he do, smuggle guns into Nicaragua? Prey on merchant shipping? Rob lobster pots?

Sometimes Rodrigue felt a greater kinship with Dominique than grandson many times removed. It came from long nights aboard the shrimp boat before his father went to work in the oil patch. His father or one of is uncles would be at the wheel on a long drag, telling the old pirate stories in phrases as practiced as a song. He was just a kid, propped in the wheelhouse door and staring off into the blackness where it all had really happened. Sailing the sea at a time when the horizon marked the threshold of a whole new world for all practical purposes—that was the most free man had ever been. He was his own nation. But it was just a sentiment, like the memory of a happy Christmas long ago. It didn't have anything to do with the here and now.

These people had some connections in Colombia—they might be on their way back there, running from their emergency fueling stop at Cay Chapel straight down to some point on the Mosquito Coast to refuel, and staying well outside the reef. If that were the case, he couldn't hope to pick up their trail by boat. He'd have to stash the skiff, buy some new clothes, and hop a plane for Cartegena, where he might be able to find them. *Might.* Every day that went by, the odds grew geometrically longer. But he could only do what he had come to do, and that was to try.

Rodrigue checked his fuel: three-quarters left in the last tank. He'd have to find Placentia pretty soon. He hoped there would be some fishing boats out in the Inner Channel to steer him. Tired of the plodding pace, he twisted the tiller and the skiff crawled onto a smooth plane.

Breakfast was a can of corned beef hash, heated by the sun, seasoned with lime juice and washed down with water. Rodrigue badly wanted coffee.

Near noon he sighted a pale triangle and steered toward it. It turned into a patched gray sail of a gray wooden lugger manned by what looked like three generations of Caribs. They eyed Rodrigue suspiciously as he fell alongside.

" 'Marnin'," he called. "Ketchin' eeny?"

"Kine abba," replied the old man, meaning they were having fair luck.

"Ah ben ahn da sea frahan day bruk. Weh happen to Placentia?"

The old man smiled. "You gwine deh?"

"Yes, maan, but me laas me one. Cud you pint da weh?"

The old man laughed and the younger man and boy

170

cracked large smiles. "Da weh deh," said the younger man, pointing.

Rodrigue asked them if they had seen a big North American yacht. They had not.

Nor had anyone in Placentia seen or heard of the *Wahoo Too*. Rodrigue hired a Carib with a wheelbarrow to piss-ant the six-gallon boat tanks to a gasoline pump beside a dilapidated warehouse while he took tea with an ancient Englishwoman who still wanted to gossip about the royal wedding. The fueling completed, Rodrigue gratefully said good-bye, replenished his water supply, and set out again.

He hugged the coast down to the settlement at the mouth of the Monkey River, where a handful of Yankees were trying to farm shrimp, and heard the same thing: nobody knew anything about a large yacht from the U.S. in these waters. He had some "bamboo chicken" (iguana) and rice with the shrimp farmers and then set out for the Sapodilla Cays—twenty miles offshore and two-fifths of the way to the Honduran coast—to test his theory.

It was still midafternoon when he pitched his anchor overboard in the lee of Tom Owen's Cay. When he had first sighted the curving chain, sand cays with scrub and a few tall palms, he turned toward the southernmost end, Lawrence Rock, and then skirted the islands curving back toward the north again. Nothing except a few local smacks. He opened a can of Spam and "grilled" it on the salt-encrusted gunwale of the skiff. Tomorrow he would head north again, looking at the rest of the Sapodillas and then back up to the cays he had missed when he veered off for Placentia. Then . . . ? Well, he'd worry about that tomorrow. He was taking the rest of the afternoon off.

He had a few rums, huddled under the tarp while the evening rain poured into the boat. It relaxed him, but he didn't feel like celebrating. He had walked out on what might've been a world-class piece of ass for a wild goose chase in a damn rowboat with no bilge pump. What was worse, he'd eventually have to go back the same way.

The rain stopped so abruptly that Rodrigue peeked to see if something was over him. The sky was clear and growing dark. The squall was rumbling on toward the mainland. He bailed out enough water to stretch out under the tarp and was quickly asleep.

The throb of a big diesel's idle woke him. There was the splash of an anchor. He felt for the machete as he peered out from under the tarp. White daylight stung his eye and made the looming form indistinct. It was a big boat with a blur of motion on its bow deck.

"'Mornin' to ya!" called the man up on the big boat's bow.

He was a tan, wiry man of about thirty in blue-jean cutoffs and long blond pigtails. He wore a long mustache that blended into his sideburns. Definitely the doper type, Rodrigue thought. He pulled the tarp aside and sat on one of the skiff's thwart seats, holding the machete out of sight beneath the gunwale.

"'Marnin', suh," he said. "Fishin'?" He would retain the Belizean Creole accent for protective coloration, yet speak plainly enough to be understood by a Yenky.

The man shook his head and the pigtails danced on his shoulders. "Divin'. Pretty good reef here." The boat was a wooden Matthews with a narrow beam and high, vertical prow. It was thirty years old at least. The cabin had been cut away for deck space and a high canvas awning installed in its place. In the cockpit two couples were donning scuba gear. The younger of the two women shot an indifferent glance forward.

"Da so, eh? Plenny lobster, eh?"

"Oh, plenty, plenty. You got some pots out around here?"

172

"No, maan. Big sportfishing baat called da *Wahoo Too* come by an' as' me to carry am some lobster out. You seen am?"

"No, man. We just left Utila—in the Bay Islands? Too much shit going on around there right now." He tugged on the line to see if the anchor was holding and glanced back to check on the progress of his clients. "Wait a minute," he said, looking back at Rodrigue. "There *was* a big sportfisherman in the lee of one of those little cays this side of Tela Bay. Big Hatteras or Viking, looked like, with a tower and outriggers and the whole bit. 'Course I didn't see the name."

Rodrigue sighed. "Prolly too far to go anyway, maan. How far is it?"

"Well, from here about fifty, fifty-five miles. On a heading of"—he thought for a moment—"about one hundred degrees, just south of due east. 'Course I'd have to take this boat south a ways before I could get through the reef, but that skiff'd slide through anywhere. But like you said, that's too damn far and they'll probably get lobster off the locals to boot. Here, man, let me buy 'em from you."

Rodrigue looked past the low island at the vast blue sea. "No, maan. A bargain is a bargain. You pick am off the battam anyhow, eh?"

"What the hell's a big sportfisherman doing down this way?" the man in pigtails mused. He glanced back at the waiting divers.

"Well," he said cheerfully, "have a nice day."

CHAPTER 20

Mexican fishermen used the kind of skiff Rodrigue had rented from Nicky to longline for sharks in the Gulf of Mexico and in the Pacific, staying miles from land for days at a time. Rodrigue had seen them leaving Guajardo, below Matamoros, with a lard bucket full of beans, tortillas tied up in a bandanna, and a cheap pocket compass on the seat. Sometimes the fishermen didn't come back. But with all that flotation in the gunwales, the boats usually did. The tar-stained derelicts on the beach were treated as shrines to the dead. The outboards were removed and resurrected by mechanics whose skills bordered on sorcery.

Rodrigue didn't have a compass but he knew which way east was by the climbing sun. He kept it over the port bow, so that if he missed his landfall, he would err toward the south, toward the mainland. The smaller cays of the Bay Islands stretched westward toward Punta Sal, he

174

knew. He would simply hail a fisherman and ask directions again.

The seas, which had been steep and threatening near the reef, were now smooth enough for Rodrigue to open the throttle. Saloming gently across the face of the swells, he figured he was getting a good twenty-two knots. At that rate, he'd be there in time to tempt them with lobsters for lunch.

If the weather held.

And if *they* held.

And if it was the *Wahoo Too* in the first place.

And if the outboard didn't break down.

The motor quit the instant he thought about it—and for the instant it took him to realize he had simply sucked one of the tanks dry, he was genuinely spooked. He attached the pickup hose of another tank, squeezed the bulb to prime the hose, and the Yamaha started easily on the first yank. Was it too early for a drink? Yeah, he decided. It was.

Land rose to starboard and he veered toward it, making better time with the following sea. But then he went and went and went for long enough to age scotch and the land seemed not an inch closer. He started trying to remember if there were supposed to be any twenty-plus knot currents in this part of the world he could be fighting—and then he realized he was looking at mountains. Angry at himself, he steered back to east-southeast as near as he could figure it.

Lunch came—celebrated with sardines in pepper sauce and soggy crackers—and Rodrigue had just started to worry when he spotted the gray-blue thickening of the horizon that signaled land at last. This time it rose quickly, rivaling the mountains still visible to starboard. And it soon spread across the horizon. It had to be the mainland.

Cays inshore would be almost invisible against the mainland until he was right on them, Rodrigue knew, so he held his course. He figured to have to swing back east again, but there was no point in changing course without something to steer for. He kept his eyes peeled for a sail, a mast, a puff of smoke, anything.

The coast grew emerald green in the afternoon sun. Suddenly it was flecked here and there with reds, browns, and tans—hillsides barren of vegetation, either cliffs or terraced fields. Those tiny dots of white could be a village. And finally he spotted boats, three of them with ancient outboards—Johnson Sea Horses, or so they appeared—painted the same faded salmon color as the boats. They were anchored within fifty yards of one another, the men gutting and gilling some kind of reef fish. The fisherman in the nearest boat leaned over the side and rinsed a fish in the alcohol-clear water, its rib-lined cavity pink and glistening.

"¡Hola!" Rodrigue said. "Is the fishing good?"

"Yes, thank you," replied the man suspiciously. He had been furtively watching Rodrigue's approach as he went about the task of cleaning the fish.

"Good. It is a fine day, true?"

"Yes, it is a fine day. Are you fishing?"

"No, no. I'm looking for a big Yankee boat, a big white one with tall poles on each side and a high place from where it is driven, you understand?"

"Yes, a sportfishing boat," the Honduran fisherman said with a hint of aggravation.

"Oh, then you have seen it?"

"No."

Rodrigue thought about maneuvering close enough to grab the fisherman by the throat, but then he thought better of it. "I have been told the boat was anchored at an island of the Islands of the Bay, a small one east of the Bay of Tela. In what direction would that be?"

The fisherman pointed eastward, where the green shoreline merged into the horizon.

"And how far, ¿por favor?"

The fisherman picked up another fish. "Many miles," he said, turning back to his task.

What was many miles in a wooden smack with a twenty-year-old outboard might be measured in minutes in Nicky's big fiberglass skiff. Rodrigue stood and squinted in the direction the fisherman had pointed. It sure *looked* a long way to anything. He glanced at his Timex, the one chink in his disguise. It was 2:17. But he still had plenty of gas. He put the Yamaha in gear and waved good-bye to the fisherman, who was no longer watching. He circled the anchored boats widely—a habitual courtesy rather than a considered one—and bore for the thin, wavery point of land in the distance.

The string of cays appeared quickly, growing out of the hazy blue-gray shoreline, clumps of mangroves that were sharply etched and colored a brilliant coppery turquoise in the fiery afternoon light. The little island chain ran east and west. Except for a slight difference in size, they all looked alike, linked by a common reef to the north. And he had found them just in time—the wind freshened, carrying the smell of rain, and the sea livened up almost immediately. Rodrigue backed off the throttle to reduce the noise of the outboard and circled southward to come under the lee of the nearest island. Then he heard the high-rpm roar of big gasoline engines.

Bearing for him from the south, toward the mainland, throwing aside curtains of spray, was a patrol craft of some sort. Rodrigue could make out a blue flag that he supposed was Honduran.

There was a crude shark's grin painted on the bow—and there was something else about that boat—something . . .

A *PBR!* It was an old navy PBR, just like he had

177

commanded most of his tour in Vietnam—thirty-one-foot fiberglass, shallow draft—it had been used mostly for night patrols in the narrow, murderous backwaters. The sight of it brought back a torrent of ugly memories . . .

Rodrigue had recklessly sped through the driving rain and into a wall of green tracers, he had boarded the other PBR, the one that had been raked by enemy fire, put thermite grenades on the radios, the engines, and on the receivers of the .50-calibers and the 60mm mortar, found the codes, and then went from body to body feeling for pulses.

While he was being so thorough, Dielgleman took a burst square in the face, and Rodrigue stepped on his body as he hauled the one living crewman from the other boat onto his PBR. He looked down and Diegleman, whose outstretched arms were supported by the rim of the pit, seemed to be reaching up at him. For an instant Rodrigue thought he wanted help getting up. Even after he saw the pulpy nothing Diegleman's face had become, he couldn't shake the feeling.

He went berserk. He dropped the wounded sailor and grabbed the .50-caliber bow gun and sprayed the dozen or so sampans and junks that had been crossing the canal. If he sank three, let alone thirty, he had performed a miracle. But in those days, miracles weren't enough to satisfy the government's public-relations effort.

There must've been a hundred VC still on the bank, waiting for a ride across. One of them fired a Russian B-40 rocket launcher into Rodrigue's boat and turned everything aft of the bow gun pit into a meat grinder. QM3 Fred Tunny of San Bernardino, California, died of his wounds a day later. The other two got Purple Hearts and wheelchairs. Rodrigue never heard from them.

*   *   *

The boat bearing down on him now was definitely a PBR, probably Vietnam surplus. From the sound of it, the diesels were gone and big-block gasoline engines installed in their place. Probably the jet drives had been replaced by props as well. The awning was gone but there was still a machine gun on the bow—and it looked like someone was manning it. Rodrigue twisted the outboard's throttle wide open and steered for the opposite side of the nearest island. He didn't feel like explaining himself to the Honduran Navy.

But the PBR gained steadily. As he rounded the mangrove to starboard, Rodrigue wished he hadn't run. He was looking down the long, narrow lagoon between the reef and the string of islands. The shoal water of the lagoon wouldn't bother the PBR anymore than Nicky's skiff. There were sure to be places he could cross the reef and they couldn't, but the sky had fallen over the sea like a black velvet curtain bordered with lace where waves dashed explosively on the coral. He had no business out there.

He could duck into a mangrove vein, one of the labyrinthine passages that wormed through most mangrove islands, but they could just wait him out. The only . . .

And just as Rodrigue was weighing the possibility of it, it came. Rain hit him like a flapping wet sail as the squall marched in from the sea. Knowing he had been swallowed up in a purple-gray wall, he steered for the first cay, pulling the sombrero low to shield his eyes from the downpour. And finding the edge of the mangroves, he slowed to look for a vein, hoping the roar of the rain would mask the changing pitch of the outboard. It would be one less clue they would have to work with, if they chose to pursue him.

He found a vein and entered it, killing his outboard as

soon as he was deep enough to be hidden. He heard the PBR's engines slow as the rain reached it. Trying to wait him out would be a long shot now—they didn't know where to wait. Sure enough, the twin engines churned on, fading until the sound blended into the roar of the reef.

Almost as quickly as it began, the rain ceased. Rodrigue hurried out of the vein before the mosquitoes found him. The sea beyond the reef was still rough and gray but the wind had died. And just as he eased around the first cay, he spotted unnatural white spires poking above the towering gray-green jungle of the second island—the outriggers and fiberglass whip antennas of a big sportfisherman, resting at anchor on the other side.

The *Wahoo Too!* It had to be. It *had* to be her. What the hell would a big sportfisherman with outriggers and single-sideband and VHF and loran and weatherfax and the whole bit be doing so far off the beaten track? It *had* to be them. Rodrigue's excitement bordered on joy.

He picked up the long pimento stalk Nicky had intended for the ridge pole of his shelter and used it to pole the skiff back into the jungle. Mosquitoes attacked so suddenly and viciously that he dropped the pole overboard and had to retrieve it with his broom after he soaked himself with insect repellent. The tide was rising and that made the poling easier.

Grasping mangrove branches and pulling himself along now, he shoved the bow of the skiff into a cove behind the cay. The fading sun cast a purple glow over the still water. The boat was out of sight around the mangrove point, but Rodrigue could hear the pop of her generator. They weren't conserving fuel, he thought. He probably could've motored through the cay unheard, but he'd had no way of knowing that.

He reached down into the forward bilge and hefted each of the three lobsters he had taken from the traps at

St. George's—still alive. He started the motor and puttered out of the hidden vein without bothering to work out a plan. He would play it by ear.

It was *Wahoo Too* all right, salt-caked and already shabby-looking from the want of Mickey Aimes's loving hand. Rodrigue put the outboard in neutral and coasted to within fifteen yards of the boat and hailed it in Spanish. Immediately a face appeared on the fly bridge—the man apparently had been lounging on the cushioned bench up there.

"You want to buy some lobster?" Rodrigue called in Spanish.

"Wait a minute, wait a minute, I don't understand that shit," the man said, swinging down the ladder to the cockpit. He was tall and thin and his unkempt hair formed a red halo around his head in the dying light. McWherter.

He slid open the saloon door and disappeared. In several seconds a shorter and much stouter figure appeared, followed closely by McWherter. "What is it you want?" he asked in badly accented Spanish. Rodrigue couldn't see them well now—the light was behind them and fading quickly—but the voice sounded young.

"I am selling lobsters. Do you want to buy them?"

"How much?" asked the young man.

"Oh, some beer maybe. I will make you a good deal if you will let me sit in that seat up there. I want to get a good look at these islands from up high."

"What's he saying? What's he saying?" asked McWherter.

Another shadowy figure joined them on deck.

"Said he wants to go up in the tower and look around." In English the voice had what sounded to Rodrigue like a Cajun accent. Leland Marchand's nephew?

"He just wants some beer for the lobsters."

"Don't you let that sumbitch on board," said Mc-Wherter. "Shit, we need beer worst'n we need lobsters."

"The guy's selling lobsters?" asked the third man—the other nephew, judging from the accent.

"Hey, man, lobsters would be great. We can get more beer. They do make beer down here, you know." This was the one who had spoken Spanish earlier, the first nephew.

"I don't like it," said McWherter.

"Man, you don't like *anything*. You! How many lobsters do you have?"

"Three," said Rodrigue. "I have three left."

"Three? There are five of us. Three are not very many for five men, true? Could you go catch some more?"

"No, señor, I have just replaced my traps in the sea. There will not be any lobsters in them yet. Maybe tomorrow?"

"How much beer do you want for the three lobsters? We don't have very much beer left. It's Mexican beer. You like Mexican beer, true?"

"It makes me very happy."

"What's going on?" a new, fourth voice demanded.

It sent a chill through Rodrigue. It was young, tough-sounding. And he recognized it instantly as the voice who had called his house for Mike Ferguson the day Mike was killed. The old rage flooded him again.

"Aw, a spick peddling lobsters," said McWherter. "Motherfucker wants to come aboard."

"No fuckin' way!" said the new voice. "Why?"

"It's no big *deal*, Leonard," said the first nephew.

Was this the blabby one? Rodrigue's mind tried to replay what Bruce Phillips had told him that drunken evening in Alabama. And all the while he stood grinning in Nicky's big Mexican skiff, holding up his lobsters.

". . . few lousy beers, bro," Marchand's nephew was

182

saying. "He just said he would make us a good deal if we would let him climb up into the tower and look around."

"What the fuck *for?*"

"It's too much night for you to see now, compadre," the nephew called down. "How many beers do you want?"

"No, no. I have very good eyes for seeing at night. I can see all the islands. What I want to see is if the way I go from one island to the other is in truth the shortest way or if I should take another way."

"What's he saying?" asked the other nephew.

"Hell, I don't know. He really wants to get up there and look around."

"Aw, let him, if it'll get rid of the son of a bitch," said the tough-sounding one, Leonard.

"Bring the lobsters," called down the first nephew. "Come."

The cockpit was suddenly flooded with intense halogen light from the aft rail of the flying bridge. He could see them all plainly: the lanky redheaded McWherter; the nephews with the dark, stocky looks of southeastern Louisiana redbones, a mixture of Cajun, Negro, and Indian; and the fourth man—hard, squinty eyes and square jaw . . .

It was the hauntingly familiar mannequin's face behind the windshield of a waiting car, tapping a rock beat on the steering wheel, as Rodrigue was being taken away and the FBI fussed over the bodies of Sandy and Mike. That was too much for coincidence. He didn't know where he had seen the kid before that bloody day at Sea Isle but he was sure now that he had found Sandy's killer. Rodrigue smiled grimly. The rest would be easy.

There was no way they would let him climb up there with his machete. He realized, too, that he reeked of mosquito repellent. A local fishermen wouldn't use mosquito repellent, but maybe they wouldn't know that or wouldn't notice. He had his damn watch on too. Maybe they wouldn't notice that either. He fumbled for a piece of twine and bound the lobsters. He remembered the knives, twelve-inch fillet knives as sharp as straight razors and racked on the bulkhead beside the bait-rigging station—and near the ladder leading to the flying bridge and the tower above that. He would pretend to slip and have all their throats cut in one sweeping flash.

"Hey, nice ones, bro!" the nephew said as Rodrigue handed up the lobsters. "*¡Muy grandes!*"

"Thank you," Rodrigue said modestly. "This is a very fine boat." He eyed the knives.

"Uh-huh, you can can the crap, Throckmorton, or whatever your name is!"

The new voice came from just inside the saloon, from beyond the blinding glare of the halogen lights, from the fifth person on the *Wahoo Too*. Rodrigue had the chilling feeling he had heard it before.

"I don't understand," Rodrigue said in Spanish.

"Can the *crap*, Throckmorton," said the man, stepping into the lighted cockpit.

It was Virgil Chapman, the Mr. Clean chopper pilot with the Roy Rogers eyes and Dick Tracy jaw. And he was pointing a .45 automatic at Rodrigue's belly.

CHAPTER 21

Chapman's Roy Rogers eyes were red-rimmed and they had dark circles under them. He had about a week's stubble on his face. His cheeks were hollow. Amber liquid swirled around ice cubes in a glass in his other hand. But he still had the military posture and his speech, while faintly slurred, still had that ring of authority. It it hadn't, there still would've been the gun.

"Inside, Throckmorton!" He beckoned with the muzzle of the .45.

Rodrigue shrugged and stepped up into the saloon of Greathouse's big Hatteras.

"I saw some tie-wraps in that tool box down below the vee berths. Go get me one, Chip," Chapman said to the quieter of Marchand's nephews.

"Who in the hell is *he?*" asked Leonard, spitting on the "hell" as though he had begun to salivate at the prospect of another kill. Rodrigue understood why he had looked so familiar. He was the image of his father except his features were smaller or his head larger. The effect was that he looked slightly Mongoloid. And certainly sinster.

"He came around the house right after Alley took off," said Chapman, "asking questions about the boat you idiots left tied to the rig. I thought there was something out of sync with him then."

"Oh, Jesus!" said McWherter. "DEA, you think? Maybe there's more!"

"No. He's no DEA. FBI was right behind him, wanting to know what the visit was about. They weren't on to me yet. Naw, he's private. Working for Greathouse, I'm sure. That right, Throckmorton? Who *are* you?"

"DEA and I've got the place surrounded."

"Hey!" said Leonard at the sound of Rodrigue's accented English. "I talked to this son of a bitch the day I iced the reporter. I did it at *his* house!"

Rodrigue suddenly felt cold. He would have to kill the kid before they got him. That's all, just the kid. But it wouldn't be an even trade in the end—not that he had any choice now. It would be like dispatching a mad dog by grabbing the beast by the scruff and diving off a cliff with it. Hell of a way to go.

"Hmmm," said Chapman, "maybe he *does* work for the newspaper." He suddenly became aware of the ice clinking in his glass and poured in more Johnnie Walker Red to silence it. "Drink?" he asked with the bottle poised.

"Never touch the stuff," said Rodrigue.

"Say, you sound like you're from Louisiana," said the senator's talkative nephew, as though they were at a college mixer.

"Belize," said Rodrigue, plopping down on the divan to see how much sudden movement he could get away with. Chapman tensed, then let the .45's point of aim

186

droop to the cabin sole as he gulped the scotch. But Rodrigue didn't feel lucky.

"This what you're talking about?" asked Chip, reappearing with a small strap of black plastic. It was the all-purpose fastener electricians used on wires and mechanics used on horses. Slip the pointed end through the slotted end and tug and you could handcuff Houdini.

"It's about time," said Chapman. "I almost had to shoot the son of a bitch. C'mon, Throckmorton, on your feet!"

With his hands pinioned behind him, Rodrigue eased himself back down on the divan. He was delighted to hear that Chapman didn't want to shoot him. McWherter paced the saloon. His sunburn was peeling and his thirtyish face was haggard. As if taking a cue from Rodrigue, the two young redbones sank into lounge chairs. Leonard perched on a bar stool; his father stood at the end of the bar with both scotch and pistol at the ready.

"Well, Chapman," Rodrigue said, stretching his legs out comfortably, "I sure never took you for a cocaine addict."

Chapman laughed bitterly. "Never used it in my life. Not even now. Isn't that funny?"

"What're you doing here, then?"

The pilot drained his glass and poured another. The gun got in his way and he handed it to Leonard. "If he moves, kill him," he said without rancor. Leonard nodded, and Rodrigue didn't feel as comfortable.

"This your boy?" he asked.

"Uh-huh. By my first wife. You met my second wife, didn't you? No, that's right, you came too late. Beautiful woman. Beautiful kids. That's right, huh, Leonard? Sparky and Samantha's beautiful kids." He choked on the words and swallowed some scotch to ease the pain.

"Why're you here, Virgil?" Rodrigue asked gently.

"Kathy—that's my wife, Kathy—my second wife—she's, uh, a little, uh, how would you say it, uh . . . expensive." He smiled broadly at the word. "Not extravagant, you understand, but she's . . . rich kid, you know. Always had nice things." He sighed deeply and it turned into a belch.

Leonard was leaning on the bar. His expression, if it could be called that, hinted at both anger and sorrow.

Leland Marchand's talkative nephew put his feet on Greathouse's coffee table. McWherter continued to pace.

"You know what a chopper jockey makes with PHI?" Chapman asked belligerently. "Forty-two thousand, tops, and that's in the air all the time. *Tops.* Unless you move into a supervisory slot, and there's only so many of those. Just like the damn navy. I'd have stayed. I would have." He stared into his glass. "But there were too many pilots. Only so many slots. So I went into business, plain and simple."

"You better shup up, Virgil," McWherter warned.

"Why? Mr. Throckmorton, here, is a corpse."

"The name's Rodrigue," said Rodrigue, suddenly feeling the urge to come clean. "And I'm a salvage diver, not an investigator. Greathouse hired me to sink that boat and when it turned up in the middle of a dope deal, I had to find out what was going on. For my own protection, eh?" It sounded funny now.

Chapman glared at his crew. "Yeah, that was outstanding. Really outstanding."

"Yeah? Well, who *reported* the motherfucker?" whined McWherter.

"We stopped in Belize on the way down," the talkative nephew interjected. His teeth shone white against his dark, acne-scarred face. "For diesel fuel."

"Did you know what you were doing when you

reported the Wellcraft?" Rodrigue asked Chapman, steering the conversation back to the abandoned boat. A falling-out among thieves was the best he could hope for under the circumstances.

"Hell, yes! We knew the boys were due with a shipment, then we found that blood-smeared boat tied up below . . . Alley said he knew someone who could get rid of it for us. Then I got word there was a big drug sweep going on and I knew if they found that boat before it could be removed and I hadn't reported it . . ." He snorted. "You know damn well we'd have been instant suspects. I had to report it fast, before I could get ahold of Alley, and just hope for the best. Then *that* fuckup hits the panic button."

"Uh-huh, uh-huh," said McWherter, getting angry. "*I* was the one selling the shit to Greathouse. He fuckin' never heard of *you!*"

"Right. Then how'd he know to send this clown to sniff around? Oh, they were onto me, all right, and if I had the slightest indication that it was you who put them on me, I'd let Leonard do you in right now."

Suddenly Rodrigue wasn't anxious for the fireworks to begin. "Greathouse doesn't know anything about you," he said. "He simply hired me to sink the boat, and that was just because Alley, here, talked him into it. Said it was for the insurance, right, Alley?"

"That's right. How'd *you* know?"

"Greathouse told me. As far as I know, nobody ever suspected you of anything, Virgil. That's why I can't figure out what you're doing here."

"Ferguson figured it out. He wrote an article about me. Said he was going to identify me to the FBI if they didn't move in on me on their own. Didn't *name* me, of course, but it was obvious."

Rodrigue laughed. He couldn't help it.

Chapman, puzzled and drunk, just frowned at him.

"Right. Then these clowns come running to me to hide them, and Alley'd gone to Mexico, so we just jumped on a plane and followed him. What's so fucking funny?"

"You know who Ferguson thought he was writing about? Buck Greathouse. That's right, the feds didn't have the foggiest idea who was getting the dope in Galveston. *I* thought it was Greathouse because he had hired me to sink the boat, so I tipped Ferguson off and he rushed into print with it. You just *thought* it was about you."

Chapman tried to assay what he had been told, but his mind wasn't up to it. At best it meant he could go home again. At worst he had left home for nothing.

"Well," he said, suddenly uneasy, "kill him whenever you're ready, but don't throw him overboard. Wait 'til the morning and we'll go outside the reef where the sharks are. 'Night." He went unsteadily down the ladder to the staterooms forward. Rodrigue imagined he would plug his ears with his pillow so he wouldn't hear the shot.

He turned quickly to the talkative kid from Louisiana. "Say, you're one of Senator Marchand's nephews, aren't you?"

The nephew smiled, then the smile disappeared. "How did you know that?"

"You told it to a DEA informant in Columbia. Word gets around." He stole a glance at Leonard, who was looking down at the .45 with a chillingly blank face. "They had the whole coast blockaded. The Republicans were kinda anxious to get something on Leland Marchand."

"Oh shit!" the other nephew, Chip, said with a giggle. "Wait'll they figure it out about Anthony!"

Leonard chuckled nastily.

"Who's Anthony?"

"Kid I had to ice," Leonard said, squinting at Rodrigue. "Pain in the ass from the word go."

"His old man owned the yacht we were using," said the talkative nephew.

"Oh, yeah. Big *Republican,* if I remember right. But this doesn't have anything to do with politics, does it?"

"Fuck no," said Leonard tiredly.

"I mean it's a family deal, ain't it? The uncles and the daddies stay at home and the sons and nephews go a-smuggling, right?"

"Hey, it beats the shit out of selling fuckin' insurance," said Chip testily.

"Let's get this over with." Leonard stood straight and leveled the .45 at Rodrigue.

"I'll stink," Rodrigue said quickly. "In this heat? You better wait 'till almost dawn. Wait'll everybody's ready to go to bed anyhow. This Cajun and I, we have some singing to do yet," he said, switching to French.

The talkative nephew lit up. "That is right, my friend," he said, also in French.

"Anymore of that shit and I'll kill you both," Leonard said, very seriously. "Speak English."

"See, Leonard's dad and Uncle Leland and this dude, Thomaston, Anthony's old man—they were all in 'Nam together, right, Leonard?" said the talkative nephew, a little nervous himself now.

"Yeah. *Forrestal.*"

"Anyway, Uncle Leland does a little coke. Cool motherfucker, if you know what I mean." He flashed the white grin. "Mostly, though, he spreads it around a little. Buys him some favors. Who knows?"

"Thomaston sucks it up pretty good," offered Chip. "At least that's what Anthony said."

"Why'd you kill him, Leonard?" asked Rodrigue. "Anthony."

"Little shithead went crazy after he killed those fishermen. Blabbed it to the fuckin' Coast Guard and everything. I iced him as soon as we got away from there

191

and dumped him in the fuckin' river. Probably found him by now."

"Anthony killed the fishermen? Why?"

"Because *this* shithead yelled that we were smuggling cocaine out fuckin' loud, that's why!" He leaned on the bar again and shot a dark look at the talkative nephew. "The kid panicked and iced them."

The talkative nephew grinned sheepishly and shrugged. "Fuck, I didn't even know they were there. It was like our sixth trip, you know, and nobody'd ever been there before. Mr. Chapman and Alley would fly out and get the stuff and Alley would drive it to Uncle Leland and this dude Thomaston on his days off. We had the range to cross over and back without refueling, so we'd make this one quick stop, pick up our cash, and off we'd go again. Pussy in Isla Mujeres! Whoopee!"

"Fuckin' guys pulled up when Oscar was up on the platform," Chip said. "Tied up and started fishing. We were nervous as shit about it, and Anthony had a Mini-14 out of sight and ready, and then Oscar leans over the fuckin' rail and before we can wave him off, he shouts down: 'The coke's in the can and the cash's in the hand!' Probably wouldn't have meant anything to them but Anthony sprayed them anyway. Then Oscar and I went down and heaved them overboard."

"Yeah, we *all* fuckin' panicked and beat feet for Yucatan," said Oscar, the talkative nephew. "Only some hose worked loose in the engine room when it got stormy and the boat sank. I mean it was just about gone when the Coast Guard got there. Wanna do a line before you die?"

"Uh, naw, you go right ahead." Rodrigue hadn't given himself up for dead yet. They were about to make their first mistake.

Chip produced a black plastic 35mm film canister and tossed it to Oscar, who dumped some of the contents on the glass-topped coffee table. With a thin-bladed knife, he lovingly arranged the white powder into what Rodrigue, bound in detached fascination, thought resembled the rippling of a sandy ocean bottom. Oscar took a clear plastic straw from his shirt pocket and plowed a deep row in the ocean bottom. Rodrigue could tell it made him happy.

"What happened next?"

"Well, shit," Oscar said, craning to look over McWherter, who was bending over the coffee table with his own straw in hand, "we didn't know *what* to do, so we called Uncle Leland, who had a fuckin' cat. He sent an attorney from Baton Rouge to get us out, I mean a guy with a *lot* of stroke, if you know what I mean. Gave us some money and told us to go poof!"

Chip did his turn at the table. Rodrigue was waiting for Leonard's turn. He would lean back and kick the murderous little sonofabitch in the head as he leaned over to sniff the cocaine. He would jump up and kick him until he was down and then stomp on his throat—that would kill him for sure. Maybe with a burst of adrenaline he could snap the tie-wrap and grab the gun. Maybe not. Anyway, he'd get Leonard.

"So Leonard iced Anthony and we hopped a plane to Houston. And then when Leonard's dad said the reporter was onto him somehow, Leonard tracked him down and iced *him* too."

"Him and some old bimbo he was fucking," said Leonard with a miniature grin.

Rodrigue's heart pumped freon for an instant. He positioned his wrists for maximum use of his muscles in wresting them apart. But he forced himself to bide his time. "How'd you track him down?"

Leonard shrugged. "Public library. He gave me the phone number where he was on his recorder—*your* phone number. When you wouldn't tell me anything, I called the library and they looked the number up in the city directory. Gives your address and the whole ball of wax."

"But if you killed the reporter—"

"Fat-*assed* motherfucker."

"So what was the problem? Why'd your dad take off?"

Leonard got off the bar stool and moved toward the coffee table like a big jungle cat. "Cops were fuckin' everywhere. I mean just like that—" He snapped his fingers. "When I told him that, he figured the FBI'd already gotten to the reporter. So we drove all the way to Miami in case they were watching the airport in Houston. Hopped a plane for Cancun, to throw them off, and then took the fuckin' bus to Cozumel."

"Jesus!" muttered Chip, evidently remembering the bus ride.

Leonard never took his eyes or the gun off Rodrigue as he reached down, took a pinch of the cocaine, and snorted it out of his fingers. His small eyes glittered in a way that Rodrigue didn't like, and he was beginning to wish he'd had a better plan—or just a *plan*. He decided to pick on McWherter a while.

"You're the one who got me into this, you skinny motherfucker," Rodrigue said with a grin. "Why in the fuck did you get Greathouse to have the boat sunk after you and Virgil had gone and *reported* the son of a bitch?"

"*I* didn't know the asshole was going to report the motherfucker!" McWherter said heatedly.

"Watch it!" Leonard warned.

Yeah! Rodrigue thought happily. *Get mad.*

"Well, I *didn't!* Greathouse had a boat and I could lean on him and that was all I needed to know. I had no idea he was going to report the sonofabitch."

"Kinda left ol' Virgil in the lurch when you took off like that, didn't you?"

The cousins and Leonard were following the conversation as though it were a tennis match.

"He knew I was going and he was glad of it. Took the heat off'a him. And I called him when we got to Cozumel."

"And you killed Mickey Aimes?"

"Naw, Leonard here done it."

Of course. Leonard was the killer. Rodrigue looked at the straight-backed young man with the square jaw and glittering, slitlike eyes, and wondered how to keep him from getting sleepy.

CHAPTER 22

Rodrigue's only regret in his final moments was not steering Ann Eller
straight to bed when he had the chance. At the same time
it was his crowning achievement. It might even get him a
stint in purgatory.

All that crap about your life passing before your eyes
was just that—crap. Rodrigue's whole life had been
approximately four days long. He walked numbly into the
pale dawn, his senses turned down low. He had given
himself up for dead when Virgil Chapman emerged,
scrubbed and shaven and grinning, just as the day was
dawning clear and rosy.

"Stand by to fend Throckmorton's boat off, there,
Chip," Chapman was barking cheerily at the other
nephew. "We'll set it adrift where we dump the body. It'll
look like an accident, if anybody cares."

Up on the flying bridge, Leonard started the engines.

McWherter, standing behind him, suddenly became

196

animated, swinging his head back and forth to find a clear view through the salt-caked vinyl curtain.

"Someone's coming!" he screeched.

"What?" yelled Chapman. "Let me see!"

He let the .45's muzzle swing clear of Rodrigue's belly for an instant. If Rodrigue had been ready, it might've been enough, but in anticipation of his death his metabolism had slowed to that of a frog in December. Chapman paused on the bottom rung, leveled the gun at Rodrigue again, and said with a grim smile, "Just what is it that you see, Alley?"

"Boat," answered Leonard. "Headed right this way. Looks like some kind of patrol boat. Got a flag flying. Machine gun on the bow."

"All right, all right, probably nothing," said Chapman inwardly. "In case they want to board us, though, Leonard, you come down and cover this clown. Stand here beside the ladder and if anything happens, shoot him first, and then any of *them*"—he jerked his head in the direction of the approaching boat—"who has a gun, got it?"

"You," he said, looking at Rodrigue, "keep your mouth shut. If you are questioned, answer in Spanish. Tell them you're our guide. Nothing more. Oscar! Get out here!"

Not that he had an option—he could at least choose to die at a most inconvenient moment for his captors—Rodrigue wanted it all. He wanted to live. His heart was pounding and his muscles were weak and jumping involuntarily. His civilian eye bounced from father to son as the weapon changed hands. He had to think of something—fast.

Oscar came blinking into the gold sunlight. He had been sleeping on the divan. Oscar had saved Rodrigue's life—up to now—merely by being his loquacious self. He had wanted to talk, mostly about the ladies of Mexico. He was a good listener too, and Rodrigue tried to sell him on the virtues, if that's the word, of the hot Creole women in Belize City. He actually liked the kid, but as cordial as their all-night visit had been, there was always the concrete understanding that Rodrigue would die at dawn. Sooner if he moved too suddenly.

Chapman leaned over the flying bridge rail to brief Oscar. "Listen up—a patrol craft of some sort is approaching from the west. They may want to board us. Leonard has Throckmorton covered. He's not to speak unless spoken to, then only in Spanish. He's our guide, you understand? If he says anything to the contrary—let's see, we need a signal . . . tell you what, if he says anything wrong, you say: 'windowpane.' Leonard'll open up and it'll be up to us to mop up. Take one of those knives there and cut that tie-wrap off Throckmorton's wrists."

"*Window*pane?"

"Don't hesitate, Ace. You don't want to spend your life in a Honduran jail."

Rodrigue heard the high-rpm whine of gas engines at full throttle. He craned his neck and saw the old PBR smiling at him through the shimmering spray, the blue-and-white flag standing stiff overhead.

"I think we should practice, Oscar," Rodrigue said loudly in Spanish.

"What? What?" said Leonard, looking back and forth from Rodrigue to Oscar.

"You better shut your face," Oscar said, smiling but no longer friendly.

"In Spanish, Oscar, in Spanish."

"Shut up!" Oscar said, loudly.

The PBR came sliding beam-to, coasting on its wake.

"Here I am," Rodrigue shouted, "trying to help you

198

bastards, and this is the thanks I get? Damn your mother, you stingy bastard."

"I'm gonna waste him," Leonard said resolutely, raising the pistol, but his father hissed at him from above to put it away, and then there was a hail from a bullhorn in an unmistakable accent from the southern U.S.:

"Everybody calm down there and stand by to be boarded. I'm a lieutenant in the United States Army, attached to Honduran security forces. Stand by to be boarded."

The old PBR bumped alongside and the little Honduran soldier in the forward gun pit automatically brought the .50-caliber machine gun to bear on *Wahoo Too*'s cockpit.

Rodrigue was as shocked as anyone to discover a U.S. military adviser aboard, but he still felt he had instinctively done the right thing. Anyway it was too late to try something else. If he were to come out now and tell the lieutenant that these men were dope smugglers, that cold-blooded sonofabitch with the .45 just might start shooting.

He had intended to start an argument—yet staying in his appointed role as local guide—in the hopes that the Hondurans would side with la raza and let him simply hop off the boat. If Oscar's Spanish was good enough to keep a translation coming, Rodrigue would be getting away without immediately threatening Chapman and crew. They would either have to let it happen or get into a shooting match with the Hondurans.

But ethnocentrism was a two-edged sword. Maybe the other edge would cut as well . . .

"Now look at this!" Rodrigue screamed in Spanish at Chapman, who was almost frantically bewildered. "A man cannot have a decent quarrel with his employer without some fat-assed, peanut-penised Yankee bastard wanting to step in and settle it!"

There was a roar of laughter on the PBR and the U.S. Army lieutenant paused at *Wahoo Too*'s gunwale to get a translation from a wooden-faced Houduran with a slightly more elaborate uniform than the others—their officer, Rodrigue guessed. At the same time, Oscar was ad-libbing an even more innocuous version for Leonard. He obviously didn't relish the prospect of dodging a cross-fire of .45- and .50-caliber bullets.

The lieutenant's fleshy jowls turned a fluorescent pink and he hurled himself over the gunwale with a burst of strength that made everyone retreat a step.

"Very good morning, pig-shit," Rodrigue said pleasantly.

"You shut your filthy mouth, scum!" the lieutenant drawled menacingly, waving aside the translation from the Honduran officer, who had swung over the gunwale behind him. He didn't understand Spanish but he had a firm handle on the gist of the conversation so far.

The Hondurans on the PBR were howling wildly, wiping tears off their faces. The officer remained solemn.

"I'll take care of this piece of shit for you," said the lieutenant, who was indeed fat-assed and sweating profusely in his dark fatigues. "But you men are going to have to move away from here."

"No, it's all—" Chapman tried to protest.

"I'm afraid I'll have to insist. We're holding some joint exercises with the Hondurans and these islands here are smack-dab in the middle of the operational site. You can stand off out yonder if you want to, but don't do no divin', now. We'll be setting off some explosives." He grinned and smacked his chewing gum good-naturedly.

"Ah," Chapman began, "this, uh, gentleman here is, uh, our fishing guide. A little excitable, like all these people are, but—"

"Yeah, well, you won't be needing a fishing guide

around here no more. Won't be a fish on this reef by tomorrow night," the lieutenant said proudly.

"Listen—" started Leonard heatedly. Chapman cut him off:

"Uh, very good, Lieutenant. Former navy myself. We'll get under way immediately, take this boy back to his village—"

"You have the breath of a burro's butt," said Rodrigue to the army lieutenant. "You—"

"Shut up!" The lieutenant slapped Rodrigue across the face with his open hand, silencing the guffaws on the PBR. It actually felt good. "I'm takin' him back myself and I'll see to it he gets straightened out. These people here don't fuck around."

"That's not necessary—"

"C'mon, shithead!" He already had Rodrigue by the shirt and put one hand on his holstered pistol for emphasis.

As he stepped down into the familiar cockpit, Rodrigue was flooded with relief. He flashed on the many good times inside gunwales just like these, the bullshit sessions with Diegelman and Smitty and Ross and Tunny. He was surprised, after all these years, that it was a little like coming home.

The way the Honduran soldier at the stern was minding the line from the skiff's bow told Rodrigue the original jet drives had been replaced with propellers. "What happened to the diesels?" he asked the Honduran officer abruptly in Spanish.

The officer looked puzzled for an instant. "Oh, you mean on the boat. I don't know, actually. These are Ford 390s. I suppose for ease of maintenance."

He meant the Fords would last longer with little or no maintenance. Diesels are more reliable, on the whole, but they're a bitch to rebuild. In any rural village in

Central America, on any city street corner, you can find somebody who can rebuild a Ford engine under a tree with just the tools in his pocket.

The men on the *Wahoo Too* were watching with numbed expressions, Chapman and McWherter on the flying bridge, Leonard and Oscar in the cockpit. They simply stood there, mouths open, arms hanging, watching him with a trace of disbelief in their eyes. As the PBR rose and peeled away, Rodrigue waved a tiny farewell wave and the men on the Hatteras exploded into action— Chapman spun around to the wheel, Leonard and Oscar stumbled forward to get the anchor, and McWherter's head bobbed between the activity on the *Wahoo Too* to the departing patrol boat like a frantic chicken.

"Lieutenant, those men are dope smugglers," Rodrigue said in English.

"Shut up!" the lieutenant said, his face registering surprise even as he lifted his knee to Rodrigue's crotch.

CHAPTER 23

The U.S. Army lieutenant, one Wayne Ledbetter of Orangeburg, South Carolina, found it hard to overcome his bad first impression of Rodrigue. He just blinked and stared. Rodrigue, bent over with pain, gasped, "The boat is stolen. Call the authorities in Cozumel. They'll tell you."

"Are you a Mexican?" asked the puzzled Honduran officer, ordering the patrol boat halted with a fanning motion of his hand.

"No, I am a North American," answered Rodrigue in Spanish. He had to catch himself as the boat settled. "I need for you to help me convince this fat-assed bastard that those men are bad ones. The boat is stolen. They are wanted for murder in the United States. Also in Mexico. They are cocaine smugglers."

The *Wahoo Too*, now some seventy-five yards away, was weighing anchor. The Honduran looked at her and shrugged.

"What's he saying? What's he saying?" yelled Lieutenant Ledbetter. "Speak English, goddamnit!"

"My name is John Rodrigue," Rodrigue said slowly, straightening and fixing Ledbetter with his civilian eye. "I'm a salvage diver from Galveston, Texas, and I was hired by the owner of that boat to retrieve it. It was stolen from the municipal marina at Cozumel and the captain was killed. Those people also killed four people in Galveston, one in New Orleans, and they're wanted for smuggling cocaine."

The Hatteras was now under way, headed for the break in the western end of the reef.

"I would've mentioned it earlier," Rodrigue said, "but the fellow leaning against the cabin was holding a cocked .45."

"Got any proof of all this?" Ledbetter responded.

"Wanted posters, you mean?" Rodrigue would argue a little longer, then he would hurt somebody. "Listen, Lieutenant, you're passing up on a golden opportunity here. You can do something real instead of just playing fucking army. Get out there and stop 'em before it's too late! Just stop 'em and check it out later."

The *Wahoo Too* was past the reef now, her bow rising at the urging of the engines.

"Interrogate the little dark guy named Oscar and he'll spill his guts. Radio a call in for the cops in Cozumel . . . something!"

Rodrigue knew it was no use to suggest they search for the cocaine. Chip had ducked inside at the sight of the patrol boat, probably to collect their dope for deep-sixing if necessary.

"Why'd you run off from us yesterday, then?" said Ledbetter suspiciously. "And what kinda accent you got?"

"My passport!" Rodrigue said, slapping himself on

the forehead. "My passport's down in the skiff. Let me show you."

"Henry," Ledbetter said to the Honduran officer, "you check it out, will you?"

"In a little plastic case taped under the aft thwart," Rodrigue coached.

The Honduran ordered a non-com to order a private aboard the skiff. The private felt around, located the duct-taped Tupperware sandwich box, and brought it unopened aboard the PBR. He handed it to the non-com, who handed it to the officer, whose name was Enrique, who popped it open and examined the contents.

"A lot of money," he said, holding up the stack of bills. "A *lot* of money. U.S. Ah, here—"

Ledbetter snatched the passport and opened it. "Last port of entry Belize *City?*" He glanced incredulously at Nicky's Mexican skiff.

"That's where I rented this boat," Rodrigue said tiredly. "That money is operating capital, provided by the owner of the *Wahoo Too*, Buck Greathouse from Houston. He can be reached at the Cabañas del Caribe on Cozumel. Listen, all this can be checked out in due time, but you'd better get this old bitch rolling if you expect to catch that Hatteras."

"Well, I'll report it into headquarters when we finish up here in the islands," Ledbetter said doggedly. "You want to ride in with us?"

Rodrigue hit him hard, squarely in the face, and Ledbetter pitched backward into a galvanized pipe that had once served to hold a makeshift top. His head hit the pipe and he slid to the cockpit sole, unconscious. One of the men tentatively raised a submachine gun, but Enrique shoved the muzzle back down. He knelt and felt Ledbetter's pulse throbbing rhythmically in his fleshy neck.

205

"An accident," he said in English, rising to his feet again. He grinned, displaying a gold front tooth, and Rodrigue instinctively felt he had found a kindred spirit.

"Let's go get them," he said.

"Impossible," said Enrique sadly. "We do not have the gasoline. It would be many miles before we caught them now, ¿verdad?"

"How much gasoline have you?"

Enrique followed Rodrigue's gaze into the small boat, where the empty six-gallon tanks were scattered among the clutter of gear and supplies. "Enough to get us back to base with some to spare. Maybe enough left over to run such a small boat as yours many miles. Do you wish to buy some?"

"Sí."

"Then I will make you a good price," said Enrique, his gold tooth flashing. He looked down at Rodrigue's Tupperware container, lying where Ledbetter had dropped it, and nudged it gently with his toe. "Half."

"Half?"

"I am not a greedy man."

It was the truth. He could easily kill Rodrigue and have it all.

"I am very grateful," Rodrigue said, taking the Honduran's hand in the Latin American fashion, fingers grasping the base of the thumb.

Enrique shrugged. "Consider it the Honduras government's contribution to the—how is it called?—the pursuit of happiness? No, the pursuit of—"

"Truth, justice, and the American way?" prompted Rodrigue, being a smart ass.

"That's it!" cried the Central American, banana-republican soldier. "Justice!"

Meanwhile, *Wahoo Too* was bounding over the open sea, tossing spray in huge shining curtains.

CHAPTER 24

With both big diesels churning wide open, *Wahoo Too* was walking away from Nicky's Mexican skiff when she disappeared in a low cloud bank and left Rodrigue on his own. Not having a compass, he steered by the pattern of the swells.

But the swells pushed him too far to the south. He missed the Sapodilla Cays and was on his way toward the mainland when he hailed a fishing boat. The fishermen hadn't seen the Hatteras. They pointed the way to the Sapodillas.

Squalls rose up and Rodrigue lost a lot of time nosing into angry seas and blinding rain on the new heading. It was night by the time he sighted the cays but the moon gave plenty of light. The sky had cleared and the wind had died and the sea lay still.

If *Wahoo Too* anchored somewhere in the lee of these islands, her lights must be out. Approaching as he was from the direction of the mainland, on the calm side of the chain, he should have the big Hatteras in sight. But all he could see were fuzzy black clumps far, far away across a black shellacked surface. Now was the time to pull out the old snapper-fisherman's trick of using an electronic depth-sounder to follow the wake of another boat to his fishing grounds.

Big, fast-turning propellers like *Wahoo Too*'s left a trail of aerated water that often lasted hours after visible signs of the wake had vanished. It would absorb a sonar signal if the signal were adjusted so that it was just barely strong enough to bounce off the bottom. When the display went blank, you were over the wake. Or simply over a softer, less resonant bottom. Like any good trick, there was a trick to it.

First Rodrigue emptied his water supply from the plastic milk jugs Nicky had stowed on board, and he fashioned marker buoys using the jugs, twine, and full cans of Spam for weight. Then he hooked the physician's depth-finder, a Humminbird Super Sixty, to the car battery and put it on the thwart in front of him, where he could keep an eye on the circular display.

With his machete, he wacked the bushy end off the household broom and fastened the depth-finder's trans-ducer—the small, disk-shaped "antenna" that transmit-ted and received the sonar signal—to the chopped end with twine. Using the broomstick as a handle (the pimento stalks would've worked as well, but the broom-stick was smoother to grasp), he would hold the trans-ducer face-down in the water to scan for traces of the big boat's wake.

He threw out a buoy as a reference point and slowly ran a pinwheel search pattern, the flashing orange light dancing back and forth between the thirty- and fifty-foot marks on the display as he circled farther and farther from the buoy. Finally, when the floating milk jug was just a pale dot on the glassy surface of the sea, the bottom display disappeared. Rodrigue instantly launched another buoy and watched the depth-finder closely as the skiff plodded on. In seconds the display was flashing again.

Rodrigue took his bearings by the moon, by the first buoy, by the dark clumps on the horizon. He had moved parallel to the island chain, it seemed. The second buoy marked where he had cut the trail left by the *Wahoo Too*, still apparently running at top speed. Bound to be headed for an anchorage, though, he figured. Using the second buoy as a reference, he ran in a broad sweeping zigzag toward the islands. The orange light on the depth-finder winked on and off predictably. Talk about plotting sand! he thought happily.

After an hour of this, an island loomed large. Rodrigue shut off his outboard and listened, and he heard the drone of *Wahoo Too*'s Onan. They may have their lights off but they aren't doing without air conditioning, he thought. That was good. That was crucial. Between the noise of the generator and the noise of the air conditioners, they wouldn't hear his outboard. He circled around into the shallow lagoon seaward of the island and beached the skiff just as the thin scratch of new light appeared on the Caribbean night.

Doused with mosquito spray, he knelt in the damp sand, in the cover of low scrub, swatting at the buzzing insects and waiting for it to be light enough to see. She was at anchor, nobody stirring, about 300 yards from the island—amateur desperadoes, quickly running out of hideouts.

They couldn't go much farther north for fear the Mexicans would nab them. They couldn't go east either, in case Rodrigue had been able to convince the Hondurans to stop them. What they should've done, Rodrigue thought, was head straight out to sea and circle wide of

209

Honduras toward Nicaragua, and from there Panama and Colombia. But if they intended to do that, they would've done it when Ledbetter ran them out of the Bay Islands.

Maybe Chapman was thinking of sneaking home again, now that he knew the FBI wasn't after him. Or maybe they were just going to stay where they were and prey on fishing smacks. A fifty-foot Hatteras was certainly a comfortable enough corsair.

It was an intriguing thought—modern pirates in an air-conditioned pirate ship. It would make a good movie. Especially the part where he climbs stealthily over the transom and slits all their throats with the ship's own fillet knife. He crawled backward in the damp sand until he was down from the low rise, then turned and jogged in a low crouch back to the skiff.

In the end it might have been the waiting that softened him. It had grown too light to do anything now. He would have to wait until nightfall. He could drink himself to sleep and kill them all when he awoke, cramped and dirty and hungry and hungover, but somehow that course of action didn't appeal to him very much. The truth was he really didn't want to kill them at all.

Sandy didn't demand it. As tolerant as she was, she probably would've regarded young Leonard's murderous ways as an affliction—no, not even that—as some kind of weird hobby. Probably want to fuck him to take his mind off it. Or to see what a cold-blooded murderer fucks like. Anyway, where Sandy was now she was beyond wanting revenge. No, *above* it. Like Edgar Samuels. That was what made the old man seem so peaceful and whole. He was sure to have been humbled a lot in his life for no reason other than his African blood. He could've been broken or bitter but he was neither.

It was as plain as the frigate bird wheeling in the sweet, salty air overhead: mere mortals do a lousy job of wreaking vengeance. It takes too fine a hand. He could've been feeding sharks at that very moment. Chasing armed killers in a fucking rowboat with a machete!

So what *did* they want, Sandy and Mike Ferguson and Mickey Aimes? What the hell was it Diegleman had wanted? Was it enough to light a candle and drop a few coins into the tin box? No, there had to be something more.

He consulted the rum bottle but his heart wasn't in it. He was bone-tired and he had nothing to drive him. No plan. Not even a purpose. This had all been for Sandy and Mike and now they didn't seem to want it. Mickey didn't want it. He, too, was somewhere unimaginable with revenge for his untimely death the furthermost thing from his mind. Untimely? By whose clock? Death comes to all of us and after you've been dead a million years, does it really matter that you died a couple of years too soon? Or in Rodrigue's case, maybe fourteen years too late.

Except he didn't die this time either, did he? Rodrigue sat up and felt himself, grinning ludicrously. *Uh-huh*, he thought, *still kicking*. He lay back down and watched the morning sun play on the clouds. It was amazing how much shit he could get into and still be kicking.

He was who it was for, when you got right down to it. Sandy didn't want it, Mike didn't want it, Mickey didn't want it. The two fishermen at the rig didn't want it. And little Anthony—he didn't deserve it. He and the fishermen could settle up in the hereafter.

Okay, so it was his party—now what? He wouldn't mind killing Leonard, but the others . . . And yet he couldn't just let them go. *That* idea never crossed his mind. Once he got started, though, he would have to kill them all, or be killed himself. He couldn't just storm aboard and take away Chapman's scotch as punishment.

Punishment.

That was what it was all about. When the victim dies,

any Good Samaritan worth his salt goes after the robbers. Not to get even but to punish. *These men gotta be stopped 'fore they kill again!* a reformed Lieutenant Ledbetter insisted in his head. Yeah, that's it: *deterrence!* It was all fine and good for Sandy to sit on her fucking cloud and be magnanimous. She was safe now. But those of us still scrambling around down here have every right to deterrence. If the robbers weren't punished until they met their Maker, we would be over-fucking-run with robbers.

Yet that wasn't it. Too—pragmatic.

It didn't matter what the scientists and sociologists and economists quoted in newspapers said, the world did not operate like a jukebox, with this button triggering precisely this little motor which engaged precisely this little arm. It was far more mysterious. What we needed here was something purer than cause-and-effect or a means to an end.

Punishment. For its own sake. What was that, vengeance? No, it wouldn't be that much fun. Rodrigue suddenly sat up in the boat. It was just what Enrique had had on the tip of his oligarchical tongue: plain old fucking *justice!* Even Edgar Samuels would want justice.

Justice! Rodrigue rubbed his knee, which throbbed dully, and he looked around as though justice might be found trying to bury itself in the sand. There must be some way to have justice without blood . . .

And then, as though he were inventing it, he thought of the law.

He hopped out, shoved off the skiff, and hurried to get through the reef and out of hearing before anyone on *Wahoo Too* came on deck. Skirting the southern bend in the islands, he opened the throttle for Punta Gorda.

CHAPTER 25

The police station was in a new two-story concrete-block building just down from the muncipal "bridge," as Belizeans call their piers. At the blotter desk Rodrigue found a black youngster with his feet up scanning a Mexican comic book. He slapped his hand on the counter and the startled youngster slammed the chair's front legs to the floor with a thud.

"I need to see the chief," Rodrigue said. This was too formal an occasion for Creole.

"Am not 'tere. Me dah me one," said the young black.

"Where is he, at home?"

"Yes, maan."

"Well, go get him. Tell him he has some dope smugglers to round up. Make the country a little money."

"Yes, maan!" The boy ran out, unconcerned about leaving the police station in the hands of a stranger.

Marijuana was the chief export of Belize, by a wide margin, and to some extent the country served as a relay

213

point for cocaine from Colombia. None of this was condoned by the government of course, but the government was too poor to deal with armed camps of Salvadorans and Guatemalans deep in the bush. Every now and then the national guard—the Belize Defence Force, or BDF—would nab somebody and the courts would fine them heavily and let them go with the intention that they be nabbed and fined again someday. The fines were very welcome to a government whose principal source of revenue was a steep tariff on imported goods—which was to say *most* goods, since Belize wasn't industrialized. Rodrigue didn't hesitate to drag the police chief away from his lunch. He expected to make the man very happy.

He came at a trot, then very calmly listened to Rodrigue's story. His name was Ian Saunders and he was a Carib (or Garifuna, as they now prefer)—blacks who came to the Caribbean so early they developed a New World tribal identity, like American Indians. He was in his early thirties, small-boned and delicate-featured. A broad smile came and went, and when it went his face was very serious. Rodrigue decided—by gut feeling, which was the way he made most decisions involving people—that Saunders could be trusted.

He, on the other hand, was forced to omit the part where the Grand Banks sank with the last shipment of cocaine. The fact that the crew was sniffing out of a 35mm film can probably meant they were light on the cruel white dust, but Rodrigue led Saunders to believe there was a big stash that would earn the men of the *Wahoo Too* large fines, and that there were families back in the States perfectly able to pay them. At least the last part was true.

"Yes, maan . . ." The chief hesitated, giving himself time to think. "But if they have indeed done all these

214

things, how in the world will I capture them with my little force here? Unless I call in the BDF."

He had obviously been well educated—in Jamaica, maybe, or even England—and Rodrigue guessed the Creole slang that had slipped into his speech meant he was excited. Or maybe he habitually used it to disarm his listeners. To be chief of police that young meant he was a damn good politician as well as a damn good policeman.

"If you call in the BDF, they're going to pull the strings from Belmopan. But if you can get a boat big enough to hold them all, one man to run it and another to hold a gun on them, you can do it all yourself."

"Yes, maan, I can gat a fine baat, but not fast enough to outrun a Hatteras. Maan, that's one fast baat now."

"No problem, maan. I'm going to *sink* the Hatteras. All you have to do is come along and fish them out of the water."

"Sink the baat? I thought you were supposed to recover it."

"If possible, but it's the only way I can see to nab them without anyone getting killed. The owner has plenty of insurance, don't worry. He's far more interested in seeing those guys brought to justice than he is getting his boat back."

"An' how will we gat the evidence?"

"Dive for it. It's in shallow water. Or raise the boat."

"An' how are you going to sink the baat?"

"That I haven't quite figured out yet. Any explosives around here we could get?"

"There might be the odd stick of dynamite, but how are you going to blow up the baat without killing am all? They are of absolutely no use dead."

"I need to make a hole in the hull, that's all. So the water will rush in."

The police chief's top lip raised like the keyboard

cover of a new piano. "Hey, how 'bout a big brace an' bit? My father has one they used to use when they made houses the old way, with pegs to hold the beams. Big auger—drill a hole an inch and a half in diameter!"

"I don't know, Ian. How could I swing a hand drill underwater? Wouldn't be able to get any leverage on it, not without something to brace myself . . ." Rodrigue was thinking out loud. "Say, I tell you wot—can you get me a couple of good inner tubes? For car or truck tires?"

"No problam."

"And I'll need a half-dozen soft wood plugs, the kind for plugging leaks, eh? An inch at the thickest."

"No problam. *Plugging* leaks? I thought we were going to make leaks."

"We're going to make leaks going in and plug 'em coming out."

The police chief looked puzzled.

"Trust me." Rodrigue patted the man's shoulder. "Just get someone to sharpen that auger like a razor." There was at least three-quarters of an inch of woven roving— tough fiberglass cloth—in the hull of a fifty-foot Hatteras.

While Rodrigue napped in a cell, Saunders rounded up the materials he had asked for, and he enlisted a shrimp boat belonging to a Chinese. The Chinese agreed to act as skipper. Saunders told him it would be a piece of cake.

Saunders believed it himself. He stepped aboard carrying a Remington Model 870, a twelve-gauge pump with a long barrel for duck hunting, and flicked a wave at the Chinese, who immediately threw off the bow line. Rodrigue looked up and down the darkening pier. "This is *it?*" he asked.

The police chief leaned the shotgun against a rusty winch and counted on his fingers: "Maan on da wheel. Maan in da wata. Maan wit da so-so muma. Dem plenty." He grinned, eyes sparkling mischievously.

* * *

As the old boat clattered toward the Sapodilla Cays with Nicky's Mexican skiff in tow, Rodrigue wished he had the same amount of confidence. It was a good plan and that alone was plenty of cause for worry. But even after lying like a rotten log all afternoon he was still tired, and the rhythm of the diesel had nearly lulled him into nodding off when it abruptly stopped.

"We gat any closer, they gonna hear us," Saunders said in an unnecessary whisper.

Rodrigue put the brace and bit in a tow sack with the rest of his sabotage tools and stepped down into the skiff. "If the flashlight doesn't work, I'll shout, but don't come in until I signal one way or the other, all right?"

The police chief and the skipper nodded solemnly. Rodrigue started the outboard and roared for a break in the island chain.

On the beach again he donned the mask, scuba tank, and weight belt he had borrowed from Brad Potts. He stuffed the wood plugs in one hip pocket and the flashlight sealed in a Ziploc freezer bag in the other. The coil of nylon rope he wedged under the weight belt, and he had added a sheath knife borrowed from the shrimper. He picked up his flippers, collected the inflated inner tubes and brace and bit, and walked over the low island.

The *Wahoo Too* glowed softly in the darkness like a ghost ship floating on the night sky. There was plenty of moonlight but little else to reflect it. He paused in waist-deep water to slip on the flippers and then began swimming, an arm looped through each tube, toward the yacht. He took it easy, knowing it would be a long, hard night.

CHAPTER 26

The *Wahoo Too* throbbed with the rhythmic noises of a diesel generator, two air conditioners, a refrigerator-freezer and a separate full-size freezer, and some staticky reggae from across the Caribbean that rose and fell with the wafting of the AM band and the gentle swinging of the boat at anchor. Noiselessly, Rodrigue paddled along the hull. He hadn't been a combat swimmer in the navy but he had thought piratical thoughts all his life. It wasn't hard to figure out how to sink a sportfisherman.

He stopped at a plastic-rimmed hole in the side of the boat, the discharge for the forward bilge pump. Because an electric bilge pump could work against only so much "head"—the vertical distance it had to pump the water—the discharges were just above the waterline, easy to reach. Supporting himself on the inner tubes, he plugged the hole with one of the soft wood plugs, jamming it in tightly. And he very quietly circled the boat, plugging the other three bilge discharges.

There were other discharge holes located higher on the hull but they were for the sump pumps for the showers and air conditioners, which would be of little use once the boat settled that much.

To solve the problem of getting enough leverage to swing the brace and bit in the near-weightlessness underwater, Rodrigue had devised a sling he could tighten under the boat to pin himself against the hull. It was based on the crude salvage trick of using empty oil drums to support a swamped craft. He had already tied the nylon line to one of the tubes, and he would loop it through the other inner tube on the other side of the boat.

Treading water under *Wahoo Too's* flared bow, the wide flippers supported him easily despite his aching knee. He was breathing through the snorkel on the mask to avoid the tinny wheeze of the regulator. He pushed the tied inner tube to his left and the line uncoiled with it. He passed the line loosely through the other tube and pushed it to his right, spit out the snorkel, cleared the regulator, and swam under along the keel, dragging the tubes into position on opposite sides of the boat.

When the sling was where he wanted it—under the widest portion of the bow—Rodrigue tied a small loop with a simple overhand knot a few feet under the first tube. He passed the other end of the line through it, using it as a single block to pull the two tubes against the hull. Then he tied another loop in the sling near the second tube, pulled the end of the line through it and back, and he had a double block, with enough mechanical advantage to pull the sling very tight when he was ready.

The *Wahoo Too's* bottom was slick with new antifouling paint. Rodrigue maneuvered himself into an upside-down kneeling position astraddle the keel and worked his flippered feet between the hull and the sling, with the nylon rope resting snugly across his upper calves. He carefully pulled the line tighter, jamming the inner tubes, now partly submerged, solidly against the sides of the boat. Then he tied the sling off with a pair of half-hitches and began the laborious process of drilling a hole through three-quarters of an inch of fiberglass. Quietly.

He was beneath the forward quarter of the boat, right under the crew quarters, he figured. The Hatteras had three bilge pumps back in the engine room but only one in the forward bilge. If there was an alarm in the forward bilge—and *if* the alarm worked or hadn't been deliberately disconnected—and *if* they pinpointed the problem in time to slash the anchor rope—forget about hoisting the anchor—and nose her aground, they might be able to save her. That was too many ifs. At sea, three ifs and you're out.

Even after the boat began to fill they could rig a means to pump her out using the engines—just shut the seacocks on the raw-water intakes, jerk the hoses off and shove them down in the bilge, then let the cooling systems on the big diesels take over. But they wouldn't know how to do that. They had already managed to lose one of the most seaworthy yachts made.

Rodrigue ground methodically with the brace.

For a very . . .

Very . . .

Very long time.

Finally he broke through, cleanly, and he heard a momentary *slup!* as water sucked into the hole. He cut himself free with the borrowed sheath knife, surfaced, and tied the ancient brace and bit to the nearest inner tube. Suddenly there was a new hum from deep within the boat. Rodrigue rested on the tube and kicked away to wait. A fine jet of mist sprayed from the plugged discharge hole.

Rodrigue watched the *Wahoo Too* for what seemed

like an hour before he noticed a difference in her trim.
That pump must be right under the forward cabin sole,
he thought. Can't they hear it running? Maybe they didn't
know what it was—just another noise. Obviously there
had been no alarm.

Suddenly the pump quit, probably burned out from
working against the pressure of the stopped-up discharge. It wouldn't be long now.

And now suddenly there were frantic yells inside the
boat. Someone had probably sat up and put his feet in
saltwater. Rodrigue saw a figure pop to attention up on
the flying bridge—it was like McWherter to sleep up
there. Rodrigue pushed the inner tube away and settled
in the water, breathing through the snorkle again.

The aft pumps kicked on and one of the plugs spat
out. No matter, she was a goner. The best thing they
could do was gracefully abandon ship.

Starting the engines and putting her in gear now
would be a mistake—probably a fatal mistake for someone. The normally upswept bow was sloping ponderous-
ly toward the inky surface. All that water rushing aft
would certainly put her transom under and flood the
engine room. She would go down stern-first and quickly.
Someone would likely be trapped.

Unexpectedly, Rodrigue was worried about someone
drowning. He even felt a twinge of alarm as the dauntless
Wahoo Too, scourge of the Poco Bueno and other big-
money billfish invitationals, rolled gently to starboard
and slipped beneath the inky surface.

Splashing swimmers remained. McWherter was
chanting *ohshit-ohshit-ohshit-ohshit* in a thin voice while
in low tones someone was trying to calm him. It was the
senior Chapman. Leonard was there too, hissing dis-
gustedly. And, off to the right, somebody—

One missing. Rodrigue hoped it wasn't Oscar. He
liked Oscar. Wait—somebody was splashing up behind

him. Rodrigue ducked beneath the surface, grabbing his regulator mouthpiece, and waited for the swimmer to pass over.

Down ten or fifteen feet, he could easily see the blackish figures against the gray velvet surface. Whoever was swimming overhead had found the other inner tube. Rodrigue swam up and jerked it away, ripping it open with his knife and shaking the air out of it. The swimmer screeched and left a trail of glowing phosphorescence to where the others were treading water.

With almost detached curiosity, Rodrigue swam just beneath the cycling legs of the men. He could easily pick out McWherter and whichever of Leland Marchand's nephews it was he had just frightened—McWherter by the length of his legs if nothing else, but both men were kicking a lot more erratically, a lot more frantically. If he were a shark, he decided, he would go for one of them.

But he wanted Leonard. The cold-blooded little bastard needed a lot of piss-and-vinegar taken out of him before he would be safe aboard the Chinaman's boat. Remembering that the younger Chapman had been wearing Levis while his dad wore khakis the last time he had seen them, he opted for the darker pair of calmly rotating legs. Grabbing an ankle, Rodrigue jerked the dark-legged swimmer under and jabbed him lightly with the point of the knife.

Underwater, the words were faint but clear: "It's *got* me! It's *got* me!" It was Leonard, all right. Rodrigue nearly laughed out loud when he saw him trying to climb on top of his father, who was fending him off with vicious kicks. He grabbed his victim again, dragging him away from the group and jabbing him more viciously in the shins, where the knife wounds would be the least serious and the most painful. He liked the sound of the killer's deep, wounded-animal bellow.

He could kill the kid right now—simply drag him

under and drown him. He could stuff him back in the boat and it would look like an accident. An unfortunate but unavoidable mishap. But his air was coming harder, and not just from exertion. He had nearly sucked the tank dry. He released him, kicked away ten or fifteen yards, and surfaced, spotting the shrimp boat in the dim moonlight, lurking on the horizon. He hoped Leonard was sufficiently contrite.

The flashlight had stayed dry in the Ziploc freezer bag, but it still didn't work so he cupped his hands to his mouth and yelled, *"Yo, Ian! Come'n gat am!"*

He recovered the brace and bit, destined to be one of Punta's Gorda's most treasured artifacts, and stood by to play shark again if any of them tried to swim away from the boat, but it wasn't necessary. At that point, the crew of the *Wahoo Too* would've pulled themselves hand-over-hand into a flying saucer to get out of that water. When the last of them scrambled aboard under Saunders's shotgun, Rodrigue swam back to the cay where he had left the skiff.

He had wanted to take a peek at the *Wahoo Too*, to see how she was resting, but his tank was empty now and he was far too winded for free-diving.

CHAPTER 27

Saunders had equipped himself with leg and wrist irons left over from the days of slavery. At some point in the distant past they had been coated with heavy grease and packed in wooden crates. When Punta Gorda's detention facility moved from the aboveground basement of a nineteenth-century house—where huge iron rings had been cemented in the brick walls to contain recalcitrant servants—to the old clapboard shack on piers to the new cement-block building, the crate of cuffs and chains was unquestioningly moved too. Now they smelled sharply of the grease and clunked heavily on the board bridge as the men of the *Wahoo Too* were led to jail in the golden glare of dawn—the very models of defeat, with the brief exception of Oscar, who looked up and grinned sheepishly at the hot Creole women Rodrigue had bragged about.

The whole town had turned out to greet them. Rodrigue merged into the buzzing crush of bodies and let Saunders and the grinning Chinese shrimper enjoy their just desserts.

As the prisoners filed by, Leonard turned his blank face to Rodrigue and communicated absolutely nothing. Rodrigue might as well have been looking into the clustered tunnels of a stack of oil-field casing chained to the deck of one of the supply vessels his dad used to run—hollow and sulking, straining at those chains—and if a link gave way, scattering into a thundering mass, killing horribly with no malice, merely obeying the law of gravity. Here was someone who needed to be chained.

McWherter was weeping and it made Rodrigue hate him. It was, he figured, the same instinct that made a shark attack a wounded fish. Not very pretty. A whole lot like Leonard, in fact.

But Rodrigue actually felt sorry for the elder Chapman. He was haggard and red-eyed—some people shouldn't drink—and he looked shabby with his khakis wrinkled and dirty. He was solemn but not grim. He still had a spark of pride that came from doing what he thought was right regardless of the outcome, and Rodrigue saluted that.

Saunders was admirably restrained, even protective of the men. He seemed determined not to turn it into the spectacle it could easily have become in an eventless backwater like Punta Gorda. At the same time, though, he was clearly excited. He finally let his emotions emerge in a joyful hop as the men were filed into the walkway along the cells in the new jail. And when it came Chapman's turn, Saunders enthusiastically followed him inside. Interrogation rooms are unheard of in Punta Gorda.

"Mind if I sit in?" asked Rodrigue.

"Not a'tall. Be pleased, in fact. You know the situation far better than I."

From Chapman came a derisive snort. "Throckmorton doesn't know shit."

"Who's Throckmorton?" asked Saunders.

"Never mind that," said Rodrigue, taking the offensive. He leveled his civilian eye into Chapman's. "Did you order the killing of Mike Ferguson?"

"Yes," Chapman said without hesitation, then he shrank onto the bunk with a sigh. "I guess I did. I told Leonard the son of a bitch was trouble and I'm not sure now what I expected him to do about it. Maybe I don't want to be sure. I was in a panicky state about that time."

Can't be more forthcoming than that, thought Rodrigue. "What'd he do with the twenty-two pistol?" That was important. That was hard evidence.

"Threw it in the bay. I couldn't go back to it."

"See here, who's this Mike Ferguson?" demanded Saunders, who wanted to talk about cocaine.

"Ferguson's the reason this is going to be a big case," said Rodrigue. "He was a newspaperman they killed to keep him quiet."

"Yes, but what about the evidence, maan?" asked Saunders expectantly.

Something about Chapman's attitude had been troubling Rodrigue. Suddenly he had a disturbing thought. "Did *Leonard* put all this together?" he asked incredulously. "The dope ring, I mean?"

Chapman smiled. "Hardly."

Leonard had been kicked out of UT, U of H, and finally the College of the Mainland at Texas City for one infraction after another, Chapman said. The boy had been working on oil-field supply boats in the summers and that was a factor in the birth of the plan, but the real spark came at a reunion of Chapman's—and Thomaston's and Marchand's—old squadron in New Orleans two years back. Sitting around in a place Marchand kept in the Quarter, they drank and reflew sorties and drank some more and brought each other up to date—*really* up to date this time, confessing failures and recalling all the Other Women—and drank some more and finally got around to snorting coke. Chapman ad-libbed around it. Even in his drunken state he was disgusted at the ritual but he instantly recognized a way to make what he figured would be extra pocket money.

Thomaston had bragged about his yacht. And he had confessed his failure in his son, Anthony, a thoroughly rotten little punk. His other old buddy Marchand had money—both of them had lots of money. And Chapman had McWherter, the sleazy pumper he flew to unmanned platforms in the Gulf.

Actually, Chapman said with a hint of discovery in his voice, it was McWherter who made him see the possibilities, just in idle chatter on the runs out to the rigs. Wouldn't it be fine, he had said, to have a stash of coke waiting out here? They were never searched coming back in.

So what would you do with it if you had it, Chapman asked after his trip to New Orleans. McWherter had started to joke but Chapman looked him coolly and seriously in the eyes and asked him if he could safely— emphasis on safely—sell cocaine. And inside of a month McWherter had found Greathouse.

Thomaston and Marchand didn't know about Greathouse. They thought Chapman was a user himself and for that reason they thought the scheme was perfect—no middlemen to trip them up. For Thomaston, the bonus was not having to pay Anthony's fines and kick dirt over all his little peccadilloes. The boy was going on an extended sea cruise and Mrs. Thomaston couldn't have cared less. Marchand enlisted his nephews in the crew, Chapman figured, as insurance he would be getting his fair share of the shipments.

The three contributed equally to the upkeep of the

boat and the expenses of the voyages. They dolled out what they hoped was a moderate amount of cocaine for the crew's use, but there was no way to be sure. Hitting the coke too heavily may have been what caused the slipups in Cartagena and back at the One Seventy-four, Chapman said.

Since the cocaine was for the private use of three men and their friends, Chapman hadn't expected nearly the volume they were soon doing. There was no way he could justify having that much cash, so except for the generous amounts he bestowed on his wife for her daily shopping, he stashed the money and wound up using it for their getaway fund. Before he left, he faked an accidental death so his wife could collect his insurance.

The story became angrier in the telling. He was angry at the way it had turned out, but also very coldly and calculatedly angry at the fact that Marchand and Thomaston hadn't been touched. He was basically an upright citizen who did what he had done, Rodrigue sensed, to get even—to get back at God or whatever engineer of fate had bounced him out of the navy and onto an airborne bus route with nose-picking rednecks like McWherter for passengers while corrupt men like Thomaston and Marchand prospered. He was especially angry at Marchand, who on top of everything was an arrogant little bayou Napoleon who hadn't even entertained the notion of getting caught. Rodrigue got the idea Chapman would make a world-class witness if he ever made it to court.

Somebody would have to talk. The Grand Banks, the shipment of cocaine, and the weapon Anthony Thomaston had used to kill the hapless shark fishermen were sitting in at least twenty-five fathoms. That certainly wasn't too deep for recovery—he'd do it himself, free— but the odds of finding a fiberglass wreck sunk in a storm

228

were pretty slim, even if the Coast Guard chopper crew had noted precise coordinates.

"And how much of the cocaine was on the baat when it went down, Mr. Chapman?" Saunders asked expectantly.

Rodrigue cringed, but Chapman, apparently thinking Saunders meant the Grand Banks instead of the *Wahoo Too,* said, "The whole lot. About forty pounds, I'm told."

Saunders smiled. That would be fine evidence.

"If you have lied to me, you are in a lot of trouble, maan!" said Saunders bitterly.

"Huh?" mumbled Rodrigue. He rose to consciousness like a hard hat diver being winched to the surface.

As his head cleared, he remembered why the police chief was angry. He had been expecting it but that didn't make it any less awkward. Here he was in the man's home, curled up on a puffy single bed on the louvered porch, enveloped in the smells of the musty old quilt and the damp tropical foliage and the wife's pungent fish soup, now bubbling to perfection in the big kitchen. Somehow he had imagined this one last little problem would solve itself.

He thought he deserved a break. He was the Good Samaritan triumphing over evil—an upracticed sensation, to be sure—and now that he had bought them all to justice, justice should damn well be done.

Rodrigue never cast Father Lynch's God as the actor in these wild, headlong careers of fate that made up his life. Maybe it was because he had been taught not to put that God in that kind of position, lest He disappoint you, and in turn be disappointed *in* you for being disappointed in Him. But his own private God, the one he only worshiped on the pale purple fringe of his consciousness, *that* God had to be setting things on an even keel from time to time. How else could you explain hurricanes?

Saunders had taken Rodrigue home to meet his family and bedded him down on the guest bed while he went back to arrange to have the forty pounds of cocaine raised. He had telephoned a dive-boat operator at Placentia who just happened to be loading a club tour from San Francisco for a trip to Queen Cays on Belize's great barrier reef. The dive-boat operator had put the phone down a minute and returned to inform Saunders that the Californians would be more than happy to dive on the wreck for him. The *Wahoo Too* was resting on the bottom about thirty-five miles south-southeast of Placentia, while their original destination was about thirty miles west. This would give them something to do besides sightsee, something they could tell their grandkids about.

"They combed that baat from stem to stern and they didn't come up with forty pounds of cocaine! They didn't even come up with one *ounce* of cocaine!" Saunders was saying angrily. "Chapman, he tells me now how they didn't have any cocaine on board. They found the one gun, a pistol, on the battam, but I don't believe the district officer will hear a charge for that since they had not officially landed there. Maan, I'm gonna look like one real fool if I must let am go!"

Rodrigue rubbed his eyes and sat up, hiding an erection with a wad of quilt. If he had been dreaming, he didn't remember it.

"Ought to have been some money aboard, Ian," he said wearily.

"Yes, the thought crossed my mind as well. Either it was lost to the sea or one of the divers has taken it."

Rodrigue cringed slightly. He himself had been accused of stealing the pocket change of drowning victims. The only thing he could figure was that sometimes the sea stole. "How long can you hold them without charging them?" he asked.

230

Saunders groaned. "I can hold am until they rot, but that's not the *pint,* maan! I've got to feed am. I've got to keep someone at the jail to watch am. All this costs *money,* maan. That is not what we're about here."

"Look, let's say you *can't* charge them with anything, eh? They've still committed murders in Texas and Louisiana and on Cozumel too. Hell, they *stole* that boat I sank right out of the municipal harbor. So even if you've got to turn them over to some other jurisdiction, you still get credit for capturing them. Bottom line is they're bad fucking people that needed locking up and you have done that. Pardon my French."

Saunders, staring through the louvers at the dark, wet foliage against the window, lifted one ebony hand in an absentminded wave. "Belize has no extradition treaty with either the U.S. or Mexico," he said softly. "That doesn't mean I cannot arrange to release the men where they will be immediately recaptured by other authorities, but . . ."

He looked at Rodrigue and smiled.

"If you were willing to chase them over the sea in an open baat, the least I can do is weather a little political storm on land," he said. "I can probably borrow from my relatives to make up the reward I promised Chin."

"Chin? Ah, the little Chinese shrimper. How much did you promise?"

"I stuck my neck out, figuring to give him my bonus from the fine—five hundred dollars."

"Five hundred Belize?"

"Of course."

"It's no problem, maan. I'm authorized by my employer to grant rewards of up to one thousand dollars for assistance in bringing these guys to justice. One thousand *U.S.*"

"Five hundred U.S.!" said Ian, almost swooning.

"No, maan. One thousand. Each."

231

"Well—as I said," said Ian, manfully recovering his composure, "what's a little political storm?"

Rodrigue ate the fish soup and stayed the night, restlessly, on the too-soft bed on the porch, and left the high, palm-fringed bluff at Punta Gorda with the first good light of dawn. It was well over a hundred miles to Belize City. Running wide-open he could make it by at least midafternoon, if he didn't run into a lot of delay refueling at Stann Creek. He would need to refuel, though. At that speed, he'd be getting about five miles a gallon.

He made the seventy-five miles to Stann Creek in three hours, refueled quickly, and started on the forty-mile final leg to Belize City with a whole lot less urgency and a stout grog-and-lime, first of many. He rounded the point into Haulover Creek at 1:10 P.M. by his Timex.

After he settled up with Nicky Fuentes and arranged to have the scuba gear returned to Brad Potts on St. George's Cay, he checked into the Fort George Hotel for its efficient switchboard and put in a call to Bruce Phillips at the Galveston County Sheriff's Office.

"Where in the hell are you at now?" Phillips's voice was cordial.

"Belize. I got your boys. They're being held by the police in Punta Gorda, down south."

"What boy're those?"

"The boys who killed Sandy and Mike and Mickey Aimes and the two shark fishermen at the One Seventy-four and I forget who all else. I'm drunk."

"I heard about Mickey. That's tough. Real tough. But that's the Mexicans' jurisdiction, Rod. And the fishermen at the rig ain't even being treated as a murder. They disbanded that task force and as far as anyone around here's concerned, Mike Ferguson is fighting for Fidel in El Salvador."

Rodrigue took another long pull of the hotel's Bacardi

232

and soda. "Yeah, I forgot. It's just politics after all, isn't it, Brucie?"

" 'Fraid so. One Anthony Thomaston turned up dead over in Marrero, across the river from New Orleans. His dad's Gregory Thomaston, who just happens to be a big Republican party honcho in Florida, if you know what I mean." Phillips's voice had dropped in volume.

"Yeah, I know. It was his yacht they were using to haul the dope to the states. The ringleader is a PHI pilot named Virgil Chapman. He told me the whole story."

Phillips laughed. "I finally came to the brilliant conclusion that he was involved after all when we found his boat drifting near Greens Cut. Figured he'd been bumped off. And here he faked it instead."

"The local law will dump him in international waters if you can get somebody to come pick him up."

"Ain't no law against going to Belize, Rod."

"I've got two of Leland Marchand's newphews down there. He's in it up to his goddamn silver eyebrows."

"The feds know that. Evidently it's too even a swap. Like playing chess. When the Thomaston kid turned up dead, there was no way they could pursue it and keep his old man out of it."

Rodrigue, Phillips knew, was often his most lucid when he was drunk. He would understand without having to be told how the deputy felt about all this.

"Forget it," Phillips said. "Let the Mexicans have 'em. C'mon home and let's go fishing. They're really turning on around here, now that the water's cleared up."

"It was Chapman's kid, boy about twenty-two or so, who killed Sandy and Mike," Rodrigue said dully. "I could've killed him but I didn't."

"I'm glad, Rod. Really am."

"What about the little girl? She all right?"

"You bet. I called a city detective in Atlanta I've known for a while and he got her to call me away from the house and she sounds fine. Sounds like she got a lot of sense shocked into her. Anyway, I think her and her old man are getting along fine now. You'll probably be hearing from her—she wanted your address."

"That's nice," he said, feeling an unaccustomed thickening in his throat.

"Listen, Rod . . ." There was a long pause. "Sorry about that rum. I spiked it with 151-proof."

"The devil sez ye! I wuz plannin' to burn Cruzan in me outboards from now on."

"There was a lot of pressure around here. Still is. We're in way over our heads on this cover-up."

"Suppose it gets out—you gonna be in any trouble?"

"Not as long as I ain't the one who lets it out."

"Well, the district officer, which is a sort of judge where they're being held, will probably try every which way he can think of to make lemonade out of these guys. So keep your shoes shined, eh?"

So it would be Mexican justice. That was okay—better, even. Rodrigue lay back on the bed and happily imagined Leonard rotting in a tropical dungeon. Once they get their hands on them, by hook or crook, the Mexicans would have no trouble proving Chapman and his crew had stolen the *Wahoo Too* and killed Mickey Aimes. McWherter would sing like Tiny Tim. Oscar too.

The afternoon rain clattered suddenly against the curtained windows. The drumming on the panes grew louder and louder until it finally drowned the coarse hum of the two-ton air conditioner above the door. Rodrigue dreamed he was dropping Sandy and Sarah at the Holiday Inn, but it became the airport. They were out on the apron. It was cool, night, and the droning of engines was in his ears. He was seeing them off someplace. They smiled and waved. He waved. Nobody was sad.

The awful jangling of the phone woke him. "Punta

234

Gorda on the line, sah," said the woman at the switch-board.

"John, this is Ian. The news is not good."

"What's wrong?"

"The district officer unofficially informed the U.S. authorities of the arrests and they unofficially informed us back the subjects are not wanted in the U.S. for anyt'ing."

"What about the Mexicans?"

"Yes, they are interested, but they will not act fast enough. No way."

"What's the hurry? Goddamn, Chapman and that bunch can't eat *that* much."

"No, maan. Where the problem lies is with the relative of the two brothers, someone apparently very powerful in the U.S. My district officer says the maan is arriving Belize City tomorrow and is expected here Monday. If he begins making trouble, we will have to release am."

"How long can you hold out?"

"I don't *know,* maan. That's just it."

"Well, hang in there. I'll see if I can get some strings pulled in Mexico and get back to you."

He put in a call to Greathouse on Cozumel. He would tell him Chapman's crew deliberately skuttled *Wahoo Too,* which ought to make him mad enough to finance a Mexican posse, pronto. Two hours later, after he had showered and shaved and shook most of the wrinkles out of his last clean shirt, the message caught up with him in the restaurant—Mr. and Mrs. Greathouse had checked out. No forwarding address.

Well, that was that. Greathouse, blissfully having nuptial miracles performed on him in Cayman or some-where, had written the whole thing off. Leland Marchand was on his way with charm and money, the two keys to any Belizean's heart. Chapman and his whole gang would be set free—probably paid off and put on the next plane to New Guinea or someplace as distant.

Rodrigue lost his appetite. He didn't really mind that Chapman would be getting off or Marchand's nephews or McWherter or, hell, even Leonard, who was as innocent in his deadliness as a lion in the jungle.

They had gotten the best of him for a while. Rodrigue was perfectly capable of killing to avenge friends—he had done it before—but it had only caused misery and death for other friends. And the government had scooped up the bodies and used them for public relations. He had taught himself to be cool, to be apart. But then he had come home and found two of his preciously few friends staring at the ceiling. And then the government had jerked him out of his life and into bondage, not a whole lot unlike Ian's and Mr. Samuels's ancestors.

When it came to killing Leonard and the others on the *Wahoo Too,* his anger had wilted. But he was still deeply angry at the government, and at those few figures he could dimly perceive to be running it. Leland Marchand was one of them—in fact, he would be elected governor of Louisiana. The consolation prize for the Republicans was that they could keep digging into Gregory Thomaston's pockets in good conscience. And Haas and Wilson could keep kidnapping and harassing private citizens with impunity. They had gotten away with it. They were getting away with it all the time. All *he* had done was sink a damn good boat. Again.

And now he was free to go back to being Rodrigue the Pirate, the blustering Bluto of Galveston—until somebody up there jerked his strings again, that is. They had done it before, they could do it again.

But not to Sandy, ever again. Or to Mike—Mike, the phantom freedom fighter. He would ride the hills of El

Salvador forever, like Emiliano Zapata. A free man indeed.

That was all Sandy had wanted anyway, freedom to fuck anybody she wanted to. It wasn't too much to ask. And it was the same with Diegleman, only what he had wanted was out. But it was the same thing, really. Freedom from lifers like Rodrigue with their endless shit details. Freedom from the Uniform Code of Military Justice.

Now Rodrigue understood what had been lost. Justice is only a means to an end. The UCMJ is perfect for keeping smart alecks like Diegleman in line, but that isn't justice. Real, true justice is the means to only one end: freedom. And there was no justice. Not in Belize. Nowhere in Central America. Not in the United States of America.

He wandered aimlessly through the hotel lobby. Bought a two-day-old Miami *Herald*. Stepped outside and sniffed the city. Stepped back in and looked up at the cocktail lounge. Didn't feel like climbing the stairs.

Earlier he had toyed with the idea of flying back to Cozumel, but now he didn't feel like doing that, either.

CHAPTER 28

Columbia's next mission is to prove the
Shuttle can haul payloads. Two communications satellites will be placed in orbit in NASA's
first commercial venture. And authorities in Honduras
deny that U.S. troop involvement in war games there is
aimed at stemming the flow of supplies to leftist rebels
fighting the government in neighboring El—

Rodrigue's big sunburnt hands crumpled the *Herald*
before his face, revealing a clear-eyed look of revelation.
He tossed the paper in a wastebasket beside the desk and
jogged to his room, hoping he wasn't too late—for a lot
of things.

First he called the TACA representative at home and
made sure he could get on the flight. Then he called Ian
and told him the plan. And finally he called the Mayan
Plaza on Cozumel and paced the room at the end of the
phone cord like a tiger on a leash while the switchboard
rang and rang and rang.

Finally Ann Eller answered with a sleepy *"¿Bueno?"*

"Hi, this is John."

She was silent for a dozen terrible heartbeats. Finally: "How are you?"

"I'd like to see you again," he said quickly. It was the simple truth. "I can be back in Cozumel Tuesday, maybe even Monday. Sorry I can't be more—"

"It's okay, I have another week of vacation."

"Great. Been working on your tan?"

"To tell you the truth, I've gone to Chichen-Itza, which I've been to before, and Tulum, and Uxmal. It's no fun just sitting around in the sun without a mysterious stranger at your elbow, you know? Is everything all right?"

"I have to go to Tegucigalpa tomorrow to make sure but I think so, yeah."

"Pound—"

"Plot. I'll call you as soon as I get back. 'Night."

He hung up, smiling a gentler smile than his usual cold-eyed display of teeth.

The next morning Rodrigue made the early Mass at Holy Redeemer and had a leisurely breakfast at Mom's, scanning the weekly *Beacon* to catch up on local happenings. He still arrived at the airport too early and had to bribe the concessionaire to open the bar before fewer than a dozen departing passengers had assembled in the small, squat terminal. Rodrigue rewarded him further by having several icy Belikins in a row.

Some of the passengers were locals, headed for the U.S. on business or to bask in the air conditioning of a Miami or New Orleans hotel. There wasn't quite the funereal atmosphere as in the winter, when the terminal would be crammed with departing dive-tourists, broke and frazzled from too much sun, too much exercise, and too much booze.

"It's Captain Rodriguez, isn't it?" said a woman at his

elbow. It was the secretary and her boss from St. George's.

"Rodrigue, ma'am. The French version." He kissed her hand and smiled at the man. "Trust you had good diving?"

"Oh, excellent," the man said. "Out-of-season is definitely the time to come."

"Definitely. Back to Toronto? Must make for a long day."

"Not too bad," said the woman in French. "You speak French, of course."

"*Mais oui,*" said Rodrigue. "The French of *l 'Acadie.*" He shrugged. "It's French."

The man frowned.

"We pause for several days in New Orleans," the woman continued. "It's not too bad."

"Ah, New Orleans," Rodrigue said wistfully.

"Well, come on, Rene, we'd better grab a seat before this place fills up," said the man, trying his boss-tone again. "Nice to see you again, Rodriguez."

"Charmed." Rodrigue grinned evilly.

Even in the summer a seat on one of the hard benches in the terminal would be scarce as departure times approached. Flights in and out of Belize International were scheduled back-to-back so that the place was jam-packed for an hour or two each day and then everybody could go home. Soon passengers bound for Houston, New Orleans, Miami, and Guatemala City were being massed in waves, like troops in an amphibious assault. Rodrigue's group was first. In line and backed against a wall to make room for the passengers filing in from the baking tarmac, he came eye-to-eye with a short, silver-haired man, an elegant-looking man he recognized immediately. Rodrigue winked and the man blandly smiled back. The silver-haired man didn't know Rodrigue

240

from Robespierre but lots of people knew Leland Marchand.

He was bold. The next governor of Louisiana down here bailing out drug runners and homicidal maniacs. And a horny little nephew. The whole Punta Gorda police force would have heard about the girls of Isla Mujeres by now. Rodrigue had a shot of rum on the rocks on the way to Guatemala City. And on the leg from Guatemala City to the Honduran capital, he had a double.

"I may not look it," he told the taxi driver at Toncontin Airport, "but I am a North American journalist."

"You look it," the driver said wearily, eyeing Rodrigue's rumpled Hawaiian shirt.

"I want to meet other North American journalists. Do you know at what hotel the North American journalists are gathering?"

"Yes, yes. They are all at the Holiday Inn."

"That figures. Let us go to the Holiday Inn, *por favor.*"

The Holiday Inn was what Rodrigue remembered as the old Lincoln Hotel, all spruced up, with a first-class bar attracting a well-groomed clientele from the downtown mall. The reporters were easy to spot by their khaki safari coats and crepe-soled shoes. Rodrigue took a back booth and watched them until he thought he had a winner, a young fellow whose gaze kept wandering outside the group of fellow Americans around the table.

He was thin, about twenty-five, with shoulder-length sandy hair, and energetic—not nervous, exactly, but the kind who walks on the balls of his feet. Rodrigue waited until the kid was coming out of the men's room and he pulled the old turn-and-*whoops* trick at the bar.

"I'm very sorry," he said in Spanish. "Did I spill on you?"

"I'm sorry, I don't speak Spanish," the journalist replied, pushing on.

"Hey, are you one of the reporters?" Rodrigue asked in English. "Why in the hell are all you guys still *here?* Shit, I guess I'm the only one in the world who thinks it's news."

"Thinks what's news?" the journalist asked, his curiosity momentarily aroused. Then he decided it was wishful thinking. "Those war games on the coast? We're covering 'em. This is how you cover war games."

"Big deal. I'm talking about the dope bust in Belize. They nabbed two nephews of the next governor of Louisiana, who's down there right now trying to bail them out. And the *son* of a big Republican in Florida was—"

"Can I buy you another drink?" the journalist said, quickly steering Rodrigue away from his colleagues at the table. "Here, let's sit over here, you want to?"

The journalist was from the New Orleans *Times-Picayune*. Pure, dumb luck. And he was perfect—he thought Leland Marchand was a demagogue but that all Republicans were profit-worshiping philistines.

"All right, when can we leave?" he said after he had heard enough.

"We? I'm afraid I have to go to Cozumel first thing in the morning. Got to deliver a fathometer for a friend of a friend."

"Shit. I thought you might come back to Belize with me."

"Ian Saunders. Ask for him. He's the police chief there. It's when you get back to the States that you better be careful."

"How do you mean?"

"The feds are serious about keeping it under wraps. A good friend of mine, an investigative reporter for the Houston *Post*, Mike Ferguson, was working on the story and he wound up dead."

"No *shit?*"

"No shit. Only nobody knows what happened to him.

242

I mean *I* know—he was shot to death in my house, along with another friend of mine who just got in the way. All this happened when I was doing a diving job. Cops were all over the place—Galveston County deputies, since I live out of the city—and yet not even his own newspaper knows what happened to him. The feds cooked up some ridiculous story about him running off to Salvador to fight with the rebels, but I know for a fact there's a medical examiner's report on him that the government has classified top secret. Figure *that* out."

"Do you know for sure the feds did the killing?" Excitement made his eyes sparkle in the darkened lounge.

Rodrigue considered the question, mischievously. "Nah," he said finally. "The dope-runners did it. Point is, it's been covered up to protect them."

The journalist stole a glance over his shoulder at his colleagues, who were laughing and talking a little loudly now. When he turned back to lift his drink in a toast to Rodrigue, he wore a small, hard smile.

Rodrigue smiled back, the wide, white shark-smile. Who said justice couldn't be fun?

Ian's job was to make sure Marchand stayed in Punta Gorda until the journalist could eyeball him. That was all there was to it. It was like setting off a bug fogger, it would reach them all sooner or later—Thomaston, Special Agent Roy Wilson, and the inquisitors of Maxwell Prison Camp. And under the doors in Washington, wherever those terrible strings led.

Of course it would probably come back around to him too, for sinking the Wellcraft at the rig. Might even end his relationship with the U.S. Coast Guard. Rodrigue didn't care. He started his vacation that afternoon, loafing in the narrow Old World streets of Tegucigalpa, with its whitewashed walls blinding against the lush emerald of the hills and the dark purple of the approaching rain.

ABOUT THE AUTHOR

KEN GRISSOM was born in Corpus Christi, Texas, in 1945. He has traveled extensively and has worked as a commercial diver and an engineer on offshore oil-field supply vessels. An outdoor writer for the Houston *Post* and a frequent contributor of articles on boating to magazines, Mr. Grissom lives in Seabrook, Texas, where he is at work on his next John Rodrigue novel.